IN THE TEMPLE OF DROOD OF THE THOUSAND ARMS

Tiana awakened stiff and cold. Her eyes focused—and rolled in exasperation. This sort of thing had happened to her before and was a dreadful bother. She was cold because she was naked. She was stiff because she was chained spread-eagled atop the altar of cold black stone.

By the Cud—what a cliché! These jackals are about to sacrifice me to their grisly God! This, Tiana realized, was an unusually bad situation: If Caranga and the King's Own were to come in and find me like this, I'd never hear the end of it!

Her chains allowed her some freedom of motion. Twisting, she could see the religious killers seated on their cushions before the altar. They looked expectant, all glittery of eye. Tiana suppressed a shudder. Whatever these evil men planned for her, it would be a spectacle they would enjoy.

GW00686268

Books by Andrew Offutt and Richard Lyon

Demon in the Mirror
The Eyes of Sarsis

Published by POCKET BOOKS

ANDREW OFFUTT
AND RICHARD LYON

THE EYES OF SARSIS

Part Two in the trilogy
War of the Wizards

PUBLISHED BY POCKET BOOKS NEW YORK

To the Grand Masters who taught us all,
L. SPRAGUE DE CAMP and FRITZ LEIBER

Another *Original* publication of POCKET BOOKS.

POCKET BOOKS, a Simon & Schuster division of
GULF & WESTERN CORPORATION
1230 Avenue of the Americas, New York, N.Y. 10020

ISBN: 0-671-82679-4

First Pocket Books printing September, 1980

10 9 8 7 6 5 4 3 2 1

POCKET and colophon are trademarks of Simon & Schuster.

Printed in the U.S.A.

BOOK I

The Leftward Eye:
SCARLET VISIONS

CHAPTER ONE

"Here, kitty kitty!"

As Darganda of Reme was not a skilled thief or even cutpurse, he specialized in the robbery and murder of drunken sailors. It was hardly a rewarding occupation; by the time his victims were drunk enough that he dared attack, they often had little left worth stealing. Indeed, Darganda had done death on five men this month to so little profit that he'd have starved by now, were it not for his second occupation or rather "occupation": cat butcher.

Once again he lurked in an alley behind a tavern in Reme, chief port and capital of Ilan. His stomach was growling, and it was too early in the evening for seamen to be helpless with drink, and Darganda was pleased to see himself approached by a cat. The wiry man fingered his knife eagerly. Keen of edge and needle-pointed, it was the weapon of a true *grub*, the street assassins that infested the city. Darganda was no warrior to keep his blade all shiny and eye-catching; it was dull and lackluster as the eyes of his habitual victims. Few had seen the blade, though many had felt it. They did not remember.

"Here kitty kitty—come here and let Darganda cut your darling throat."

He saw that the animal was sleek, well fed, without scar or blemish. Its fur was pure white, long, and rich as sable. Clearly this was no alley beast, but the pampered pet of some aristocrat. He waited. It continued to pace toward him mincing with tail high while it stared at him with big luminous eyes green as gems. Musing that the pretty thing would yield a tender stew indeed, Darganda was startled to note that it wore some sort of necklace.

7

This'll be the first time I ever robbed a cat!

He reached forth his arms and the cat, obviously expecting to be petted, hopped into them. Darganda cradled the animal in one arm while he drew his knife. It was then that he received the next to last surprise of his life; he looked closely at the cat's necklace.

The grub expected a cut glass trinket worth a few coppers. Instead he gazed, intoxicated, upon a faultless diamond of a thousand winking facets, wide as a man's thumb and blazing with internal fire. *A king's ransom,* Darganda thought, for his thoughts, like his sparse converse, went little beyond the most standard of clichés. The sale of this treasure—here, in his arms!—would bring more gold than a man could carry! The feet of the wiry little thug of Reme were set on the road of Empire, sure!

Like many another worthless harbor rat, Darganda imagined himself a great man denied opportunity by cruel circumstance. Now destiny seemed to open its door. Bustling to enter, he saw himself as a successful bandit chieftain, and then as a robber baron; general of a vast conquering army, he burned, pillaged, enslaved whole nations. He dreamed of himself as emperor. He visualized scores, countless beautiful slavegirls to do with as he pleased. No no: noblewomen, for was he not emperor?

The myriad vainglorious dreams burst like bubbles, in the alley behind the Wayfarer Tavern.

All this was provided he was not killed and robbed of the jewel before he departed this alley! With his new wealth, every men was his enemy. *Every face that of an enemy,* he thought; *every hand raised against me! All will want to steal* my *treasure from me!*

His rat's eyes ranged their gaze up and down the alley to assure himself that it remained deserted. A bit of lamplight crept from a high rear window of the tavern. The only other source of light was the full moon, a silver skull suspended high in the sky. The tavern's rear door represented a threat; at any moment it might disgorge attackers. Hugging his cat, his prize and his treasure, Darganda moved deeper into the shadows. It was imperative that the white cat die silently.

"Nice kitty, kitty . . ."

Darganda petted the cat, which purred luxuriously. Its large green eyes stared luminously into the grub's. Like the diamond, the cat's eyes seemed to hold cold fire prisoned within. Staring into them, Darganda did not notice that the diamond was changing. One by one, each of its thousand white facets was turning into a blood-red star.

The cat stared, the diamond blazed, and the thug raised his knife. He placed sharp edge to pulsing throat.

"Nice kitty, this won't hurt you a bit."

His words were entirely true. A single swift movement drew knife's edge across throat, severing the jugular vein. Blood bubbled. The cat sprang from the man's arms and Darganda collapsed into the filth of the alley. It was then that Darganda made his tardy discovery, the last surprise of his life: the throat he had just cut was his own.

While his blood poured forth onto the ground, he saw the cat clean itself of the few droplets that had spattered its gleaming coat. Though Darganda's eyes closed then, his ears heard for another moment. The last sound he heard was the cat: it was lapping and purring as if drinking the finest cream.

Its meal finished, the cat turned from the corpse. Fastidiously it cleansed its whiskers and button nose of scarlet stains and, with the easy natural grace of its kind, paced down the alley until it was beneath the tavern window. An effortless leap carried the animal up onto the sill. There perched the white cat, surveying the tavern called Wayfarer.

The scene within presented a paradox. The tavern's patrons were pirates, hard and gristly. Grizzled sharks of the sea. Yet seated in the place of highest honor at the very head of the Table of Captains was a woman of both youth and beauty. Her hair was misty sunset and her eyes flashing emeralds; a black cloak was furled back to display a superb body sparsely clad in a tight green shirt and short skirt, both of silk.

A newcomer might well wonder why this choice morsel remained untouched in the very midst of a hungry wolf pack. A more discerning eye would provide the answer: those round arms concealed muscle and the woman's beauty drew attention from strength and speed. Too, the hilts of the rapier and dagger at her belt were worn from use. All were wolves here; one happened to be she-wolf.

It was a measure of the daring of Tiana, Captain of *Vixen*, that she left her crew behind and came alone to such a den. This night she was manifestly enjoying herself. Her fellow sea-wolves listened with awe to her adventures,

roared at her jests and ribald jokes, and were fervently dil-
igent in keeping her wine-cup brimmed. This homage she
accepted as her due, for Tiana knew she was the best of the
pirates who sailed from Reme.

She knew what she looked like, too, and was well pleased
with the knowledge; naturally these men cherished some
childish plan to get her helpless with drink and rape her—
for after all, she thought, who did not!—but she knew too
that she could and would drink them all under the table.
They were only men.

All laughed at someone's joke, and their host nervously
wiped his hand in his apron. The trouble with these damned
boisterous murderous scarred hard-drinking sharks was that
their money was so good!

Tiana lifted high her mug without spilling a droplet of
wine, despite its just having been filled to the brim by a
hairy-chested ox who had lusted after her for years—and
who now watched not her face or arm or the mug but the
interesting lines of stress that leaped up in her blouse with
her movement.

"Ha!" she cried. "I know not about your ship *Black
Sword*, Mandias, but as for *my* ship . . . I am the vixen of
Vixen!"

Again laughter rose loud, and the white cat completed its
observations.

It jumped down and walked unnoticed toward a dark
corner of the inn. There squatted Arond, former pirate
turned beggar by one swordcut several years agone; now
he waited for such food as fell to the floor. This he did by
smell and touch, for his eye sockets were empty pits of
darkness. The cat halted before the beggar and stared up at
his face. The diamond at its neck was a shining silvery
white—that was slowly turning red in the way of a crystal
goblet being filled with crimson wine. Somehow the blind
man sensed the cat's silent approach. Had anyone noticed,
he'd have seen that Arond was frightened by what he
sensed.

None noticed. Tiana held all attention; Tiana and the
goblets and mugs on the Captains' Table. She had been
asked to relate how she had despoiled the Tomb of Kings
up in Calancia of Nevinia. Captain Tiana Highrider did
love to tell that tale, assuring all that she had known no
fear even when buried alive and later menaced by the
bestial ghouls that awaited her within Nevinia's good earth.

No one saw Arond's ugly face while his fear became terror. He drew breath to scream, but his face went blank and his cry emerged only as a muted whimper that was hardly as loud as Mandias's sudden burst of laughter, across the room. Rising slowly, Arond walked to the rear door of the Wayfarer. The white cat followed closely, tail high. Arond was not feeling his way; he walked as swiftly and surely as a sighted man. He opened the door unerringly and he and the cat passed into the alley. No one saw. The cat's tail-tip twitched as it followed the blind former pirate to the bloodless corpse of Darganda.

Even a sighted man could not have detected the grub's knife in the darkness and filth of the alley; Arond picked it up without hesitation.

As he walked back to the inn's door, the cat sprang onto the windowsill. It sat once more surveying the tavern, tail moving only at the tip. The Wayfarer's vein-faced proprietor was just taking away the empties in exchange for the new crocks and jugs of wine and ale he set upon the Captains' Table.

"You were entirely naked?" This from Cap'n Barkis, called the Weasel.

"I had a ribbon in my hair," Tiana said blithely, and eyes rolled.

Three doors holed the inn's walls; front, rear, and side. While Tiana continued her story, a man entered by each door, simultaneously. By the rearward exit Arond returned. He moved toward the Captains' Table in an uncanny manner: unseeing yet unerring. Truly his walk had become the old confident swagger he'd affected as one of the sea's boldest pirates. He'd been a bold one, aye, before he had several years ago forgot himself and sought to seize the ship of his fellow corsair Caranga, whom Arond had dared call Black Caranga.

In by the side door, meanwhile, came a man unknown to the pirates of Reme; a tall, slender, hawk-faced fellow he was, with dead eyes cold as a virgin's bed. He walked with an oddly liquid limp. The lean body shifted ultra-lithely from side to side as though he were powerless to control it.

He went unnoticed, as did Arond, because of the advent of the third man.

This one thrust himself boldly through the front doorway, where he stood a moment to survey the place. Though he was not over-tall, his broad powerful shoulders seemed to fill the doorway. Gray traces gleamed in his black, tightly curly hair. Otherwise he was as a slice of night confidently entering the Wayfarer; this man's face and bare chest, loose leggings and boots were all black as coal.

Striding into the tavern as though he were its owner, he bellowed greeting to fellow pirates. They called back in happy camaraderie: "Ho, Caranga! About time!"

The white woman and the black man could not have been in greater contrast save had she been blond. Yet she smiled and called, "Father! You're just in time! Do try Cartro's roast beef—it's truly excellent tonight!"

The newcomer thus addressed glanced at the inn's host, smiled, and nodded. Cartro bustled to his kitchen. The flame-haired pirate queen was starting to create a place for the black when an expressionless voice spoke, from her right.

"Captain Tiana Highrider, I have something for you."

She turned questioning face to the stranger. While his eyes looked at her with neither emotion nor recognition, he extended a scroll of parchment. Tiana automatically reached for it—and the attack came, a sudden and complete surprise. Arond sprang.

The stranger had no chance to evade the knife the blind man thrust unerringly into his heart. Whirling, the beggar stabbed at Tiana. She was just able to twist aside and grasp his wrist. She forced the arm down while her knee shot up. An audible snap accompanied the breaking of Arond's arm. Yet his fist remained clamped around the knife while with his other hand he reached for the woman's neck.

Tiana dared not release the knife-hand, broken or no. She stepped toward her attacker. As Arond's left hand closed about her throat, she kicked him in the groin with a small foot shod in a large, square-toed boot. The murderous beggar showed no sign of having noted the blow that was a standard part of Tiana's fighting repertoire—and always effective. Not this time. Arond's fingers contracted about her neck like iron bands while his broken arm strained to drive the knife at her.

While Tiana fought horror and death, the man she'd called father was far from idle. He charged with a bellow, scattering men and tables like a bull elephant on the rampage. As Arond's fingers squeezed more tightly about Tiana's throat, the burly man's heavy cutlass flashed up and down to sever the beggar's arm just above the wrist.

"I should have killed you that other time, damn you! My sweet Tiana told me I—Susha's paps!"

Without the slightest expression of pain, Arond dropped like a puppet whose strings had been cut.

His fingers, meanwhile, continued to contract about Tiana's neck. She tore at the severed hand while her face darkened. If anything, the thing's strength and lust to kill had increased with its disconnection from its arm. She could not breathe. Her lungs were afire and the lights of pain flashed before her eyes.

With the world a swimming blur, she somehow managed to force her fingers beneath the crushing thumb. Only by pulling back with all her strength did she break the strangling clutch. Instantly the hand was limp and lifeless.

Immediately Tiana squatted by the body of Arond. Her considerable skill at battlefield surgery was of no use, she swiftly ascertained; no life remained in the beggar.

"This death," she muttered, "is as unnatural as the life of his hand."

He showed no wounds that should have proven instantly fatal; in any case she knew that the body always struggled to retain life, if only briefly. The beggar her foster-father had once blinded—in self-defense, without having sense enough to give him another stroke, damn it—had shown no pain, no struggle. The moment he could no longer attack, his life had ended.

"It's almost as if . . . as if he was discarded," she muttered; "a broken tool no longer useful to . . . the owner." She looked up, frowning, as two big black hands came down to her.

Caranga helped her up. "Well, daughter, your sweet old father saved your life this time!"

"*Thank* you, father. I do wish you'd just . . . waited."

"But this dog attacked you!"

"He'd not have done, if you'd killed him years ago instead of letting him go because he was blind and . . . *helpless?* Besides, if you'd just given me a minute, I'd have disarmed him. Then he could have answered my questions. It wasn't as if I was *afraid,* after all."

"Of course not. What questions?"

"To begin with—how does a man without eyes see so perfectly?"

"My dear nosy daughter," Caranga snorted, "stick to

honest piracy like a good fellow, and leave black mystery alone!"

"You're a fine one to use 'black' as an adjective, my dear interfering fa—"

"Captain Tiana," the flat expressionless voice said, from behind Caranga, "I have something for you."

The reformed cannibal turned respectable pirate whirled; he and his adopted daughter stared at the stranger. He still stood upright, despite Arond's stab wound—which was bleeding only a little. With a "Here," he placed the scroll in Tiana's hand. "For you. It's a map of possible interest." Then he lay down on the floor on his back. He straightened his legs with the thighs together, closed his eyes, and folded his arms over his chest. And he was motionless.

"G'night Caranga, Tiana," Captain Mandias of *Black Sword* said, and in departing he started a general movement throughout the Wayfarer.

Caranga did not answer; swearing under his breath, he had squatted to examine the supine messenger. He heard his daughter's awed voice.

"Has all the universe gone mad? Arond should not have died and did, on the instant. That one's wound should have been instantly fatal. For that matter—father? Why did he bleed so little?"

Caranga ended his examination and straightened. "Did you note this man when he entered—how he walked?"

"Only as he approached me. He had an odd limp. His upper body seemed to—to slip from side to side."

"Ah yes. So I'd expect—his spine is broken. *Was* broken. To answer your questions: if the universe has not gone mad, this inn has. I for one will no longer be a patron. Your, ah, message-bearer's wound was *not* fatal, and he bled so little because . . . this man has been dead for several hours." Caranga watched her face closely. She took what he said; he had raised her well to join the family business, and she was strong, for all that she'd been born a duke's bastard and left to die. "Now, daughter, if you will take my advice for once: burn that scroll, unopened. Whatever this evil affair is, we're best out of it. And here. The Wayfarer's gone as bad as the Smiling Skull we used to frequent—till you burned it."

The roast beef she had praised was a cold heavy lump in Tiana's stomach. Although the night was cool and three doors hung open, she was sweating and her mouth was dry,

Tiana was vain of her courage, far too vain ever to make conscious admission of fear. Her voice emerged angry.

"I'm not about to hoist the surrender flag. We've won. There's an explanation, somewhere."

"In the mind of a sorcerer or demon!" Caranga gestured sweepingly to show her an empty tavern. "Who's to see the flag of surrender? These flea-bitten curs have run away with their tails between their legs. White men were never cut out to be pirates—they know it's ill to see what we've seen and they flee lest the dark powers ensnare them. I've no curiosity about that scroll."

Tiana said, "Dung!" And then, "By the mud on the back of the Turtle that bears the world . . ."

Then her voice and face softened. "Dear father. As usual you are doubtless right . . . but do tell me this: were you alone, which would be stronger, your prudence or your curiosity?"

"The dead do not walk for friendly purpose, Tiana!"

"No, and you didn't answer me either, old fearless."

"Oh all right, open the Susha-blasted thing and *then* we'll burn it!"

The scroll was sealed with wax and before breaking the seal she examined it. Some figure had been impressed on the wax, but the impression was poor and not recognizable. She broke the seal and unrolled the scroll. It was completely blank.

CHAPTER TWO

"By the Great Cow's Cud," Tiana swore, "what madness is this?"

Caranga started to reply, but his ears pricked and he stood silent. His hands made a rapid set of signs. Tiana nodded. They continued to talk but neither paid attention to what was said.

The Wayfarer Tavern's only doorless wall housed a large open fireplace. Since no fire had been laid tonight, the tavern was lit only by three candles on tables about the room. Both Tiana and Caranga stood facing the fireplace and neither seemed to glance back or to the side. While she spoke banalities, Tiana rerolled the blank scroll and placed it in a pocket of her cloak.

The room behind them was silently filling with King's Own Guardsmen. Oddly they were not in the normal Guard uniform tonight; they were barefoot. Helmets and short swords were standard issue but instead of steel body armor, each man wore hard leather. The guardsmen were equipped for stealth, and their captain was well pleased with the surprise they were achieving. Tall, proud of bearing and countenance, Captain Despan watched as his men entered. Now he had twenty inside the tavern, grouped about the three doors, and a like number outside. That female pirate had a reputation for being slippery but Despan was confident she would not escape his grasp. Now his men were in perfect position. Captain Despan, from the northern province, called out in the nasal accent peculiar to that region.

"Captain Tiana, in the name of the King I arrest you on charge of treason and witchcraft. Surrender or be instantly slain."

Despan should have realized that in a pirate tavern,

16

lights were readily extinguished. Caranga kicked one table, sending it flying into the soldiers' faces while extinguishing the candle it bore. Tiana's rapier swept with a *wheep* and the other two candles died. The darkness was sudden and total.

"Quick, father," Tiana called, "up the secret ladder in the fireplace."

Caranga had moved so that he was not far from the captain. In a reasonably good imitation of Despan's nasal voice, he shouted, "Quick men, after them! They're escaping up the chimney."

The captain tried to countermand this false order but as soon as he opened his mouth, Caranga's sledgehammer fist slammed into it. Most of the King's Own were jamming themselves up the chimney. Though it did not contain a secret ladder, it did contain a great deal of soot.

The pirates hied themselves to the back door where Caranga grabbed a short guardsman. "Here," he called, "I've got her. Help me hold her."

He then threw his victim into the arms of the soldiers who guarded the alley. While the alley guards industriously beat one of their fellows, Caranga and Tiana slipped into the alley and ran. Tiana's black cloak made her no less a nearly invisible shadow than Caranga. Nevertheless, behind them came the roar of pursuit. Tiana took the lead and dashed down a side stret. After they had run a few blocks, she turned a corner and stopped. Gesturing to Caranga for silence she peered around the corner, back the way they had come. The guardsmen came racing pell mell down the street—and were abruptly reduced to a howling mass, hopping from one foot to the other, seemingly unable to stand on either. They gave forth an intense chorus of profanity.

Caranga whispered, "What happened to them?"

"They were barefoot. Gormansot the fruit merchant is having a little war with the street urchins. The boys steal his fruit, so he retaliated by spreading these about." Tiana held up a small object with four short prongs. No matter how it fell, one of its projections would be pointed upward. "He thought these jacks would not bother adult customers wearing boots, but would be rather hard on barefoot small boys."

"They did rather well on barefoot King's Own Guardsmen too," Caranga murmured.

"What makes soldiers such lackwits?"

"Maybe they put something in their food so they'll obey orders better."

"You think? Well—best we gather our crew and leave Reme behind us. Where did you leave them?"

"In Zolgis's House of Heavenly Pleasure. Come along."

Zolgis's House was the scene of a recent battle. Blood gleamed in the gutters and the unconscious bodies of sailors were stacked in heaps like cordwood. Tiana saw no dead and none of her crew. Zolgis's girls were running around like a decapitated flock of chickens while acid black smoke poured from the windows. Tiana spotted plump Zolgis and grabbed her. The woman was highly agitated but the sight of a large gold coin in Tiana's hand calmed her.

"I want to know what happened here."

"It was awful! The monsters! How dare they do this to an honest business woman?"

Tiana continued to display the gold coin in her left hand —and now she held her shining dagger in her right. "Just tell me what happened."

"It seemed chilly tonight, so I built a fire. The monsters must have climbed on the roof. As soon as my fire was burning well, they dropped a great length of oily rope down the chimney, then stopped it up. We couldn't breathe or see in that terrible smoke. They had nailed shut all the doors save one, and that one they'd blocked so that the men must stoop to leave. They were clubbed down as they emerged."

"Where are my men, Zolgis?"

"They loaded your crew into wagons and drove off with them. They must be in prison by now, Captain."

Tiana glanced at Caranga. "You mean the King's Own did this, Zolgis?"

"A squad of about twenty of them."

"By all the mud on the Great Turtle's back! Our crew numbers eighty good fighting men, as well as a host of other sea reavers, all in your house! You're telling us that a handful of men treated them like a sweet herd of penned cattle?"

"Yes, father, it would appear that not all the guardsmen are fools." Tiana tossed the coin to Zolgis, who hastened away. "Now, father, we have a problem."

"Truly. To storm the prison and free our crew, we'd need at least two thousand well-armed men. There might be half that many sharks in port, but they're drunk and most of the scurvy dogs wouldn't fight to save their own mothers anyhow."

"This whole thing makes very little sense. The Guard acts on orders from either King Hower or the Duke of Reme. The king is a harmless cipher—why should Duke Holonbad suddenly attack us? His share of our plunder helped make him wealthy."

The black pirate considered, then slowly replied. "The duke is a greedy man, Tiana. I see only one possibility: for some reason he now fears us. I adopted you many years ago but your natural father was Sonderman, Duke of Reme before Holonbad. Perhaps there's been some change in the law and you could now inherit . . ."

"No, father; once a bastard, always a bastard. Besides, why did the Guard take our men alive? It would have been less work to kill them. Too, why didn't the duke use treachery? If he had simply summoned us to his castle, we'd have walked into the trap."

" 'Tis a night of puzzles. No doubt the duke would explain it, if we asked him politely, while holding a knife to his sweet throat. Daughter, you grew up in the castle. Seems to me you once said there were secret passages the duke did not know about."

"Yes! Let's just visit my lord Holonbad."

Although the city was filled with Guardsmen searching for Tiana and Caranga, they arrived without incident at the outskirts of the castle. It gloomed down on them from atop a rolling hill. A corner of the hill had once been subject to erosion and a stone retaining wall erected long ago.

Tiana pointed to the wall. "My thrice great-grandfather planned that if the castle were stormed and taken he could escape via a tunnel. The exit is a hidden door right here."

"Does it open from the outside or do we have to force it?"

"My twice great-grandmother liked to sneak out at night, so the door opens from both sides. The release is hidden in a small hole in the wall."

"I'm surprised no one found that in all these years."

"The wall's full of holes and vipers use them for lairs. If memory serves, the release is in here." Tiana thrust her rapier several times into the hole. "There doesn't seem to be a snake in residence," she said, and started to put her unprotected hand into the hole.

Caranga stayed her. "Best you let me do this."

"No, the hole is small and your arm is too thick."

While Caranga looked nervous and disapproving, his foster daughter's bare right arm slipped into the hole. Slowly it went deeper and deeper. Suddenly her face convulsed with terror and Tiana whipped forth her arm.

Caranga saw what she held, and his face went blank in horror. "A death adder. Where did it bite you?"

Tiana sat down and laughed heartily. "Look again, father. It's not a live adder, only the long-dead remains. Now I remember. When I was nine, I killed this snake and put it in the release hole as a joke, to scare my brother Bealost."

Tiana put her hand back into the hole. With a snapping sound, a section of the wall shifted slightly. Caranga placed his shoulder to it and with a groan of rusty hinges the door opened. After lighting a candle filched from Zolgis's, they hastened along the tunnel and thence through a maze of narrow passageways. Tiana's memory and sense of direction soon led them to a peephole. She peered through it—into the duke's bedroom.

Plump Duke Holonbad was sitting up in bed, talking with a tall blond man. The latter wore shining torso armor, gorget, and no helmet. He was armed with a light straight sword. Though he was pale, as if he had recently lost blood, his movements had a graceful easy flow about them. Tiana heard Holonbad call him Kathis, and knew she was looking at a dangerous opponent, combining speed and perfect coordination. She let Caranga replace her at the peephole.

He soon whispered, "This is the best chance we are likely to get. It will take speed to keep the duke from pulling the alarm bell, so that is your task. I should be able to take the soldier by surprise—the door opens behind him."

"It might be wise not to kill him."

"Aye. Likely the dog's reporting how he clubbed our crew like cattle. When we open the door, he'll turn. While he's at it, I'll knock his sweet head in with the flat of my cutlass. We'll see how he likes his own medicine."

They held no hope that the secret door could be opened silently. Caranga kicked it in with an awful crash and the adventurers leapt into the duke's bedchamber. Caranga rushed at the warrior Kathis—who did not turn. Instead he stepped rapidly back and to the right, while swinging his left elbow backward. Caranga's cutlass struck the other's armored shoulder at the same time that the point of Kathis's elbow slammed into the pirate's unprotected stomach. The warrior whirled, driving his mailed fist into Caranga's face. The pirate shot backwards, smashed an ornamental chair, and lay motionless.

Tiana saw it happen; she was halfway across the room, and the jowly Holonbad was close to the alarm bell rope. Faced with the need to fight on two fronts, she acted rapidly. Her dagger leaped into her hand and flew at the duke. It pierced an untenanted fold of his robe and pinned it to the wall. She now had a moment or two to kill the warrior. Now that they faced each other's shining steel, Tiana saw Kathis's face for the first time. The warrior's were a calm handsome set of regular features, clean-shaven—and bright green eyes. The eyes were cruel but without conscious evil and now they burned with a lust to kill.

Tiana's attack was rapid and furious. His armor was hardly perfect protection. There were plenty of places her strong slender rapier could pierce and take life. Kathis's blade, however, was a perfect defense. Her every thrust was stopped by a smooth easy parry. His sword was a shimmering wall of steel that she could not penetrate. He was not quite as quick as the pirate; no one was. Yet his every motion possessed a perfect unhurried accuracy. He was poetry in motion, speed without haste.

Tiana's peripheral vision told her the duke was free and had sounded the alarm. It did not matter, for now her antagonist was taking the offensive. Kathis had taken her measure, and his attack was as calm and smooth as his defense. Desperately she parried the thrusts of a sword that sought her life. With each exchange, she was driven back and off balance. Each thrust she deflected or avoided by a slender and decreasing margin. Abruptly she realized that her opponent was playing with her: Despite her speed he could kill her at any time, but was prolonging the agony. Killing was a sport this man savored.

A door burst open and archers boiled into the chamber.

"Tiana!" Duke Holonbad called. "Lower your point and surrender or my archers will feather you."

Tiana was willing. Kathis was not. He gave her no opportunity to surrender. Instead he pressed for the kill. It required all of her fading reserves of speed and strength to stop him. Before the deadly efficiency of the warrior's attack, her defenses were rapidly crumbling.

"Last chance, Tiana," shouted the duke. "Archers: pull and aim!"

She threw her rapier into the warrior's face. Though he easily deflected it with his sword, she had gained a chance to leap beyond his reach. He raised his sword and started toward her. The green eyes were ugly.

"Kathis!" the duke snapped, loudly. *"Stop!"*

The soldier's eyes turned toward his lord and they blazed with an almost tangible green fire. Holonbad gasped as this psychic force hit him. One of the archers panicked and his string twanged. The bolt struck to glance harmlessly off Kathis's chest plate, but it broke the spell. He lowered his sword and turned his eyes from the duke. Reassured of his command of the situation, Holonbad straightened to stand in manner ducal.

"Kathis: you're the best fighting man in Reme, but unless you learn to take orders, I'll have you drawn and quartered." Turning to his servants, the duke continued, "Chain these pirates and bring them to my council chamber at once. I'll hold court and pass sentence on them tonight."

The council chamber was a large room, decorated lavishly in poor taste. The duke, in a fine brocaded chamber-robe, looked down on Tiana and Caranga from a high throne chair. "Because I am a just and merciful lord, I am giving you two a completely fair and impartial trial. I shall act as prosecutor and fair and impartial judge. I have appointed as your advocate my trusted advisor, Illdabar. Thus you shall have the best possible defense, although you clearly deserve to be executed out of hand."

Caranga's voice rumbled from his big chest: "May we know the charges against us?"

"High treason and witchcraft."

"What specific acts did we commit and what is the evidence?"

"There is no need to delay these proceedings with those details, pirate. Your advocate has already been informed." The duke turned toward his advisor. "Illdabar, what defense can you offer on their behalf?"

The advisor bowed. "Your Grace, their crimes are such that no defense or well-founded plea for mercy may be offered."

"I see," purred Holonbad. "Before I sentence you to

death by slow torture, do you wish to say anything?" Holonbad stroked his overly pointed beard.

Tiana ended her silence. "No, we have nothing to say."

"Nothing?" Holonbad repeated, clearly surprised.

"No, not a thing." Tiana stood tall and clear-eyed. Caranga glanced frowning at her.

"But surely you can find *something* to say," the duke said, practically pleading.

"Yes, but I don't need to say anything."

"Explain yourself, girl."

"Look about you at all the wealth displayed in this room," Tiana said coolly. "I suppose you decorated it yourself. I can tell because the room is done in such extremely bad taste. A council room should give the impression of grace and wisdom, rather than make you look the greedy pig you are. Still, that's beside the point. The point is that we pirates stole most of this wealth for you. I personally . . . *acquired* the ermine robe you're wearing, those cloth-of-gold-bordered drapes, and these silk rugs. The pirates of Reme are a river of gold flowing into your pockets and you would never harm us."

"Then why," thundered the duke, "do you suppose you're here?"

"Obviously you have some dangerous errand you want us to run. This trial is just a charade you staged to gull us into working for short pay."

The duke sighed. "I pass over your impertinence, for there is a slight element of truth in what you say. There *is* a service by which you may earn my gracious pardon. I shall hold your foster father hostage till you've completed your mission."

Now Tiana was positive the duke was bluffing; that he was in fact bargaining from a position of extreme weakness. She decided to push him. "My father and I work for gold, not threats. If you harm him, I'll take vengeance, full and bloody. I love him far too much to pay ransom."

My lord Holonbad's face showed his discomfort. "That makes no sense. Paying ransom is an act of love."

"It's an act of folly. The willingness to pay ransom is what incites kidnapping in the first place. Surely even such a lackwit as you can see that if I paid you not to harm my father, his life would forever be in danger from every greedy knave we meet."

A section of the magnificent gold drapes parted and a

slender man stepped forth. Tiana gasped and bowed before Hower, King of Ilan.

The king spoke in a mixture of anger and despair. "My orders, Holonbad, were that you should obtain *Captain* Tiana's cooperation. Instead you have aroused her hatred."

The duke groaned. "Your Majesty, as I told you before, there is no problem getting this girl to help. The only difficulty is that she is certain to demand an excessive payment."

"I'm no slave," blazed Tiana. "Or girl either. Why do you think I'll be eager to do your bidding?"

"My dear," pleaded the king, "we are prepared to reward you. In addition to your share of the treasure, I'll elevate you to the minor nobility, in spite of the . . . unfortunate circumstances of your birth. You can be Lady Tiana."

"Thank you, King, but I'd rather be a rich bastard. What's the treasure?"

"The jewels of the wizard Ullatara. His collection included the pearls called the Tears of the Gods, a set of matched rubies known as the Blood of Astorloth, the emerald Sky Island, the Crown of Aldavar, the diamonds named The Eyes of Sarsis, the—"

"King Hower," Tiana interrupted, "any one of these would be a king's ransom, but they've been lost for ages."

The duke snorted. "You are behind the times, girl—uh, Captain. The jewels were found and lost anew this past month. Moreover, prices have gone up. Together the entire collection failed to ransom a single princess. Come, sit down and I'll tell the story from the beginning."

The lord Duke Holonbad rose and led the way to the back of the chamber where there was a number of comfortable chairs. He turned to a servant. "Bring wine and—"

Holonbad stopped. He was going to order the chains taken off the guests. Instead, the so-called Pirate Queen had produced a pick from somewhere and opened her manacles. Caranga had apparently found a weak link in his own manacle chain, for with sudden violence he pulled it asunder.

The king only sighed. "Dismiss these guards and others. This must be heard and held in strictest secrecy."

The duke obeyed while trying to maintain a calm exterior. Inwardly he was atremble. Things were going badly. He had incurred King Hower's displeasure, no light matter. Worse, he had begun this bargaining with threats, and must now finish it unarmed and unguarded, facing a huge and ferocious-looking black pirate whose bare hands were obviously deadly weapons. Holonbad's distraction was such that he failed to notice the white cat that had entered the room soundless as mist. It sat quietly under a table, watching attentively. And listening.

CHAPTER THREE

The duke started to speak but King Hower raised his hand.
"This is my disaster and I shall tell it."

His thin white hair trembling, he began.

It all started at my daughter's birthday party. Princess
Jiltha loves puppet shows and I had arranged a very
elaborate show, a complex play with dozens of characters.
Since I had four skilled puppeteers, eight characters could
be moving on stage at any one time. The puppets were
extremely lifelike in appearance and natural in their mo-
tions. The play concerned a battle between a brave warrior
and an evil wizard. I started to protest when I saw that
the wizard was obviously patterned after *Pyre*. It is ill to
mock that great and dread one, but I was ashamed to show
fear before my daughter and her guests and Pyre is far to
the north in his Keep called Ice. What harm could our puppet play do? At the climax of the play the warrior rescues
the princess and beheads the wizard. There is a scene of
dancing and rejoicing, involving eight puppets. Nevertheless a ninth puppet moved; the wizard rose and put his
wooden head back on his shoulders. While I was thinking
that a clever trick to frighten us, the puppet took up a
sword and cut its own strings.

Freed of any control, the "puppet" walked off the stage
and stood before me. Its face was still carved wood, but the
eyes were alive. Tiny black dots, gleaming with anticipation,
like a snake which has trapped a bird.

"*Greetings, King Hower,*" said the puppet, "*I am your
friend, Pyre.*"

"How can we be friends?" I stammered. "We have never
met."

"*We have common enemies,*" replied the puppet. "*What
other kind of friendship is there?*"

26

My terror—uh, nervousness overcame me and I shouted, "Begone, demon! I want no part of your black intrigues."

The puppet moved its sword so that the point rested on my bare hand. I saw that the tiny blade was smeared with a green substance, poison.

It said, "Lord King, you shall be a useful ally or a dead one. Now hear my warning. In Naroka to the east dwells the wizard Ekron, a subtle man of dark learning and darker nature. Here in Reme dwells the wizard Lamarred, a monster vulnerable to no mortal weapon. Both are my enemies. Now they have formed an alliance, each to give the other certain things. It is a true wizard's bargain; dark unnatural acts in exchange for equally evil deeds. To keep his half of the bargain Lamarred will need your cooperation. He knows you will not help willingly and will seek to enslave you. Guard yourself and your young daughter, King. When your barber trims your beard, have him burn the hair at once. Let everything which has been part of your body be destroyed with fire. Take the same precautions for the Princess Jiltha. Both of you must stay in the palace at all times. Let the sacred lamps of Theba burn brightly day and night throughout the palace. Destroy every mirror in the palace. Search every visitor. If any one carries a mirror, slay him, wrap the mirror in black cloth and have your sailors sink it in the deepest part of the ocean. Do these things and perhaps you shall save yourself and your daughter from harm."

["All this the *puppet* said," Tiana commented.

"Yes," King Hower said, and continued his story.]

The puppet turned and started to walk away. I had to know more so I grabbed it to shout angry, frightened questions at it—and I found myself holding a piece of wood. People were staring at me. No one had seen anything out of the ordinary, save that their king had seized a puppet and shouted at it.

That afternoon I ordered all the precautions the puppet described. From then on, the palace lived in a state of siege against a danger of which I alone knew. Many of my most loyal subjects thought me mad. Perhaps I was. I have hosts of fighting men at my command but I lived in fear of a single man, not daring to order an attack on him. I did use my spies. The King's Ears are an efficient service, but they could learn little about Lamarred, and what they learned made no sense. Lamarred conducted all his business in the Inn of the Smiling Skull. He was never seen elsewhere in Reme, nor was he seen to enter or leave that inn. Yet most of the time he was not to be found inside the inn. He appeared and disappeared there without trace.

Concerning the inn, again little could be learned. The food was excellent, yet few dined there, because the inn's patrons often died, suddenly without apparent cause. I lost two of my best men that way. There was little that could be done save to keep a close watch outside the place.

Six weeks ago, Tiana, you were observed entering the inn late at night. Several sailors followed you inside, carrying a coffin. They left empty handed. Voices were heard coming from within, then the crash of breaking glass and fire. The inn's outer walls are solid stone, but a man, or something man-shaped, smashed through the wall and ran down the street toward the ocean. This figure was on fire and in agony. You were seen running after the burning man. You harassed and mocked him until he was completely consumed by the fire. My spies reported that the Inn of the Smiling Skull was burned to the ground, and that you had slain the wizard Lamarred—and departed on your ship before they could question you.

That day I was drunk with relief. In my gratitude I would have given you anything. Jiltha asked permission to go shopping. At last seeing no danger, I allowed it. She left with a normal complement of guards. My daughter has not been seen since. The guards were found dead, most by sword and arrow. But three bore no wounds, though their faces were contorted in terror.

Thus my day of joy ended as the day of disaster. I cursed myself for my folly. In hindsight it was very obvious I should fear both wizards, but Ekron had seemed remote and no direct danger. Now I was trapped and must give this evil being whatever it was he so coveted.

I spent the next week in grief and mourning. Were my daughter held by men of any western nation, I should not have despaired so. But the men of Naroka are not as our folk. They claim to be the most civilized people of the world, and if civilization means subtle cruelty it is true. They do not worship the gods of the West, nor do they swear the same oaths. They do not believe the world was created by the ruminations of the great Cow, hence they do not swear by the Cud! Neither do they believe the world rests on the back of the Great Turtle, so they swear not by the Back! Instead they hold that the world was created and is sustained by the spinning of a great Spider, and make their oaths accordingly. In my youth, before I was king, I visited Naroka's capital, Shamash. In its evil way it is a beautiful city. The buildings are complex, elaborate, ornamented with exquisite workmanship. Yet still—the city is built without regard for public safety or convenience. The streets are a maze. Their order is a false one that one may more easily become lost. Side streets and alleys often end in hundred-foot drops, with no rail or warning sign. The main streets are decorated with lovely flowering trees. There is nothing to hinder one from reaching up and picking the lush fruit these trees bear. The fruit is poisonous! Many of the buildings are decorated with sharp projections on which running children may impale themselves. They do! Indeed it is a popular game among the children to trick their comrades into such death. The Narokans in word and deed worship the Spider, who slays by cunning and deceit.

These people, subtle beyond western measure, held my daughter. I could do nothing but await their demands.

A Narokan warship sailed into Reme harbor and discharged a single passenger. He demanded immediate audience which I granted. The man was Thetoora, acolyte of Ekron. He gave me the ruby turtle ring my daughter always wore—my gift on her thirteenth birthday. My anger hid my fear. "Dog!" I roared at him; "I should hang you and declare war on Naroka!"

"True," he replied, with maddening coolness, "but if you were the sort of king to do that, we would not have kidnapped your daughter in the first place."

"Be warned, the mighty *Pyre* is my friend and ally."

"Good, simple, King Hower! Pyre is a safe enemy and a dangerous friend. Did he not warn you concerning the bargain between my master and Lamarred?"

"Yes. That proves his friendship."

"Pirates stole those things my master sent to Lamarred. Thus was the bargain made void. You were in no danger from Lamarred, which Pyre did not deign to tell you."

I had neither hope nor strength and the man before me could read my face as though all my thoughts were written in large print thereon. Pretense was useless.

"What do you want of me?"

"Only a small favor . . . a trifle for such a lovely princess as Jiltha."

"Stop torturing me! Whatever you ask you shall have, but name the price."

"All my master requires is two holes in the ground."

"You have mocked me enough! I am a king, and I think your master would still bargain with me if I sent you home minus an ear or two!"

"Perhaps. But you misunderstand, King Hower. All Ekron requires is that you provide laborers to dig two large holes. And, of course, permission to remove what shall be found there."

"Ah, the ramson is a buried treasure?"

"True, but the cost to you is only two holes in the ground."

"Where?"

"At places I shall point out in the Holy Groves of Syrodan."

"But to disturb the trees of Syrodan is blasphemy; an act forbidden."

"If Your Highness doesn't believe his daughter is worth a little blasphemy, there are other buyers. I believe the King of Thesia expressed an interest in adding her to his harem despite her youth."

I knew I was becoming part of something monstrous—and that I had no choice. I agreed. The acolyte designated two sites for excavation. I paid scant attention to the digging, for I had neglected the affairs of the kingdom and devoting myself to this work eased my worries slightly. I was at the digging site when the first temple was found, some forty feet beneath the earth. The workman who came up to report it told me that it was a small shrine. Its only carving or decoration was on the brazen door. The door depicted the world as a small green sphere. A great snake poised, jaws open wide, about to swallow that sphere. The workman had come to tell us these things while his comrades freed the door and opened it—and as he spoke, ghastly screams rose from the pit. I ran to its edge and stared down. It was high noon, and that pit was filled with blackness! The screams soon stopped.

Thetoora only smiled. "I see the digging goes well." He looked at the horror on my face. "Perhaps I forgot to mention it. The treasure is guarded. No matter; there are plenty of workmen left to continue the other excavation."

He walked to the side of the pit and started to descend. "If Your Highness or any of the King's Own wishes to come down with me, please feel free. Of course, I shall come back up alone."

When that mocking jackal was gone, I trembled with fear. If he did not return, how could I recover my daughter? My spies confirmed her presence in the labyrinth city, Shamash. She was alive, unharmed—and well guarded. I had no hope of a rescue by force.

The acolyte returned after a very long hour. He carried a heavy chest as proudly as a young man carries his bride. "Behold!" He put down the chest and opened it. The display was crystal fire. I have seen the crown jewels of many wealthy lands, but compared to this treasure, all I had seen before was a handful of broken glass. Thetoora laughed at me.

"These are not baubles to ornament foolish women, O King. They are means of power. Each is useful in one spell or another, and this"—he held up a piece of steel, shaped like an egg and as large as a man's head—"this contains the Left Eye of Sarsis. When my master has both Eyes, he shall crush Pyre and all who oppose us."

"But it's a plain piece of steel without joint or seam," I protested. "How can you open it?"

"My master will attend to that detail. Take the treasure chest back to Reme and guard it well. I shall attend to the second excavation."

I did as I was . . . ordered, though it is bitter for a king to take orders from another man's servant. To a king the greatest achievement is accurate foresight and this time I saw the disaster coming. When he returned from the first pit, Thetoora had been joyful, proud, like a warrior who has fought and easily won his first battle. Before he descended into the pit, he had insulted me. Why? Probably to salve his own fears. Perhaps he was inexperienced in these matters, and now was grown overconfident with too easy a victory. Such men often die in their second battle. I doubled the guard at the second excavation and sent my best soldier to command it: Kathis.

As soon as the second temple was found, the laborers fled although they were receiving triple pay. I had to offer pardons to the scum in my prisons to obtain men willing to finish the digging. They cleared the way around an unmarked silver door, which they were most careful not to open. I cannot reconstruct the disaster accurately. All the survivors agree that Thetoora descended into the pit and opened the silver door. After that some claim that a great snake came forth and swallowed men like field mice. Others swear the sky was blackened and arctic winds froze them in the middle of summer. The only certainty is that we found many dead bodies. Some had fallen by their own hand, others at the hands of their fellows. Despite the slaughter, there was little spilled blood on the ground. Kathis was not found. Of Thetoora, little was found; some burned bits of clothing, a melted blob of gold which might once have been his ring, and his shoes with his feet still in them. Beside the pit we discovered a second chest, filled like the first with fabulous jewels. But it did not contain a steel egg. There were fragments of steel on the ground beside the chest. The egg was shattered and the Right Eye of Sarsis was gone.

I had lost half my poor daughter's ransom! Ah, that day was a waking nightmare. I saw the things Ekron might do to my helpless Jiltha in his rage; an endless series of visions of horror. That night my courage returned and I resolved to play the cards fate had dealt me. I took up my quill and wrote the message myself.

Ekron, Arch Fiend

I, Hower, King of Ilan, hold your evil life in my hand. Know you that Pyre has stolen the Right Eye of Sarsis. Should he gain the Left Eye, he shall have power to crush you like a worm beneath his feet. You may buy the Left Eye and your life from me. The price is the safe return of my daughter. Give no thought to treachery for my spies are everywhere and your every act is known to me. I have gold as the sunshine and it buys every secret of men. If you would live, take my daughter, at once, from the Tower of Vargan where you have prisoned her and place her on board the large fishing vessel which is now in Shamash harbor. You may send a few soldiers and a trusted acolyte with her, but you must stay behind. Let no other vessel leave the harbor today or three days hereafter. The fishing vessel is to sail to a point fifty leagues due east of the Isle of Red

Stone and there drop anchor. My ship will meet it and trade the Left Eye for the Princess.

Obey my conditions and you shall have the Left Eye and your life. Disobey and die.

Hower, King of Ilan

Next morning two ships sailed forth. One carried my letter, the other the steel egg. They were scarcely out of sight when word came that Kathis had been found, weak as a kitten and so pale I doubt he had a cup of blood in his veins. He was not able to give a coherent account of the disaster. Thus there is no knowing whether it was Pyre or another who took the Right Eye.

When the first ship returned, her captain reported that Ekron read my words and sweated greatly though it was a cool day. He was in haste to obey my instructions.

The second ship did not return. Neither did the fishing vessel which carried my daughter. It is as if the ocean has swallowed her, the two ships and the treasure.

King Hower finished his narrative and sat staring at the floor. Sad eyed, he looked up at Tiana.

"My daugher is lost at sea and lost in a black maze of witchcraft. There are many I could order or beg to hunt her, but I fear they would die to no purpose. You, Tiana, are both a wizard-slayer and a sea warrior. You are my only hope."

CHAPTER FOUR

Moved by the king's plea, Tiana said, "Your Majesty, I am a loyal subject and will gladly do what I can. I ask only fair payment."

Relief showed strongly in his face. "If you succeed, the nation will owe you a debt beyond recompense. As to that payment. First there are the Jewels of Ullatara. Whoever has my daughter must also have them. I propose that these should be yours free and clear without the usual shares to the harbor master, the Duke and the Throne. Further, such operating capital, supplies, men and aught else you need, is yours for the asking. Bearing in mind that my treasury is depleted, do you require more than this?"

"Yes, much more. I require justice."

The king frowned before her level gaze. "I don't understand."

Duke Holonbad remained silent while his face showed his discomfort.

"While it is true that pirate captains are safe in Reme, the common seamen do badly. There's a gang of grubs who rob and murder them. The King's Own Guard does nothing because the grubs divide the loot with milord Duke. When I return with Princess Jiltha, I want to see the heads of the entire gang decorating posts in the harbor. Further, before I leave I shall prepare a list; the name of every tavern and innkeeper who robs sailors with drugged wine or crooked gambling games. I want these dogs flogged and banished and their businesses given to honest men."

The duke opened his mouth to protest but under the king's angry eyes he wilted. Hower said, "These things shall be done. This is no payment, but my clear duty as sovereign."

Holonbad still sat silent and motionless. Though his share

of the dishonest gambling was a large part of his income, in the king's present mood it would cost the duke his head to offer a protest. There was, however, one thing he could say. It would not recover any of his losses but it would hurt Tiana.

"Gracious Majesty, if you are to trust this woman with the princess, you must have some guarantee. I suggest Caranga remain as our guest."

Tiana had no illusions as to her father's well-being as the duke's prisoner. Fear tinged her voice. "That's absurd. My lord King can trust me without guarantees because I'm a perfectly moral person."

The duke snorted. "You're a pirate. You make your living by robbery and murder."

"Yes, but I only rob and murder people I don't like."

When the laughter subsided, Caranga said, "It is true that my daughter is loyal. Forcing me to stay behind would be like locking up half the army to make the other half fight better. The best hope *your* daughter has is to send the strongest possible rescue force, us. And, since Your Highness thinks well of him, Kathis. We would command *Vixen* and her crew, while he could command a picked company of soldiers."

"That," the duke snarled, "is hardly a proper guarantee."

"It's a guarantee adequate to the trust," Caranga said calmly. "Your Highness is not trusting us with his daughter, or her ransom, or even the secret of her location. In truth my lord King has very little with which he can trust us. Now that's the important question. Have your sweet spies found no clue?"

Hower looked unhappy. "We were hoping you could tell us."

"I fail to understand Your Highness."

"Captain Despan reported that when he tried to ah, fetch you two in the Wayfarer Tavern, he found two dead bodies inside and a third in the alley. The last body was that of a cutpurse whose throat had been cut. Yet there was no blood. That news disturbed me—men died in that manner in the disaster of the second excavation! One of the bodies inside the tavern was a beggar, while the other was one of my spies. He returned to Reme three days ago, saying he had found a clue which led here. Before he died, did he say anything to you; give you anything?"

Tiana made an unpleasant face. "Not before, but after."

"*What?*"

"It's true. He walked into the tavern and gave me what he said was some sort of map. At that time he had been dead several hours."

"Theba protect us." The king made the sign for protection against evil. Then hope conquered his fear. "This map . . . it may be a clue to my daughter's whereabouts."

"I fear not, lord King." Tiana spread the scroll on a small table. "See, it's completely blank."

All this time, the cat had sat motionless, listening. Now it moved, pouncing soundlessly into an empty chair and thence to the top of a massive oaken cabinet. From this vantage point it peered down at the blank scroll.

The king's voice was hard. "The gods are cruel. First they light a beacon of hope, then when I approach they plunge me into blind darkness."

Tiana snapped her fingers. "Blind! That could be it!" She shut her eyes and ran her fingers over the map. "Yes, by the Cud, it's a blind map!"

King Hower moved closer, staring. "Explain."

"When I saw the map was blank, I thought of invisible writing, but that made no sense. People write so that others may read. Since I know no secrets to make such writing visible, why would anyone send me a letter in invisible writing? Now I know why, and I think I can make it visible."

She hurried to a fireplace in which no fire burned. Three men and a cat watched her intently. Reaching up the chimney, she drew back her hand black with soot. She rubbed the scroll carefully, slowly coating it. While they watched, white lines and writing appeared.

"Whoever drew the map was either blind or working in complete darkness," Tiana explained. "Since he could not see what he was doing, he drew with something he could feel—either white wax or soap." She finished developing the map and looked at the two noblemen. The king was extremely worried about his daughter and demanded that others share this worry; the duke would not dare mention a less important subject. Accordingly, Tiana turned, and wiped her dirty hand on Holonbad's silken, cloth-of-gold-bordered drapes. As this failed to cleanse her hand satisfactorily, she picked up the half-finished bottle of vintage wine, poured it over her hands, and meticulously wiped her fingers on the wet drape.

My lord Duke watched this gross act in silence, and with no small amount of pain marring his meaty face.

Tiana spread the map before the king. "Lord King, this appears to be the Kroll Isles. Here is the castle of Storgavar."

"The so-called King of the Kroll pirates?" Hower asked.

"Almost. As I am so-called Pirate Queen. The Krollers are far too lawless to recognize a king or any other authority. They do respect Storgavar and take his advice because he's a powerful and cunning leader. Besides, he kills anyone who disagrees with him. Ah, now this is very interesting. These markings, Your Highness, indicate the tides and currents—and, by the Cud, these markings are their lookout posts!"

"This writing at the bottom of the map—can you read it? It contains my daughter's name!" King Hower trembled with excitement.

"Father, this is Simdan, and you never taught me to read your native language."

Caranga leaned in. "That's because I read it so poorly myself. Reading is a thing I learned only after I came to civilization. Still, it may be I can make this out. Hmm . . . 'Chieftain Tiana, I send you on a—' well literally this means 'hunt for thornbush berries.' Young men of my tribe gather such berries as part of their wedding ceremony. Perhaps it means to send you on a sacred quest. 'The Kroll pirates came upon a Narokan fishing vessel and an Ilani war galley. Having attacked and overwhelmed both crews, they thus had captured the Princess Jiltha and the shining stones of Ullatara. I send you a guide to this rich plunder, but you must, 'walk naked among tigers.' That means, uh, accept danger. 'You may do as you please with the Princess Jiltha and most of the shining stones of Ullatara, but there is an egg of a steel bird. Fools say it contains an extremely valuable diamond. In truth it holds the last treasure which once gained may never be taken from a man. It holds death. You must take the egg to Sulun Tha. He may be able—' I can't read this part, daughter. It's blurred. 'Beware, the Right Eye of Sarsis is free and—' I'm sorry, the rest is illegible."

The king's face showed both relief and new concern.

"The Kroll Islands—are they vulnerable? Could the Royal Navy attack and conquer them?"

Tiana shook her head. "I'm sorry, Your Majesty, but other kings have sent their navies against the Krolls and have been driven back with heavy losses. Storgavar's castle stands at the center of a maze of islands—a well-guarded maze."

"But how," Hower demanded, his voice trembling, "can we rescue my daughter from this shark's lair?"

"Majesty," Caranga cautioned, politely raising a hand like a black glove, "we don't actually know Jiltha is there. Remember this map is merely the promise of one we've no reason to trust. 'Twas delivered by a dead messenger and those who use such means are seldom friends to mankind."

Anxiously Hower looked at Tiana.

"My father is, of course, right. Still." She paused, thinking. "If this map can be confirmed, there's a chance. Knowing the location of the lookout posts, a fast ship could sneak past and land a raiding party."

"And what," her foster father asked, "route would you use?"

The king watched in growing hope while the two pirates planned the raid. Duke Holonbad glanced about angrily. This night had been a total disaster. He had planned to make Tiana work for a small share of the treasure. Instead he was going to receive no share of the treasure and had lost a substantial part of his income. To add insult to injury, she had ruined his finest drapes. His anger needed an outlet, but there were no servants he might beat. He looked up and saw the white cat sitting atop the oak cabinet. Holonbad raised his hand to strike it for no reason save that it was there. He stopped and his eyes narrowed in suspicion. He did not allow pets in the castle. What was this pretty beast doing here? He could not help staring into those glowing green eyes. He was only vaguely aware of the brilliant diamond at the cat's throat. Slowly the diamond's white fire turned red.

The duke's eyes dulled even more than usual.

He turned and said, "My lord King, good and trusted friends, this map and the high hope it promises calls for a bottle of my special wine. I have it here." Holonbad opened the cabinet and drew forth a sealed crystal bottle of amber. Unstoppering it he said, "With all due respect to Your Majesty's wine cellar I'm sure you never before had wine of such a subtle and marvelous bouquet." The Duke of Reme filled all four goblets, raised his own, said "To success," and drank deeply.

Tiana stopped King Hower's cup at his lips. Caranga raised his glass to his lips, stuck out his tongue so that its tip touched the wine. He dropped his glass and spat repeatedly.

His voice came in a roar: "As I suspected, poison!"

The duke tried to speak but could only stammer. His face had gone pale green. He swayed unsteadily on his feet. Tiana snatched his goblet, dipped a finger in it and touched the fingertip to her tongue.

She too spat. "By the Cud! He's poisoned *himself!* Help me, father."

Caranga held the duke upright and forced his mouth open. Tiana pulled the duke's ermine robe off his shoulders and tore it to shreds. She forced a long narrow strip of fur down the duke's throat. Holonbad promptly discharged the wine and his supper onto the carpet of woven silk.

"If Your Highness will summon the servants," Tiana said coolly, "there are some things I need to save the duke."

"Unless you'd prefer not to bother," Caranga said rather hopefully.

The king did as she asked. In the excitment no one noticed that the white cat hopped on the table, inspected the map carefully, and departed.

After Tiana had, for the fourth time, forced warm water down my lord Holonbad's throat and made him return it onto the rug, she straightened to stand over him, tall and piratic and competent.

"There's no poison left in his stomach. Some has doubtless already entered his blood, but nothing can be done about that. We can but put him to bed and see whether he lives or dies."

When the servants carried off the unfortunate duke, Caranga whispered to Tiana, "Before we leave, shall I set the castle on fire?"

"Father! Why should I want to do such a terrible thing?"

"Well, you've ruined the gold-bordered drapes, the ermine robe, and the silk rugs. I thought you might want to make a clean sweep."

"Father." Her eyes danced. *"No.* Besides, the ermine

robe isn't completely ruined. There's still enough left to make a fur trim for my cloak."

The king returned from seeing the duke to bed. "What could this event mean?"

"Well, the logical explanation would be that someone poisoned a bottle of the duke's wine and we happened to be with him when he opened it. I don't believe that. Truly fine wine needs the protection of storage in a good cellar. Both my father and I were suspicious when we saw the 'special bottle' was stored in a cabinet in this chamber. That's a foolish thing to do with good vintage, and such men as the duke often keep a bottle of poisoned wine handy."

"Are you saying my lord Duke Holonbad deliberately poisoned himself in order to poison us too?"

"No, lord King, I doubt he had any idea what he was doing. What this event proves is that we've an enemy— unknown, unseen, and passing deadly. Whoever or whatever this foe is, it clearly is seeking to stop us from saving your daughter and gaining the treasure."

"What can we do?" Hower asked, his voice heavy with fear.

"It all depends on the map," Caranga said. "Until we know whether 'twas sent by friend or dire foe, I see naught we dare do."

"But my daughter . . ." Hower began, and his voice trailed away. He looked at Tiana imploringly.

In the silence Tiana felt as if the world awaited her decision.

"By the Cud," she swore, "you two have a talent for making simple things difficult. How far do you think a dead man can walk? Especially one with a broken back!"

Caranga nodded slowly. "By Susha's . . . lips, yes! Since this mysterious map-sender has to be somewhere here in Reme, we need only find him to know if his sweet map is to be trusted."

"Which we will do tonight if we have to turn the city upside down!" Tiana turned to King Hower. "Your Highness, if you would help, free my men and give Bardon—he's our second mate—whatever he needs. I want *Vixen* ready to sail with the morning tide."

Before Hower could reply, the duke's butler interrupted, "Majesty, forgive me, but I must speak to someone in authority. What shall I do about this disaster?"

King Hower replied brusquely. "Carry on as usual. Surely your master has been ill before."

"No Your Majesty, not that disaster; the kitchen disaster."

"What's happened in the kitchen?"

"The cook asked one of the maids to get him a chicken. He planned to kill it for my lord duke's breakfast. Later I was surprised to find the chicken walking down the hallway. I caught it and took it back to the kitchen. There I found the cook, sitting motionless and staring straight ahead. Nothing I could do would make him move or speak. In his hand he still held his knife, red with fresh blood. He's a neat worker. When he kills an animal, he never makes a mess. He slits the throat and catches the blood in a pan. I found the maid's body on the floor. Her throat had been cut and she had bled to death, but the pan was empty, as clean as if it had just been washed. Save for the blood on the knife, the kitchen and everything in it were clean."

Tiana stared at the servant while Hower and Caranga stared at her.

CHAPTER FIVE

The House of Seven Delights employed a unique means to attract patrons. A set of large gilded cages was suspended above the street, before the House. From these cages precariously "clad" girls called provocative taunts and promises to passers-by.

Just now they stared down at a flame-haired woman with a form as good as any of theirs, but none showed any particular interest.

"You up there," she called. "Who dangled there during the Hour of the Rat?"

They continued to stare down at her. A large silver coin gleamed enticingly in her left hand, while her right fist held a dagger. Her meaning was clear enough; useful information would gain the one, insults the other.

Misnavella decided to answer. "No one at that hour, except Irinda. And you can't see her."

"What? And why not?" The shapely redhead's green eyes flashed. What was she doing with that considerably older black man, for Theba's sake?

"Because she's entertaining an aristocrat."

"Dung."

"We can wait," the man said quietly; a burly one he was, shining as if cut from basalt. Not tall, with a bit of gray in his tightly curly black hair. He'd enough chest and arm to give pause to a bear, Misnavella thought, in her aerie. She smiled at him. He paid her no mind.

"No," the redhead snapped. "Time's fleeting, father. In we go!"

Misnavella blinked. *Father!* The only way such a man could have fathered such a woman was—well, there wasn't a way! Those two were—Misnavella blinked, and swallowed again. By the Cud of the Great Cow! Those two . . . those were the *pirates,* Caranga and his foster daughter Tiana Highrider, captain of *Vixen* and called pirate queen! She craned to see their attempt at entry.

An ex-Guardsman dealt with unruly visitors to the House of Seven Delights; at sight of the two sea-wolves he wilted even more than the breasty beauty who swung above. Rushing in and upstairs, Caranga and Tiana commenced kicking in doors with their square-toed seaman's boots. The first four employments of this profoundly rude entry interrupted only sluts with common sailors. One Tiana recognized, and she smiled and winked.

The man behind the fifth door sat straight up, belly wobbling. "I demand to know the meaning of this incredible and unconscionable impertinence!"

"Oh my good *lord,*" Tiana said, and bowed, and Caranga walked past her and knocked his lordship quite unconscious. Tiana straightened to face the cowering young woman who'd been entertaining his lordship, who obviously liked companions who appeared barely nubile. Had a fancy for his daughter, mayhap.

"Tell me, whore," Tiana snapped, "during the Hour of the Rat while you swung outside in your gilded cage of tin . . . saw you a man in a long-sea-green cloak, and him tall, thin, hawk-faced, forehead back to here, and with a gap just at his chin to separate his sideburns?"

Anger and fear even unto terror flashed across Irinda's girlish face.

"Answer Captain Tiana, you silly slut," a rumbly voice ordered her, "or by Susha's circumcision I'll shave you bald as your loins."

After a brief bout of blinking and shuddering at Caranga's words, Irinda replied. "Aye, C-C-Cap—aye, Captain T-Tie-anna, he frightened me. I saw him. He *looked* at me, and what awful eyes that one had! He—he appeared to have come from the old warehouse district —Wharf-rat Street."

Tiana nodded. The street was in truth named Wortrav, but everyone who knew anything—meaning all but the nobles of Reme—called it Wharf Rat.

"You're a good girl, Irinda, for a girl. When that old piece of dung wakes up, tell him we're agents of the king and he can check with Hower himself! As for you—once you grow up and start looking for woman's work, come see me."

Irinda stared wide-eyed, looked around the ornately appointed room, at the noble lord's discarded clothing, at her silken bedsheets; again at Tiana.

"Give up this for the bunks on a *pirate ship?*"

"Irinda," Tiana said with regal austerity, "you'll be a girl all your life. Father?"

Tiana paid the girl and the pirates departed. The old warehouse district was more than half deserted and few of the buildings had watchmen. Tiana laughed as she saw the face of the one they found.

"Allato, you old thief! What are you doing here?"

"Earning an honest living."

She laughed. "More likely you're casing the district to find something worth stealing. Have you seen a tall, slender man who walked oddly tonight?"

"No, I did not," the watchman replied, with heat.

"Allato, I've known you since I was a child. Remember when we burgled the high priest's wine cellar? You couldn't lie to me then and you can't lie to me now."

"Tiana, let the matter be. Oh, I saw him all right, and I knew he was one of the walking dead. You've been at sea and don't know the evil flowers that have growed in Reme. There's a big building at the end of this street. Black stone. I seen the dead man walk out of there. It was only the latest of a lot of unnatural events having to do with that building. It was abandoned for years, full of rats and spiders. Then two months ago it started. Late at night sounds come out of it. Screams of agony. Insane laughter. Chanting and obscene music. Strangers come and go from that building, but no native Ilani has entered and come out."

"Who has entered and not returned?"

"Two good thieves. They'd heard rumors of treasure there. They went in, one by a door, and one by a window. No more's known of them."

Tiana turned to Caranga. "It's clear we need to attack in force. Fortunately we can get the King's Own to help us. I'll stay here and watch the building, while you fetch the soldiery."

Caranga looked sharply at his foster daughter. The plan was quite reasonable, but he knew Tiana. Would she be content to wait or would she become impatient and launch some foolhardly singlehanded attack? It had always been useless to forbid Tiana to do anything. He sighed.

"Well . . . maybe I can get back before you get yourself into trouble." And he left before she could reply.

Tiana was annoyed. Caranga had spoken to her as if she were a foolish child. Of course, she'd prove him wrong. She had lots of patience. She moved silently through the shadows and found a good vantage point. From here she could sit in fair comfort and watch the front door of the mysterious building.

She did.

However, the front door just stood there. It did nothing interesting. A bored Tiana decided to circle the building. The rear door and windows she found all boarded up, but three quarters of the way around she noticed a high window. Open, radiating a faint light.

Oh well, then. Child's play! No use waiting.

And with her padded grapnel and silken rope, it was. The hook caught the high sill on her second throw. The padding stilled the sound of steel against stone. She went up the wall light as a cat.

Natural with time and most appropriate, cobwebs laced the window. She could hardly see within. Besides, it was dark. She could cut through these webs and lower herself . . . *Cobwebs?* Tiana goosefleshed. Ever had Caranga been at her to see things not as they were expected to be, but as they truly were. For that reason, she was alive. This, she realized was no ordinary web that nigh filled the window space. Each strand was thick—too thick. And the interstices were too wide.

Whatever spun this web, she thought, *planned to catch something a lot bigger than fleas!*

Watchful waiting was forgotten. This was a challenge and a problem to be solved, by the highly skilled thief Tiana was. Hmm . . . the slightest touch to this web should bring a very large spider indeed. If she was to enter, it must be fought. Fighting on its own territory was absurd. She frowned, pushing her lower lip in and out while she pondered. In this web, a human would be as a fly in a normal one. She considered. As an alarm, the web was only half clever. Regardless of size, a spider was a silent and solitary hunter. *Why, they're almost as patient as I am!*

An attack by it would bring no other spiders or human guards, surely; it would move silently and without warning to assault, immobilize, and devour.

Tiana was debating whether to summon the thing and slay it or attempt to slip in, when beneath her, within the darkened building, she noted faint movement. She saw nothing . . . stared . . . and slowly, the shifting shadow resolved into a definite shape: presumably black, and large as a hunting hound. Lots of legs. Its compound eyes seemed impossibly large topazes—cracked. They did not focus, so as to give her possible hint of the thoughts this dark thing had. If it thought.

Of course it didn't think. Not thoughts: intentions. Intentions required no *thought*, any more than the web-spinning of a creature directed by instinct.

Yet—Tiana considered. There was a big difference between planning to slay an overgrown bug, and facing this eight-legged monster! She watched it climb until it was a few feet below her. It stopped. Instinct warned it not to leave its web, she assumed, however tantalizing the prey just beyond web's edge. Human and spider stared at each other in a long, long moment of fragile truce.

She saw that its huge jaws were equipped with big fangs, which drooled a yellow-green slime. *The monster must deliver enough venom to kill an elephant,* Tiana mused cheerlessly.

Too, it did not walk on eight legs like its smaller cousins. This outsized arachnid's two forelegs, thicker and more powerful, were permanently raised for combat. Anything caught by those "arms" would never escape the envenomed jaws. It was armored too; it wore its skeleton outside the squishy body within, like plate mail.

Surely a good thrust from a blade as slim as mine will pierce that carapace, Tiana mused, but . . . *where to strike a mortal blow?* Where were its heart and lungs— did it *have* such organs? Behind those staring eyes . . . was there a brain she might pierce and destroy? She remembered once having completely beheaded a wasp, which she picked up to carry triumphantly to Caranga. It had stung her painfully, just as if it were alive. And when she tried to fling it away, the legs and feet *clung*.

Tiana not only refused to admit fear even to herself, she never remembered terror once she had whelmed its source. Now—now *it* moved, and her arm quivered with gooseflesh. That settled that.

Since this ugly huge thing frightened her, she must kill it.

A glance at her grapnel showed it firmly in place. Her rope of silk was coiled about her left hand. Using a fold of her cloak as glove, she could quickly slide to the ground without getting rope burns. That was swift retreat, after . . .

She shifted position slightly and her rapier flicked out and down. Its needle point slashed across the spider's antennae. The thing lunged up at her, and she braced and thrust: straight and true. Her rapier plunged in between the great cracked-yolk eyes. The armor snapped. The slender blade went in. Tiana held her arm steady; the beast continued coming; a foot and then two feet and then nigh the rest of her sword vanished into the creature's body. Because of the angle of spider and its stabber, the blade's tip emerged, dripping, from its lower body—and for Tiana it was let go the hilt or lose her arm.

Tiana let go and swung back, squatting with most of her body outside the window so that anyone below would have had a most fascinating view. She stared at the spider, which had stopped. Good, then. Surely such a transpiercing wound would swiftly prove fatal.

It did not. With great speed the spider lunged. Tiana dropped, barely evading the grasp of its hairy forelegs. She slid swiftly down her rope, back into the alley, while the spider gained the windowsill. A thread of pallid white dropped from its body and Tiana felt a cold, sticky touch on her right arm. A few feet from the ground, her downward slide was arrested with an abrupt jerk. It hurt. And that was not all.

Her right arm was twisted above her head—and she was being pulled steadily upward. The spider had ejected webbing, snared her, and was . . . reeling in, or something like. Did spiders do that? Tiana didn't know. Nor did she care; this one did, and was!

Now that her weight was on the spider's line, her own rope had gone slack. Desperately giving it a flip, she tugged hard. The grapnel hopped free of the sill and tried to fall on her. A great spider-leg was in the way. The beast was toppled forward to plunge past Tiana. She groaned, trying to hang onto her own rope and being pulled by webbing and—

She hit the ground hard, and rolled. The webbing that had snared her had been scraped loose. Her arm, abraded on the hard-packed earth of the alley, oozed blood. She threw herself up, whipping out her dagger, and—*where was the accursed beastie?*

It should have fallen near her. Yet it was nowhere in sight. She glanced around again, her heart pounding, and then came the slight sound and she hurled herself flat. The black monster shot through the air above her. Apparently a hastily-extruded strand of webbing had prevented its falling all the way. Now it was swinging back and forth in the alley, a pendulum of death. She had no place to go. The narrow alley ended a few feet behind her, and the old temple's rear door was barred from within.

The spider whooshed past again.

Fighting down panic, Tiana tried to think her way out of the trap. If she moved to the end of the alley, she *would* be trapped. The enemy need only drop on her. Just now, it was at the top of its arc; now it was falling toward her. . . . She ran toward it, and at the last moment dived to the ground. More pain, but she hardly noticed, hearing those venom-drooling jaws snap within a hand's breadth of her body. She was clear, already up and running. Her abraded leg tried to buckle, and held. The thump behind her was shocking, as the creature landed on the ground, six-legged, and pursued her. She heard the point of her rapier scrape the ground, still thrusting from the monster's lower body. The thing was gaining on her!

Why did the fates decide that I, with only two legs, must race a fiend that runs on six? What disadvantage does the Drood-sent thing suffer to pay for its four extra legs?

She stumbled, and had her answer: balance.

It was too late to worry whether her flash of idea was good or no. In another instant the dog-sized spider would run her down. She swerved leftward, stopped, and sprang to the right even as she whirled around. The spider's headlong rush carried it past her; it too had swerved to its left. As it scuttled by, Tiana slashed, but her dagger glanced harmlessly off an armored leg.

Stopping almost instantly a few feet beyond her, the spider started to turn.

In an act that would have looked insane to any observer, she pounced—at the beast. Before it could come around to face her, she struck again, and this time with force and accuracy. Tiana was accustomed to thrusting; she was swift and could never be so strong as many male warriors. Therefore she had long ago chosen the swift, light rapier—and now, with her dagger, she made a rapier-like thrust.

Just as a mailed knight might be stabbed in the joints of his armor, so the spider's armored leg possessed vulnerable joints. Into one of these spots her steel bit deeply. Feeling triumphant but trying to backpedal too rapidly, Tiana sprawled, and the spider was now facing her. Big multifaceted eyes gleamed. The monster lunged—and toppled over in mid-stride. Before it could regain its footing and compensate for its one useless leg, she swiveled on her backside and stabbed another leg joint. Then she *rolled*, with all her might.

A filthy pirate stared at her wounded enemy.

Though the spider struggled, it could no longer stand up. Tiana grinned. Rising, she moved about it. Calmly and carefully she destroyed the use of another leg, and then one "arm," and then, though barbs brought blood from her own arm, she daggered its other armlike leg.

The spider was helpless. Not without some difficulty, Tiana regained her rapier. Arachnid blood gushed.

Her own legs made it emphatically clear that they wanted a rest. Rather suddenly, Tiana sat. The hard earth felt fine. Her heart was pounding furiously and her lungs burned. Little shudders came and went.

In retrospect, she was surprised that she had not sooner perceived the solution. The spider walked with a gait like that of a horse's trot: the right front and rear legs moved forward along with the left center leg, while the other three remained down, and then the left front and rear legs and middle right, and so on. Since the creature was always propped on three legs even when rushing, it never had need for a sense of balance. Losing the use of a single leg proved a fatal disadvantage for a creature without balance.

Rested and rearmed, Tiana stared up to the lighted window. Now that the way into this building was clear and unguarded, she remembered her resolve to stay out of trouble. Still, there were several good reasons for entering, now that she considered the matter. If whoever sent the map was a friend, he must be prisoner inside this building. In that case when the King's Own broke in the front door, the prisoner's guards might slay him. On the other hand if the map's sender was an enemy, he might lock himself up and pretend to have been a prisoner. On balance, Tiana thought, the occasion called for some discreet spying.

Again her grapple flew. It dropped silently onto the windowsill and Tiana went up. The spider web was an advantage, now. If a human guard heard some slight noise he would not dare come to investigate. A few moments' dagger work and a path was clear for her to lower herself to the floor. She slid down.

The warehouse was a single great room. Around its dingy walls were scattered large bales and packing crates, behind one of which she now hid. A check of a few crates showed Tiana that they contained a variety of valuable merchandise. *The rumors of treasure are at least partially true,* she thought, with a pirate's interest. The front door was invisible; that portion of the room had been curtained off. The center of the floor was bare of goods. A large number of small cushions lay before a carven dais of black stone.

Tiana stared. *An altar!*

Sight of what stood behind the altar gave her the sensation of her heart's skipping a beat. A single up-reaching arm, ending in a hideous taloned hand in the act of clutching.

Drood! she thought with a shudder. *It's a cult devoted to Drood of the Thousand Arms, dread Lord of Death . . . and patron of murderers! Oh this is charming; Tiana m'dear, you are in the den of those creatures calling themselves Arms of Drood—I thought this mischief had been stamped out of the city about the time I was born!*

She had known the Arms had been more active in Reme of late. It had not occurred to her that the creatures would dare establish a shrine for their bloodthirsty rites here in the capital!

Still Tiana had yet to see the most sinister aspect of the . . . shrine. While much of the warehouse was filled with dark shadows, the blackness in one area did not result from lack of light. To the left of the altar, numerous lamps had been placed on the floor. Each burned with a cheerful bright glow. At first glance the lights appeared to be votaries arranged in a circle around some black object. Such, Tiana soon realized, was not the case. There was no object within the ring of lamps. There was simply blackness. A total blackness that admitted no light whatever. Tiana stared at the impossible and eerie.

Feeling gooseflesh, she considered. *Best to see what's behind that curtain and get out before the Arms return to their mangy temple.*

She crept silently forward to peer around one edge of the curtain. In deep darkness she could just make out motionless figures—many. Scores of them. Statues? No! She could hear their breathing and she concentrated on stilling her own. She saw that the front door did not open directly into the warehouse, but into a long entrance hallway. An ambush, she thought. A superbly designed one too! The Arms lurked in darkness outside the entrance hall. Archers' ports had been cut into the hall, which was well lighted. Shooting out of the darkness, the disciples of Drood could easily massacre Caranga and the guardsmen.

Tiana knew she must warn Caranga swiftly and—her eye caught movement to her right.

Her sword flashed and an Arm of Drood died, his warning cry a faint gurgle in his throat. It was enough; the murdering horde heard, turned and saw her.

"Dung!" Tiana fled, pursued by men who murdered as a matter of religion. An Arm swifter than his comrades overtook her just as she reached her rope. Leaving her rapier in his stomach, she threw herself up the rope. Above, the spiders' web would provide haven. She was nearly there when she saw a man throw his knife. Recognizing a true throw, Tiana dropped a few feet down her line. The knife passed overhead. But not harmlessly. It cut the rope. Tiana's weight was enough to sever it. She knew a brief sensation of falling, then splashing light-flashes of pain, and blackness.

Tiana awakened stiff and cold. Her eyes focused—and rolled in exasperation. This sort of thing had happened to her before, and was a dreadful bother. She was cold because she was naked. She was stiff because she was chained spread-eagle atop the altar of cold black stone.

By the Cud—what a cliché! These jackals are about to sacrifice me to their grisly god! This, Tiana realized, was an unusually bad situation: *If Caranga and the King's Own were to come in and find me like this, I'd never hear the end of it!*

Her chains allowed her some freedom of motion. Twisting, she could see the religious killers seated on their cushions before the altar. They looked expectant, all glittery of eye. Tiana suppressed a shudder. Whatever these evil men planned for her, it would be a spectacle they would enjoy.

The altar consisted of the black stone slab on which she was chained, and the raised platform behind it. Tiana knew that she was but one character who would perform on this stage, and turned her head to see the other. He stared down at her. A tall gaunt man, wrapped in black robes. His face was a grim skull under a thin film of skin. Eyes like glass. He smiled, sort of.

"Welcome to the temple of Drood of the Thousand Arms. I am Uldrood, child of the Lord of Darkness and his First Arm. Now that you are awake, we may begin the sacrifice. Long have I practiced my art, but never before have I had such a choice subject." Before Tiana could spit words, he turned and raised his head to the idol.

"Hear me, O Dread Lord of the Thousand Arms! Grant your blessings to your faithful worshippers. Let our knives be red with blood and our pockets full of booty. Accept this our sacrifice. In your honor I break her bones." The priest turned back to look down on the assembled devotees. "The God is pleased to accept this unworthy creature's death. It is a sign of His singular favor that in a vision, Drood told me this shapely defiler would come. Thus I prophesied to you, and thus it came to pass."

From among the Arms rose a man of medium height and powerful build. "Uldrood! I thought no prophet could be wrong all the time. Yet you have been. Your prophecy was that a troop of royal guardsmen would come through our front door. Instead, this lone woman entered through a high window!"

"Orgar," roared the priest, "sit down and stop blaspheming!"

"No. It's time for a reckoning." Orgar strode forward and bounded onto the altar, a big man whose shoulders strained his black robe. He faced his fellows. "Brothers! Do you know what has been happening to us? Do you want to know why a night-demon habits our temple?"

A general shout of approval rang in the sprawling room. Uldrood raised his hands in an attempt to command silence. To no avail. It was clear that Orgar would have his say. Tiana watched these events with interest, knowing that Orgar was walking a thin line. He must hope to displace Uldrood and assume leadership of these idiots. To do that he must destroy confidence in Uldrood's leadership—without saying that which would justify the priest in ordering his execution. For Tiana the fight for supremacy was a most welcome distraction. Her picklock was where it always was—masquerading as an eardrop. Was there enough slack in her chains to enable her to reach it?

Slowly, hoping no one would notice, she twisted, squirmed, reached for the pick. Chains clinked. . . .

"You want to know!" Orgar shouted. "I will tell you! It is a *war!* A war between dark and unknown powers. The gods alone know what the shadow dwellers struggle over, with men and kingdoms mere expendable pawns in their game! You have all heard the stories. Fools die in every back alley of the world, fighting for they know not what. Thanks to this so-called priest of ours—and his visions—we have been sucked into this unholy business!"

Tell them about it, Tiana urged mentally. *Tell them, boy!*

Now she had her pick. Her hands above her head, she worked on the lock of her right manacle.

"You remember Uldrood's first vision. Last week he said it was the will of Drood that we capture a blind old man who had just come to Reme. We brought him here, not dreaming he was really a black demon. Uldrood ordered us to slay him—and then the darkness came! There it lurks still, in the middle of our temple. A piece of Night that no light can penetrate."

Tiana's right hand was free. To free her left she must work with the pick in plain sight. It was painted a dull dark red, of course. Still . . .

Orgar ranted on. "How did Uldrood deal with this

disaster? Did he work magic to clear our temple? He did not! You remember his words, brothers: 'This blackness is but a trick to frighten you. Go into it and slay the old man.' Four good men plunged into that ensorceled dark—and how did they emerge? From time to time the demon throws out one of their bones . . . well gnawed!"

Tiana's left hand was free. She lay on a high altar with her left side toward the devotees, who stared at Orgar the fiery. Keeping her left arm above her head, she allowed the unlocked manacle to remain on her wrist. Her right hand reached down. By pulling her legs up, she could just reach the manacle on the right ankle. *Don't run dry, Orgar,* she urged mentally. *Rant on!*

Orgar did. "Uldrood's second vision brought us worse disaster," the big fellow shouted. "Despite my protests, one of the King's Ears was captured. He was laid on the altar" (Tiana froze) "and Uldrood broke his spine. The priest swore Great Drood was pleased with that death. Then why did the dead man *rise?* His broken body shifted from side to side as he lurched into the pool of blackness. *He* emerged—bearing a scroll in his left hand and a knife in the other. He slew men paralyzed in horror and walked out into the streets of Reme."

Tiana had freed her right leg. To pick the lock on her left, she must sit upright. Such an act could not even partially be concealed. She lay quietly. Perhaps a chance would come to pick the final lock; perhaps not. She must wait.

Orgar knew he had succeeded. The cultists' fear had become hatred of their priest, First Arm Uldrood. To become the new leader Orgar need only slay the old. He looked at Uldrood, his triumph written on his face.

Uldrood's smile was sardonic. "Orgar, why do you not say what you want? All these words, when really all you want is to kill me? I am a fair man. You are more than welcome to try."

Orgar wasted no time in accepting the invitation. His arm snapped down and a knife dropped from his sleeve into his waiting hand. He charged Uldrood, blade poised for a disemboweling stroke. The priest stood motionless until the last instant, then twisted to his right. Orgar shot past and tripped over his intended victim's outstretched foot. He broke his fall with his left hand and his knife hand flashed in a throwing motion. The priest ducked. Before he realized the throw had been faked, Orgar was up and at him, knife gleaming.

This time Uldrood met the challenger's attack squarely. As the knife sped up at his belly, the priest's right hand struck down, past the blade. The hard edge of his hand hit Orgar's wrist and there came the snap of breaking bones. The knife spun through the air to fall a dozen feet from the combatants. Orgar turned and ran to retrieve it. The priest kicked him in the ankle. Again that hideous crack of breaking bone.

Unarmed, without the use of one leg and one arm, Orgar strove on, but it was a futile attempt. The priest systematically beat him to death.

"Now you," Uldrood snarled as he hit, hit, "make full penance for your blasphemy. I am Uldrood, son and First Arm of Drood, Lord of Death! He gives me strength to break men's bones to His glory. Fool, to pit your puny normal strength against mine! I have served the Dark Lord for many years, and I have slain mighty warriors and fair princesses, kings and commoners—all die beneath my hand!"

While Uldrood was so delightedly killing Orgar, Tiana picked the lock on her last chain. *There are few occasions,* she mused, *when anyone so beautiful as I may reasonably hope a roomful of men will not watch her—but one man slaying another is such an occasion!* All her chains were unlocked. All still rested on her limbs as though secured. The only way out was the front door and the Arms were between it and her. Again she must wait for the right moment.

It did not come. Uldrood rose from his victim and walked to the black stone block where she lay. He smiled down at her with a definite unpriestly relish.

"Now it is your turn, defiling slut. I hope you do not mind if I make a spectacle of you."

"You could at least give me a bit of clothing to preserve decency."

"Any man would be a *fool* to offer clothing to a woman who looks the way you do!" he said, and the hand with which he had just slain a powerful man sped down at her.

"He'd be a fool to think I'm just for looks, too," Tiana said, and rolled off the stone block. Uldrood struck the black stone with all his strength. The loud cracking breaking sound did not come from the altar stone. Uldrood

made a horrid sound in his throat and looked perfectly
ghastly. Tiana, having fallen at his feet, kicked both his
legs. As she rose, the priest fell to a kneeling position.
His hand was a mess. The point of her elbow crashed
into the back of his neck.

Tiana had no time to check her kill. Though the Arms
of Drood were astonished by the death of their leader,
the paralysis of surprise would last only an instant. She
saw no way through them to the front door and there was
no other exit. There was no hiding place. Except the pool
of Blackness . . .

The disciples of death would not dare follow her into
that place where no light could shine. If whoever or whatever was prisoned there was a friend, well and good. If
not, she would be presenting herself to the dweller in
darkness as a free meal. Well, she thought piratically,
any port in a storm.

Tiana jumped off the dais and raced toward the patch
of utter darkness on the floor. The dazed Arms of Drood
watched her leap over the ring of bright lamps into the
Blackness beyond.

CHAPTER SIX

Caranga ran through the indigo-shadowed streets of Reme, cursing under his breath. As usual, he was sure the mess was his own fault. Yet even in hindsight it was impossible to see how the problem could have been avoided. The philosopher Saphistran had been right. Many years ago Caranga had met him and, over a bottle of wine, queried the revered scholar concerning human destiny.

Quoth Saphistran, "Every man is completely the master of his own destiny, the captain of his fate. If a man is dissatisfied with the outcome of his life, he has only himself to blame."

The great philosopher then with brilliant argument proved this conclusion to Caranga's satisfaction. However, the wine bottle half consumed, Saphistran declared that men were the helpless puppets of circumstance. Whatever should befall them, he solemnly advised, was written in their foreheads at birth. Caranga objected. With equally brilliant arguments the scholar proved his new conclusion. By then the wine bottle was empty, and pirate told scholar that he was completely inconsistent.

"Nay," the learned man replied, "both things are true. It is the world, not I, which is inconsistent." As Saphistran then passed out from drink, no further enlightenment could be gained.

Now Caranga knew the philosopher had been right. On the one hand Caranga's problem was of his own making. Of his own free will he had adopted an orphan and raised her as his son and as a pirate. The forseeable result was that his daughter was a reckless trouble-hungry hellion. While Caranga could accept the idea that a brave son might perish in some foolish adventure, he could not bear the thought of his beautiful daughter in danger.

Inconsistent, yes—and fully in concert with society. Caranga redoubled his speed. He must find guardsmen and return with them before Tiana got into trouble. Given that the whole problem was of his own making, how could he have avoided it? He'd had no idea how to raise a daughter. The deck of a pirate ship seemed a rather poor place to teach the maidenly virtues. . . .

His brooding ended when he sighted a mob of the King's Own. Why, there must be two score! Could he persuade them to follow him? The king had given him no written commission, no token of authority. For a moment Caranga cursed his lack of foresight in not asking for such. Then he remembered that he had relieved the duke of his emerald signet ring after that misfortunate lord poisoned himself. Drawing the ring from his pouch, Caranga ran toward the soldiers.

"In the name of King and Duke I command you! I am Caranga, this day appointed Friend to the King. In token of my authority I bear the duke's signet. I'm sure you all recognize it."

"Indeed I do," replied the troop's commander. Though he spoke from the shadows Caranga recognized the voice; the captain who had tried to arrest Caranga and Tiana in the Wayfarer. "Tell me, how did you steal the Duke's ring?"

"Obviously, I couldn't have. I understand your surprise, but what I said is true. The kingdom is in grave danger, and to deal with the emergency I am given special authority."

"Again, you lie well," Captain Despan said, "but I have just come from my lord Duke. He ordered me to find you and Tiana and execute you both outhand."

The soldier's tone was sincere—and the duke was lying near death and surely could not have given anyone orders. The pirate stood almost dazed with puzzlement; what madness assailed him? Now Despan pointed at the burly black.

"Seize him! I'll behead him with his own cutlass."

That proved more easily uttered than implemented. The first soldier to leap at the pirate found himself lifted, turned in air, and thrown back. He crushed into his comrades and most of the troop collapsed into a tangled heap.

This gave Caranga a fair head start. He was faster than most of the guardsmen, but not all. Though he dodged and turned through dark alleys, the guardsmen were like hounds on his trail, mail chiming and jingling. The more Caranga thought about his problem the worse it seemed. He needed time to elude his pursuers; more time to reach the castle. If the king was there, could he gain audience or would he be arrested? How many other squads of guardsman had received similar orders?

Caranga had found King's Own—and they wanted to cut off his head! Nevertheless they were the only help he could find tonight, and a man must use what fate provides. Caranga circled back to the mysterious building in the old warehouse district. By now the swifter of his pursuers were well ahead of the slower. When Caranga slowed his headlong pace and brandished his cutlass, the foremost guardsmen also slowed. As Caranga intended, that allowed the slower men to catch up. As they neared the mysterious building, the guard was in good formation, weapons ready. Good, good. If Tiana were waiting outside the building, seeing him pursued by the guard would warn her. If she was inside, he must do what he could to rescue her.

The main door to the unknown building shattered into kindling when Caranga's hurtling body smashed into it. He staggered in a narrow hallway lighted by several lamps; at the end was an oak door banded with heavy iron. This one Caranga could not smash—and the guardsmen were right behind him.

First striking a loud blow with the flat of his cutlass against the wall, Caranga leapt up and caught hold of a beam. Gaining only a poor foothold, the pirate flattened himself against the darkness at the ceiling. Black vanished into blackness. The guard poured under him, jingling, helmets aflash.

"That bang was the black dog slamming that door against us. Break it down, men!"

The door was strong and resisted the soldiers. Caranga, clinging to the ceiling, had no worry of being seen or heard. Although he was in plain sight, he was sure they would not look up, and no small sound he might make could be heard above the racket the soldiers were making. The problem was that his handholds were slipping. In a few moments he would fall into the midst of the soldiers. Silently cursing his age, Caranga *clung*.

A moment more—and with a snap the lock mechanism failed. The oaken door swung wide.

From the ceiling Caranga shouted, in his best imitation of Despan's voice, "Inside men, and slay!"

Ignoring or not hearing the protests of their confused captain, the excited soldiers poured into the building. Despan was left alone with Caranga. The pirate dropped to the floor. Cutlass in hand, he faced the outraged captain.

"You black demon! I'll cut out your lying tongue before I chop off your head."

"You could try," Caranga replied evenly. "But listen." From the building came the sound of battle, the ring of steel against steel, the scream of men dying. "This building houses some hostile power. I have tricked you into attacking that power. We may spend our time fighting each other, while your men die leaderless, or we may lead them to victory."

"You are a devil. You force me either to betray my men or disobey my orders."

"We're alone now—why lie? It's obvious there are no orders. You want to kill me out of personal malice, because my daughter and I made a fool of you at the Wayfarer."

"No, by the Cud! I swear the duke came to the armory and ordered me to find and execute you. He gave me an official death warrant, signed by the king. Here it is." Captain Despan reached into his tunic and pulled out a candle. "I—I can't understand—this was a . . . a scroll with the king's signature and seal."

Caranga did understand. "The, ah, *duke;* he was wearing his emerald signet?"

"Why, yes."

"But when you met me, immediately thereafter, I had the real ring—this one. Since the man who gave you those orders wore a false ring, it's clear that he is an impostor."

Despan's face was ashen, his brow covered with sweat. Though a brave man in facing physical danger, his voice trembled. "This was no common impersonation, but black sorcery. I have obeyed false orders and no doubt my life is forfeit. In the meantime—you speak for the king."

"Then come on, man; we've wasted too much time already!"

Caranga turned and led the captain toward the battle. He was relieved by this turn of fortune, since he had feared he would need to rescue Tiana during the confusion of a three-cornered fight. His relief ended when Caranga saw the interior of the building and the conflict. A glance at the idol told him this was a temple of Drood. Forty guardsmen battled the Arms of Drood—religious assassins—outnumbering them three to one and were getting the worst of it. Despan barked sharp orders, getting his men back onto an orthodox formation. The fact that they wore armor, and the foe none, worked to their great advantage in sword combat. Unfortunately several of the Arms had bows, and the orthodox, close-packed formation was painfully vulnerable to arrows. At this range guardsman after guardsman dropped to zipping shafts.

While all about him was a fury of frantic action, Caranga stood silent. Watching. Thinking. Although the soldiers were better armed and trained fighters, they were up against fanatics. It was clear that the odds were too great. Conventional tactics must result in defeat. The cultists were fighting with the courage of trapped rats and clearly lacked leadership. They were a mob, blind in fear and rage, and Caranga knew ways to destroy such a foe. He caught Despan's mailed shoulder in a big hand.

"Six good men, quick, armed with spears!"

Caranga explained the rest of his plan as he led the six lancers back through the doorway. They took up positions in the middle of the corridor, Caranga in the center and slightly in front of the soldiers. Inside, Captain Despan shouted an order, and again. In tight formation his men shifted away from the door. The way out of the temple was apparently free and the leaderless mob of Arms rushed to escape. The archers leapt from their vantage points to join the rush. The disciples became a tangled mass, pushing and shoving each other, struggling to force their way through the doorway. Some stabbed their fellows while all clawed their way toward escape.

Having allowed the Arms to cluster about the door, the guardsmen attacked.

They moved in perfect formation, a solid wedge of armor and swords. Heavy booted feet struck the floor in

unison as they marched forward. They were no longer a
group of men but were becoming a single killing machine.
The floor shook to their tread. Some of the cultists turned
to fight, but most redoubled their efforts to force through
the doorway. Those who fought died quickly, some
bravely with their wounds in front; others, fleeing, took
coward's wounds. With the swords of the guardsmen at
their backs the fratricidal fighting spread rapidly among
the Arms. Every man's knife was red with the blood of
his fellows. Remorselessly the soldiers moved forward,
wasting the Arms of Drood.

Meanwhile, he who was the stopper in this bottle
waged unequal combat. Caranga from head to foot was
now a red man, and some of it was his own blood. His
right leg had been stabbed by a man he'd thought dead.
The man whose dagger projected from his side had been
dead, but the press of bodies had kept him from falling
and impaled Caranga on the weapon. The hallway was
deep with corpses, the floor slippery with blood.

Still the Arms came. To them, Caranga appeared a horrible primitive god of slaughter, but he knew himself to
be failing rapidly.

Every stroke of his cutlass slew a man—and forced
fresh blood from the great wounds in his leg and side as
well as a host of lesser cuts all over his body. The world
was a graying haze before him. Was he seeing double or
were there two identical cultists facing him? A swift underhand stroke disemboweled the rightward twin, but
Caranga could not recover in time to evade the other's
knife. The last spearman impaled the attacker before
himself collapsing. Had one of the Arms of Drood thrown
a knife, or had the man collapsed from his wounds?
Caranga could not tell. Nor did it make any difference.
He was alone.

Every breath was an agony. His head spun and his
arm was gone heavy as lead. The next disciple was a tall
blur. Caranga aimed a thrust at the man's chest. The
wight twisted slightly, and the cutlass glanced off his
steel armor. Caranga saw a flash of steel and his cutlass
was smitten from his hand. Next moment he was grabbed
by several men he could not see and his arms pinned to
his sides.

The tall blur slapped Caranga's face and shouted,
"Wake up, man. It's over. We won."

Caranga relaxed, and allowed himself to be almost carried back into the temple. Though the temptation to faint was great, there was something he must know.

"My daughter! Did you find her? Is she safe?"

A figure, dressed in an ill-fitting black tunic over large pants, spoke. "I'm here, father. You rescued me from great danger. Sit down; I'll bandage your wounds and tell you about it."

As Tiana worked, she related her adventures. She told in great detail of killing the spider, then related seeing the Arms gathered around the wall of the entrance hall. "I'm sure you will find concealed archer's ports all along that hallway, Captain. It's a clever device to slaughter helpless men. Someone knew we might be coming here, probably with guardsmen to help us. That someone ordered the High Priest of Drood to ambush us."

"Why should a high priest take orders?" Despan asked.

"He thought it was a vision of his god."

Captain Despan made the sign for protection from evil. "That same *someone* came to me in the semblance of the duke and ordered me to kill you both!"

"I'm glad you had the wit not to obey such an order. You over there, look under the altar! If you find wine, bring it here. As I was saying, I saw the dogs lying in ambush, and I decided the best plan was to kill their leader. Since he was famous for killing men with his bare hands by breaking their bones, I broke his arm and his neck." Tiana thought her story was not injured by omitting irrelevant details such as her capture. "After that I took refuge in the circle of darkness over there. I knew the cultists would not dare follow me, since they suppose there's a demon in the darkness."

Caranga half raised himself to see the circle of lamps and the blackness that no light could penetrate. "What's hid in that . . . in *that?*"

"Nothing dangerous," Tiana replied, almost airily. "Several dead bodies I found provided these clothes—and something else. Here father, drink some wine and I'll show you." She opened the bottle the soldier had brought, handed it to Caranga, and ran toward the darkness. She vanished, to reappear a moment later dragging something. "Captain, give me a hand."

She and Despan carried the form to Caranga. He started to rise, but Tiana pressed him back. "No father,

I want you to stay off that leg until we get to the ship and I can properly sew it up."

She and Despan placed a dark figure on the floor. The old man was black as Caranga, save for his white hair. He was tall and very thin, his hard face showing suffering and great nobility. The black body was not a corpse. The flesh was hard as marble, and cold, far colder than ice.

Tiana related what she had heard Orgar say. "Father," she concluded, "can you make sense of these events?"

"Yes, I think I can," Caranga muttered thoughtfully. "Susha's sweet . . . eyes! It appears our unknown enemy used the Arms as cat's-paws by sending false visions to their priest. The first such vision ordered them to capture this man. They brought him here, blind and apparently helpless. But he is a mighty ju-ju man. His powers allowed him to conjure darkness, and so fight his enemies on even terms. The Arms lacked the stomach for such a fight, but he was still surrounded and powerless to leave this sweet place. So—he drew a map with soap. But how could he deliver it?" Caranga smiled and nodded at his daughter's O-shaped mouth. "The second false vision ordered these plaguls to capture and slay one of the King's Ears, who had found a clue to the whereabouts of the king's daughter. They killed the spy on the high altar. It was then this man used his greatest and most dangerous magic. He sent forth his soul, out of his body, to reanimate the spy's corpse. Using this dead messenger he sent us the map."

"But . . . father . . . why didn't he come back to life? Why is his body frozen and hard as stone?"

"I know not, though I have heard stories of these things. The soul moves from body to body through a void of outer darkness. The live body it leaves is in contact with the darkness, and cold of the darkness enters it. As to his soul, perhaps it is lost and will yet return; perhaps it is destroyed." Caranga tried to shrug, and winced. "There is a danger here, for this empty body is a gateway to our world. Captain, we'd best place this trust in your hands. If this body fails to wake before the new moon, burn it. Should it wake, look most closely into the eyes. If a true man looks back at you, do whatever he bids you. If not, destroy the thing as best you can, preferably with fire."

"But my life is forfeit, because I obeyed false orders and attacked you, Sir."

"Nonsense, boy, all's well that ends well. In a few days orders will come from the king to destroy this sweet nest of assassins. Have your report of killing them ready but just don't turn it in until after the orders come. The army is a little . . . touchy about that sort of thing."

"Father," Tiana interrupted, "you've explained much but the key question is still unanswered. Who was this man? Can we trust the map he sent us?"

"Do you know who Saint Theranos was?"

"He was an ancient hero in a war against snake worshippers."

"No, he was a hero in the war against the Snake. I know not the full truth of these matters, but I have heard many grim legends. Of this much I am sure; the world is old and man is not the first lord of the earth. Humans gained the world by war and that war is not over. Now it's a shadow war against an enemy unseen. Night can come upon a kingdom, and its rulers be men only in outward appearance. Those that were before us seek to come again. These things are seldom whispered of, but I have traveled the world and I know them to be true."

Tiana nodded slowly. "What has all this to do with this man?"

"His name is Voomundo, Tiana. Like ancient Theranos, he is a hero of the war against the Snake. When I was young, not yet a warrior proven, there was a time of trouble. It started far from my home and spread slowly through the countryside. There were no changes one might see, but in village after village the spirit went from the people. The change was as if a herd of wild animals suddenly became tame. Fattened animals, awaiting slaughter. I traveled and I often saw large villages with but a few people in them. Where had the rest gone? No one seemed to know or care. Those of us who were not yet under the shadow were frightened and leaderless. We'd no idea where or how to strike. Then Voomundo came and the warriors rallied to him. O Susha—with fire and iron we cleaned our land! There were many battles, and in the last battle we followed Voomundo into a cave. We went deep into the earth and well it was that our leader was blind, for all light failed and we groped our way down. We met and fought a scaled and coiled thing.

Many of us died but we slew it. Voomundo said he had other battles to fight, and he left before we could celebrate our victory."

Tiana raised her hand. "Father, I think you should rest now. You've lost much blood."

Caranga started to protest but the wine and blood-loss were too much for him. His heavy eyes shut and he went to sleep.

While the guardsmen prepared a stretcher, Tiana made a rapid search and found her rapier and dagger. Soon she was leading the stretcher-bearers through the night-shrouded streets of Reme. A ridiculously clothed redhead, lithe as a cat and erect as a sapling, leading a score or so blood-splashed soldiers—who bore a large man on a litter—a man as red as he was black.

They arrived in the harbor as the first rays of dawn struck the land. The change seemed symbolic to Tiana. She was leaving the tangled maze of the city for the bright open sea. She was leaving an unseen enemy who struck from darkness. From now on her foes must face her openly and taste her steel.

She was pleased to find that Bardon had *Vixen* fully provisioned and ready to sail. Kathis and forty picked soldiers of Ilan were on board. *Vixen* would be crowded, though not terribly, since there was no cargo. The ship was ready; the tide had come; Tiana was eager to sail. And there was an obstacle not easily removed. King Hower, in link-mail over tunic and mailed leggings. Tiana met him eye to eye.

"Your Highness, I realize you want to know what has happened, but tides do not wait for kings."

"Then sail." He stared right back, hands behind him, legs braced.

"But I can't take you on such a dangerous voyage, lord King."

"The royal barge is standing by and can take me back to shore after our conference is complete, *Captain Tiana*."

Tiana sighed. She wanted to be in command while her ship cleared the harbor. She wanted the clean ocean breeze in her face—and Hower was her king. He had a right to know what had occurred. Briefly Tiana summed up the events of the night.

When she finished the king frowned thoughtfully. "We

may need wizardly aid before this affair is ended. I have never allowed such in my court, for I believed an untrustworthy friend is worse than an enemy. If Voomundo does not revive, who will help us?"

"Perhaps Sulun Tha. He is a white wizard, although I have no wish to meet him again." Tiana hesitated, then decided the king was entitled to the whole truth. "The other possibility is Pyre."

"*Pyre!* But he cares nothing for us."

"He has an obligation. I have not told Your Highness how I killed the wizard Lamarred. When I learned that he—or rather it—had murdered my brother, I resolved to take vengeance. Pyre told you that Lamarred was a demon, vulnerable to no mortal weapon. That was true. It could be destroyed only by a dangerous means, one that might unleash the fiend on the world. Pyre feared to take that chance, for he knew he would be the first target of the released monster. Pyre tried to kill me, to prevent the killer's loosing. When that failed, he tried to argue me out of my vengeance." Tiana gazed asea where dawnlight gilded amethystine swells.

"Fascinating, but how does it help us? Pyre will not be grateful for a favor he did not request."

"He was sure my plans would fail, that I would be slain, and Lamarred unchained. His pride was hurt, you see. I had shamed him as a coward who attacked his friends rather then his enemies. Accordingly he swore an oath to avenge me. 'Twas an act of bravado, to salve his vanity."

With one finger the king scratched under his chaplet. "But that oath is void, Captain. Even if the wizard Pyre were a man to keep good faith to his word, which I doubt, this vow carries no obligation since you weren't killed."

"The exact words, lord King of Ilan, were 'I shall avenge your death,' with no qualifications. Moreover, Pyre swore not by the Cud which is the First Oath by the means which Created the World, nor did he swear by the Back, the Second Oath by the means which Sustain the World. He swore the Third Oath, by the Fires which shall Destroy the World."

King Hower's face showed shocked surprise. The Third Oath was seldom sworn and the consequences of such swearing were never pleasant. "In that case, he is bound.

It's a grim comfort, but whatever foe slays you, Pyre must attack."

"Exactly, lord King. Of course this is no promise of aid for the Princess Jiltha, but there is no reason for Pyre to go out of his way to harm her."

The king nodded, turned decisively with a *ching* of armor. "I fear there is little I can do other than send messengers to Sulun Tha up in Collada. Your foster father spoke of a hidden war . . . do you think it true or the ravings of a wounded man? From your account he said these things with much wine and little blood in him."

"I'm sure he recognized Voomundo and that the map can be trusted. The rest may be but a tale or may be true. It does not matter, for all we want is your daughter. The war, if war there be, is not our affair, King Hower."

"No, Tiana. I sinned in disturbing the Sacred Grove. I do not want that sin compounded into black disaster for all humanity. Save my daughter if you can, but do what is best for all men."

"And women," Tiana asked innocently, "lord King?"

"Figure of speech," Hower grumped, giving her a look.

"Very well, Your Majesty."

Tiana's face showed dutiful obedience while inwardly she cursed. This was typical of Hower. First create a mess, then order strict adherence to noble principles while cleaning it up. If he ran true to form, he would now demand that she do her job with impossible perfection. Best she change the subject.

"Lord King, I just remembered. I've had no chance to prepare that list of dishonest innkeepers."

"Bardon attended to that. I must go, but first I must explain certain things. If I were simply a distressed father, you would need only return my daughter in good health, Tiana. But I am a king and Jiltha is the throne princess. In the normal course of events in a few years I would look among our neighbors and choose a king's son, a boy both wise and good. I would arrange Jiltha's marriage to him. Such orderly succession assures continued good government."

Oh, absolutely, thought Tiana.

"If Jiltha is brought home dishonored, no marriage can be arranged. With no lawful heir the throne will belong to him who can seize it by force. The histories of wars of succession are grim. Often the victor is the pretender who gained foreign assistance by selling his country into slavery. You must find Jiltha before she can be dishonored, *and* you must guard her most carefully during the return voyage. Jiltha is a child. Unfortunately she is also old enough to think herself a woman. Her mind is full of romantic nonsense and she resents the prospect of an arranged marriage. Kathis is handsome, brave and very ambitious. You will need his aid in the coming battle, for he is the finest warrior in Ilan. Still, sending him to rescue the princess is akin to setting a wolf to guard a sheepfold."

Tiana mumbled assurances that she would do her best. Soon she had bidden farewell to her king.

The sea breeze blew her red hair and salt spray was a fresh clean taste and scent that she loved. Glittering treasure beckoned, and danger; time was come to sail in quest of both. Of course when and if she rescued Jiltha, hers would be the awkward role of nursemaid to a willful and doubtless spoiled teenager. Well did she remember what that was like! One good aspect was she'd surely have no problem in returning the princess to the king with maidenhead intact.

"All I need do," Tiana muttered cheerfully, "is find any men who might prove or dare say aught to the contrary and kill them all."

Big Rarn, ship's cat of Vixen, *prowled through the hold in a fury worthy of his mistress—as both vanity and his territorial sense approached hers. Another cat had dared to come on board his ship! Though Rarn had not yet had opportunity to slay the interloper, he'd smelled it and caught a fleeting glimpse as well. When he did find the beast, Rarn would make short work of someone's pampered, bejeweled white pet!*

BOOK II

The Rightward Eye:
CRIMSON PHANTASMS

CHAPTER SEVEN

Hartes, King of Thesia and Conqueror of Bemar, Paleran, Narf and Thunland, chose his steps carefully in his descent of the dark dungeon stair. The ruler's clothing was ordinary, his hair grease-slicked. There was nothing about the face or form of this plump man—who had crushed whole nations under his iron foot—to catch the eye or make him stand out in a crowd of four.

He who walked so quietly behind the king was a dweller in nightmares. The short bloated body was topped by a yellow toad's head whose eyes were pools of dark wisdom. Since it walked on two legs, it could, for want of better term, be called a man.

Hartes strode to a scarred oaken door banded with iron. Smiting it, he bawled out, "Zark! You lazy plagul, open this door for your master!" The king blinked then, for at his blow the door swung quietly open. "Hmp! That's odd; Zark normally locks the door when he has a victim to play with."

King Hartes stepped through the doorway and glared about. The shadowy, pain-haunted room was littered with the instruments of Zark's filthy trade: clamps and pincers; the large cradle whose inside was lined with spikes, an Iron Maiden; the pails and funnels for various water tortures, and other ugly apparati. A couple of toes strewed the floor, and the walls were darkly splashed.

On the rack in the chamber's center was stretched a man. His mighty limbs were distended by the evil machine.

Tall and powerfully built was this victim, fair of hair and complexion. Welts and burns pocked his body. Icy blue eyes fixed their gaze on Hartes with primitive hatred unmitigated by any hint of begging for mercy. Hartes was

73

uncomfortably reminded of a wolf he had recently helped slay for the sport of it; every aspect of this outsize man was that of a trapped beast. The animal had fought with intense fury to the very end, determined to wreak what harm it could before its death. Hartes saw the same mentality here.

Not unnatural that this man reminded the Thesian ruler of a wolf; he was of that race of sea-wolves of the far north whose rapine and savagery made them a terror to the southern coasts.

Staring at Hartes, the Norther shook his head so that the tangled blond mane flew. "Well, jackal king," he roared, "I see you brought your pet toad to watch my 'execution'!" He had a bull's voice to match his neck.

"Silence there, northish plagul! Show respect for your betters. I am still your lord. And this man is the mighty Ekron, chief wizard of Naroka."

"Titles, titles. I do humbly beg pardon, my lord Carrion Eater! But—why should a man under sentence of death mind his manners like you enlightened civilized folk?"

"Because, Bjaine," the king sighed, "I've come to pardon you and grant you an exalted position." Hartes raised his voice. "Zark! Come free this man."

"You're lying," Bjaine said. "Exalted position, is it? Aye—you've come to laugh while Bjaine rides the one-legged horse!"

For a moment both ruler and pirate gazed upon the bloodstained post several feet from the rack. Rising up out of the floor to a height of some four feet, the pole was three inches in diameter, and sharpened on top.

"By the Cud and by the Back," Hartes said, "I swear I have come here to pardon and to free you."

Bjaine, blinking, thought on that. "What, uh, persuaded you of my innocence?"

Hartes snorted. "Bjaine, Bjaine! I doubt you will ever understand the ways of civilized men! I—"

"I hope not! I might begin to act the same way, if I understood!"

"Um. Yes. I knew you were innocent of the charge when I sentenced you to be broken on the rack and ride the horse."

"Oh," Bjaine said equably. "Now condemning an in-

nocent man I can understand! Even uncivilized folk do
that, sometimes."

Hartes shook his head, smiling. "My sister, dear
Luquila, accused you of trying to rape her."

"Anybody who'd believe that would suck eggs in the
henhouse!"

"Precisely, Bjaine, and I would not. Had you possessed the wit to plead guilty and beg mercy—"

"Plead? Beg!"

Hartes sighed, glanced at Ekron, continued as if he'd
heard nothing: "—on the grounds that her great beauty
inflamed you, why then I'd have ordered you flogged and
let it go at that." Hartes raised his voice above Bjaine's
laughter. "I would not waste a useful man for my sister's
vanity. But Bjaine, Bjaine! You *denied* it! In front of
my entire court and council you stated that a charge even
of attempted rape was absurd for—how charmingly you
put it!—'for when I want a woman I take her and there's
naught she can do save to enjoy it!' Now I might have
passed over your calling my royal sister a liar, Norther.
But not your saying that she is so ugly she frightens
gryphons and no man would want her unless he was blind
and leprous!"

" 's true," Bjaine said, and shuddered at thought of
Luquila's face.

"You claim that what truly happened was that you
ordered the *royal princess* to fetch you wine. When she
naturally did not obey, you beat her! That shocked my
court and council, Bjaine—naturally. Then you proceeded to discourse at length on the natural superiority
of men over women, whose place is to serve man, while
every man has the right and duty to beat any woman to
teach her her place."

"So I did. I'd said so plenty of times before, and you
laughed and never disagreed!"

"True . . . but what you did and said day before yesterday was in public, and was a direct public insult to my
sister's birth, and her royal blood—and thus my blood."

"Ah!" Bjaine's blue eyes brightened and stared in-
genuously at the king. "I see. Was *you* I insulted, then.
Now I understand. If Bjaine apologized, Hartes, I would
apologize now. As I don't, though . . . I still don't understand why you have come here. With ole hop-toad,

there." Bjaine winked at Ekron. *"K'gung!"* he said, in a fair imitation of a large frog.

Ekron stared levelly at the bound Norther and slowly blinked—from the bottom up. Bjaine's eyes widened still more. He was about to invite the wizard to repeat that fascinating act, when Hartes answered his question.

"I would put my hand in any cesspool to extend and protect my empire," Hartes said, low and intense. "I pardon you because I need your services." Again the king glanced around. "Zark! You lazy pig, where are you?"

Bjaine smiled boyishly. "I doubt whether he hears you. He is entertaining a lady."

"What? I pay the knave to work at his trade, and he dallies with whores? I'll have that Narfese plagul rocked in his own cradle!"

For the first time, the wizard spoke. "I fear, my lord king, that rocking Zark would be . . . somewhat redundant." He gestured at the Iron Maiden.

With a start, Hartes took note that the device was closed. Normally it stood open, displaying its spiked interior to impressionable subjects of Zark's art, to be shut only when occupied. Now it was both closed, and leaking scarlet at its base. Hartes started to speak; instead he stood open-mouthed.

With a sudden muscular effort that was hardly credible even to staring eyes, Bjaine stretched himself even farther—and slipped his wrist-chains off their hooks. Apparently the chains at his feet had never been secured to anything at all, for he stepped forward unhindered. He bowed to the ruler, very slightly.

"How may I serve the lord king and what will he pay?" As he spoke, smiling so boyishly, he reached behind the rack to draw forth a long and shining sword.

"I—I do not understand," Hartes stammered.

"I believe I do," Ekron said. "Your torturer underestimated our friend here. In consequence, Zark is in the Maiden's embrace. Bjaine, doubtless expecting you to come and witness his horse-ride, laid himself on the rack with his sword hidden to hand. A most clever ruse, and trap."

This time the smiling Norther's bow was more profound.

"B-but Zark had four strong assistants!" Hartes protested.

The ruler's voice was weak, for he realized the gravity of his situation. He was unguarded. He had previously admired this warrior's stature and mighty physique—as he might have admired a caged beast. Now the beast was free. Its claw was of steel, and three feet long. Though Hartes was no short man, his head rose just above the corded plates of muscle that swelled the Norther's broad chest. And Bjaine's bright blue eyes stared down at the king.

Yet those eyes contained, not hatred, but calm speculation. Hartes had wondered at the seeming rule that all Northers had to be unconscionably tall. Now he wondered if they were all barbars after all. Civilization was as a patina on this man, and when he spoke, his words were smooth. Suddenly he did not seem so manipulably stupid. And his grin was that of a wolf.

"True enough," Bjaine said, "there were four assistants. And do not forget the three Thesian army guards, lord King! One of them thought it would be humorous to torment me with my own sword. Those are his toes, there, and his ugly little organ is lying about someplace. I fear your Kingness will be at some small expense to replace those men. But—no use weeping over cracked eggs. Let us discuss the service you want of me, and my payment."

The yellow toad of a man spoke in a calm and buttery voice. "I am told a session on the rack can create a . . . great thirst?" From within his robes he produced a wine pottle which he deftly unstoppered and put into the Norther's eager hands.

Bjaine handed it back. "After you, topaz."

He watched while the wizard tilted up the container. Once his adam's apple moved, Bjaine snatched it away. "Here, not all of it, you damned greedy Narokan toad!" And without a word of thanks, Bjaine drained the leather-clad pottle in a few mighty swallows. "Ahhhhhhhh."

"Now, my friend from the far north, it is well known that you handle a ship better than almost anyone asea."

"Hmp! No almost about it."

Ekron asked, "Be it true you spent some time among the Kroll Isle pirates?"

"Oh, aye. Bjaine knows the Isles and their defenses well."

"Good. We want you to lead a raiding party. Within Storgavar's keep are two things we want. For me there is a chest of jewels which includes the Left Eye of Sarsis. For King Hartes there is Jiltha, throne princess of Ilan."

"Why should you want to rescue an enemy's daughter?"

The king smiled thinly. "As I said, I want to extend my empire. If I add Jiltha to my harem, King Hower will have two choices. He could announce that the marriage is invalid, that his daughter is dishonored. That's equivalent to telling the girl to commit suicide. Hower is too soft to do that. He will recognize the marriage and accept me as the lawful heir to his throne."

Bjaine laughed. "That's as good as a cannibal I once knew. He claimed to inherit a farm because he'd eaten the owner! Well. How soon can you have a ship and crew ready? Treasure seldom remains in one place long, you know, and I'd hate to reach the Krolls only to find someone had robbed them first."

"The *Stormfury* is already provisioned," Hartes said with some smugness, "and a picked squadron of Imperial Dragons is boarding her, in addition to the best of crews. All have instructions to follow your orders."

The King of Thesia felt ready to join the Thespian's Guild. Having managed to maintain a calm front, he was now relaxing, sure the barbarian would not be difficult. Doubtless the giant was angered by the abuse he'd taken, but like any other sensible man he put his ambition ahead of his feelings.

Again Bjaine laughed, and shook his head so that dirty, sunny hair flew. "Well then King, there's only the matter of my recompense, and I sail."

"I said an exalted position for you, and I meant it: the throne of Paleran. A rich land, but rebellious. I need a man to rule it with a hand of iron. Bring me the Princess Jiltha, *alive,* and you shall be King over Paleran."

"Why thank you, Kingness. That is a most generous offer. But Bjaine did have his heart set on the payment given me by the cannibal I mentioned."

"Above a crown? What payment was that?"

"There is but one payment for a blood insult: my dears, I am going to take your heads." Bjaine took a pace, the great sword coming up. "So sorry you are allergic to blood, wizard."

"But—I offer you a *throne!*"

"Bjaine does not sell himself to be tortured, Hartes, even for a throne."

The Norther's sword caught the torchlight and reflected on his face; it seemed the personification of Drood, lord of demons. King and mage stood motionless. The former was quite unmanned by this eventuation, and ready to kneel. Ekron, strangely, seemed amused. The sword's blade was a flash of lightning as Bjaine whipped it high— and dropped it to ring on the stone floor. Bjaine followed, toppling stiffly like a great tree struck by lightning.

Ekron chuckled at Hartes's amaze.

"The wine, of course, was drugged," the toadish mage said in his soft voice. "I am proud of the drug, a most unusual one. The victim feels nothing until he makes any violent motion, at which point he is instantly and completely paralyzed. Naturally I am immune."

With a grunt, and then another, the wizard turned over the Norther's huge body. Beads of sweat stood forth on Bjaine's brow and his eyes were blue fire.

"I know you can hear me," Ekron said. "You are going on this mission and . . . I am taking a small guarantee that you will return Jiltha and the box of sorcerous gems back to us."

Kneeling beside his victim, Ekron removed various small jars and phials from his robes. "Yes, yes . . . good . . . I have all the staples I require. The only perishable needed for the spell is a cup of blood from a freshly murdered man. Hartes, do be a good fellow and fetch me such. You should encounter no difficulty, since from our bearish friend's account there should be no less than eight corpses secreted here and there."

An angry reply died in the king's throat and he swallowed the curse. He resented being first-named and treated as a fetch-boy. Yet he was also aware of the realities of power in the present situation. He moved off on his grim task, taking the tin cup used to water—or more usually to taunt—this place's temporary residents. Ekron, smiling down at the stricken Norther warrior, held before his eyes a small bottle of black liquid.

"Ink," he said equably. "The formula is a mite unpleasant and some of its properties odd, but it is essentially ink like any other."

First showing the prostrate man a brush, he commenced to draw on Bjaine's stomach. "Damn these muscle ridges! These marks are far from indelible. If you have care, they will last a reasonable time—long enough for you to complete your mission and return to us with the dear princess and the valued chest."

Just as Ekron finished the drawing, Hartes returned with the cup of blood, not quite cold. Appearing more than ever a great yellow toad, the Narokan mage added to the blood from this jar and that phial. He stirred, muttering, and painted a few strokes on the muscular stomach of his human canvas. Again he added arcane ingredients to the blood, muttering words Bjaine could not distinguish. For the Nor'man could hear, and feel. When he tried to focus on the mage's voice, however, it remained an impossible blur.

Bjaine stared up at the Narokan. He was sure it was no longer a resemblance he saw; the wizard was a great fulvous toad. In its black robe it squatted crouched beside him. Making obscene noises while pointing with its hand-like forepaw. The torchlight paled. It seemed to shiver while whispers hissed from the shifting shadows. Bjaine knew the stones beside him formed an outside wall, beneath the very earth. Nevertheless he heard a knocking, as if *something* on the other side of that wall sought admission.

From the 'toad's horrid throat croaked a single clear word: *"Come."*

What came was total darkness, and Bjaine thought he was falling into an abyss. *If someone wearing white gloves,* he felt, *was to hold a ball of snow an inch from my eyes, I'd not be able to see it!* He strove to move. He could not.

And then the dark was gone. Again the chamber was lighted and normal in appearance—as normal as could be such a place of torturous horror. Ekron was only an ugly misshapen man in a voluminous robe. Bjaine discovered that he was able to move, though he was weak as a child of civilization. And Hartes was staring at Ekron with horror-filled eyes.

"You—you changed."

"Ohly an illusion, lord King. Sometimes, during a

Summoning, the inner nature, the *soul* . . . becomes visible."

Bjaine tried to rise and was too weak. At least he could move his lips: "Wizard . . . *what* did you summon?"

"Why, look at that so-muscular belly of yours, and see."

The Norther was just able to raise his head and look down. On his stomach a pentagram had been drawn, in black ink. Within it had been painted, in blood and only gods knew what else, a demonic face. A fanged red thing whose eyes were filled with an avid hunger. For a moment Bjaine thought his sanity had fled. The eyes of the painted image moved to stare back at him—and its lips parted in an evil grin.

"You . . . have painted a . . . a devil on my stomach!"

"In a way. It is a real enough demon. When you bring us Jiltha and the little box I require, I shall remove the demon. Serve us and you will live to be a king. Otherwise . . . before very long, time and wear will do away with part of the pentagram that *holds* the devil there, and it will be freed. And hungry. I don't believe that you will enjoy feeding it. Your ship awaits, loyal Bjaine."

CHAPTER EIGHT

Tiana's sleep was sundered by a scream of anguish. She was full awake, out of her bunk and armed with her rapier, all in seconds. Ready for anything, she found nothing. Her cabin was lighted by a single suspended oil-lamp whose shadows concealed no enemy. What had awakened her? Another scream, close by and filled with pain. Somewhere on her ship there was a catfight—and she knew that made no sense. The ship's only cat was her redoubtable tom, Rarn. While it was not impossible that another cat had chased a rat aboard while *Vixen* lay in port, two weeks had passed since their departure from Reme. Rarn would surely have met and attacked an intruder long before now. Nor had he ever made any noise killing rats: Rarn was a silent efficient killer. *Could one of those verminous soldiers be baiting* my *cat?* Last year a fool tried that and paid with his eyes. A long eerie howl undulated on the night. One thing was clear: Rarn was in trouble. Tiana would learn nothing by remaining in her cabin.

She hurried out on deck. The night was all salt and cold black iron, so that her crew and the Ilani soldiers were sleeping below decks. Fog was a noiseless wet coverlet. Of course, a ship's deck was never completely deserted.

"Helmsman! Where's that catfight?"

The only answer was the sound of the sea and wind in the sails. Tiana raced to the helm and was horrified to find it deserted. Her ship was adrift. She grabbed the rudder-oar and dragged it, hard. Cording creaked.

"Bardon!" she yelled, "get up here on the double!"

Her second appeared in moments, looking amazingly

alert. Tiana demanded to know who'd been assigned to the helm.

"Garnis, Captain. What happened to him?"

"I don't know. Take the helm and get this ship back on course. I'll relieve you after breakfast."

Tiana searched for the missing helmsman. Of him she found no trace; in the forecastle she found Rarn. He had fought his last battle. His wounds had clearly been inflicted by another cat. Judging by the spacing between scratches, that opponent had been smaller than Rarn. Tiana carefully examined the dead cat's paws. Much of the blood there was not his. Good, then; he had done some damage. Tiana considered. While Rarn's coat was coarse and black, clinging to one paw was a tuft of soft white fur. It was not the hair of an ordinary wharf cat, but of a purebred. A pet. Tiana swore under her breath. Another cursed mystery! A reliable sailor gone from his post; a tough ship's cat apparently slain by a pampered little pet.

Tiana remained squatting beside the dead animal staring at the dark waters ahead. Dawn was not long off. Had she used the past two weeks wisely? Caranga's wounds were healing well, but he was still weak. She had put her own pirates and the guardsmen through endless drills and mock battles, chiding them for their mistakes: "The idea is to do the job without getting killed!" She had maintained an even-handed discipline, never favoring her own men over the soldiers. She had practiced her surgery, sewing up the victims of personal fights and accidents.

All these were good in themselves and served a second purpose: she was winning the loyalty of the guardsmen away from Kathis. Since he ruled by force, displaying not the slightest concern for his men's well being, it was an easy thing to do. After the battle, Kathis might wish to court the Princess Jiltha—and discover that none of his men would support him.

Odd, Tiana mused, that the very handsome fellow completely failed to attract her! Indeed—and far more inexplicable—she didn't seem to attract him! Well, let that rest; she'd other more important concerns.

The preparations she'd made satisfied her but what had she left undone? She rubbed poor old Rarn's fur while she reflected. In Reme an unseen enemy had tried to kill her. She had sailed away, confident of leaving that danger behind. It did not seem possible that even a supernatural being could hide on her ship. Yet a white cat was somewhere aboard.

My deadly enemy a small white pussycat?

The thought was absurd. Still . . . She hastened to Caranga's cabin. Nigh invisible in darkness, he was awake in his bunk, sitting up.

"Daughter, what in the name of Susha's sweet paps are you excited about?"

"Father . . . when the duke tried to poison us—wasn't there a white cat in the room?"

"Why yes." He scratched the hairy mat of his chest. "A beautiful animal. I remember thinking it was a coincidence, seeing two white cats in one evening."

"What? Where did you see the other?"

"Sitting in the window of the Wayfarer Tavern, watching the room."

"You mean twice in one night a white cat watched an attempt to murder us!"

"You make a coincidence sound mighty sinister, Tiana."

"Three times is no coincidence." Rapidly Tiana told of the missing helmsman, and Rarn.

"Daughter, you're making a blanket out of a few cobwebs. The world is full of cats. Too many cats. Twice during a night when we were in constant peril, we saw a white cat. Now we have a cat on this ship. It has some white fur—and may or may not be white."

Tiana sighed. "That's logical, but I can't quite believe it."

"If our enemy is on board, why hasn't he attacked?"

"I don't know, father. Perhaps you're right—but I'll feel better after we find that cat."

Dawn had arrived in pink and gold, and Tiana insisted on putting her hair to rights before she left Caranga's cabin. He sat in the bunk he had not left, shaking his head.

"Vanity," he muttered. "Your vanity will be the death of you yet!"

"My vanity! Who is it traded the price of a good horse for this fine Stigilatan mirror I'm borrowing!" And she gave herself a last appraising look, also flashing her foster

father a mirrored wink. "It's light now, father. You look amazingly good naked, for a man of your years."

Emerging into pearly light and the pleasant savors wafting from the galley, Tiana mustered crew and soldiery.

"There will be no drill today, for tonight you fight in earnest. By noon we should sight the Kroll Isles. We shall drop anchor and wait for darkness. At full dark we must sail through a maze of reefs and shallow passages without being spotted by any of the lookouts. Up until now any man who spoke during our silence drills got extra duty. Tonight he could get all of us killed. If we are spotted, there is some small hope of killing the coast-watch before he can light a signal fire. You've been through those drills. All of you know the dangers we face. If we succeed, each of you will be a hero, savior of the princess. I make this promise to you King's Own: you shall receive equal shares of the treasure with my own men. You will be rich heroes."

This brought roars of approval from the men, and Tiana posed smiling. Then they fell to for breakfast. Tiana ate hastily and went to relieve her second, a youngish fellow, well born.

"Bardon, I want you to take five good men and make a thorough search of this ship."

"What do we seek, Captain?"

"Anything out of the ordinary. Any sign of Garnis. Above all, you are looking for a cat. If you find one, kill it and bring me the body."

Bardon could not conceal his puzzlement, but the rather morose second mate left without question. The water through which *Vixen* moved was gilded blue crystal, her wake an endless stream of pearls. Farther back Tiana saw a triangular fin knifing through the blue. A shark—no, a whole pack of sharks was following *Vixen*.

Tiana pushed that thought into a corner of her mind while she saw to the normal cares of running a ship. She was thus busy while crew and soldiers ate breakfast, in shifts. At last she was able to pace hungrily to the galley where the cook had hot porridge and sausage waiting for her. Despite her attempt to relax while she ate, the stored-away observation returned to nag.

"Virakoka . . . how much food have you been throwing overboard?"

"I don't understand, Cap'n." He gnawed his droopy chestnut mustache.

"Table scraps, spoiled food, leftovers, Koka. How much have you been chucking overboard?"

"Practically none, Captain," the high-voiced Nevinian told her. "There's been no spoilage yet and the men eat everything I cook. At least they did until today."

Odd; a pack of sharks was following the ship. A few was normal, but the cook had done nothing *extra* to attract them. "Today? This blood sausage is good, Koka. I appreciate the basil. Adds a little sweetness. What was the matter with appetites this morning?"

"Thank you, Captain. Oh, they all seemed to eat hearty; no battle nerves, but there's a lot of food left. I must have misjudged and fixed too much."

Bardon interrupted. In shining leather mailcoat, he looked tired and worse than nervous. Though he was hardly ugly, her second mate's perpetually morose expression served to guide the eyes of others from him. The lean man with the lank tawny hair always looked as if he'd just lost his best friend.

"Captain: the results of our search. We found no trace of Garnis on board, or of a cat either. Captain . . . we also found no trace of five others of the crew, and fifteen guardsmen."

Tiana was profoundly glad that she could pretend to be chewing. The news was a jolting shock. Its enormity made any reaction inadequate. Twenty men—*gone?* She swallowed, otherwise showing nothing. When confronted with circumstances frightening or worse, she tended toward a superhuman calm—else she'd have been dead years ago. Besides, she was ship's master. If she showed anything approaching panic, so would the crew. Or Bardon, who appeared to be poised on the edge, right now.

"Oh yes," she said in a natural tone. "Did you find any sign of struggle?"

"No, none." Bardon showed his puzzlement at her bland reaction, and even so she *saw* him relax a bit.

"Right," she said, and dissembled further. "Well, mention that five men are sick. That way no one will wonder about someone he doesn't see—and I'll keep them busy!

Sorry, Virakoka. Maybe it was breakfast." Inside, she seethed: *Twenty men! No wonder poor Koka has leftovers!* "Why don't you each quietly have a measure of wine. Sit down and have some breakfast, Bardon. You'll need your strength this night." *If not before,* she thought, and hoped not.

She returned on deck, trying to think through the problem of the white cat. Just as the facts seemed promising to fit together, the lookout bellowed *"Land Ho!"* That drove away all other thought. Tiana mounted the rigging for a better view. Land? She saw three ugly jagged rocks rearing out of the water. If Voomundo's chart was accurate, those things were outlying portions of the Kroll Isles.

"Rat dung!" Considerably off course, she descended to turn *Vixen* eastward. That required some fairly tricky sailing; the Kroll Isles as landmarks, *Vixen* out of sight of the several lookout points. The sun was low by the time she reached her goal. Tiana gazed toward those dim rocky points and the full green sleeve of her shirt rustled as she gestured.

"Drop anchor. Into the rigging and be quick about it. We have less than an hour to lower sail and raise the black ones."

She moved to the rail. There, occasionally calling an order to hasten the raising of black canvas, she directed her mind back to the mystery of the white cat.

It's on this ship but it can't be found. All right then, it's not a natural creature. It's a—Something Else that takes the form of a cat. Though events hardly made sense, they had begun to form a pattern. The blind beggar Arond: striding through the Wayfarer as if he were again a pirate going to battle. Duke Holonbad, drinking his own poisoned wine as if it was an excellent vintage. Uldrood and his mad vision—and Captain Despan faithfully obeying orders that had never been given.

They're all in the same pattern, Tiana mused. The cat never attacked directly. Its power was that of illusion, which it used to trick others into doing its will. After each use of that power, a bloodless corpse was found. *This accursed cat is a king vampire! It needs to drink blood each time it uses its power*—and it must want either Princess Jiltha or the Jewels . . . ! Fate had made her the cat's rival for both, she realized now, and it had naturally tried to kill her. Failing in that, it had found a way to join her expedition.

By the Cud—it hadn't attacked during the voyage because I am taking it where it wants to go!

Tiana trembled, practically dancing in excitement. She was solving the riddle! Another few minutes and she would have the pieces together—and her thoughts were interrupted. It was the handsome and thoroughly competent Kathis of Reme. Strange that the man failed to attract her; there was something . . . cold about him.

"Yes, Kathis," she snapped coldly, "what is it?"

"It is the eve of battle. There are many details we need to discuss, Captain. First though I want to thank you. I understand the king's original plan meant that I and my men would be fighting for no more than our regular wage as soldiers. Your generous decision to share the treasure means I shall be a wealthy man."

Tiana looked narrowly at the warrior. Was this ever-armored stick really so naive that he failed to see the larger stakes in this game? "No thanks are necessary, Kathis. I wanted to avoid setting our men against each other." *And can't you see that I have also robbed you of your command?*

"I have known many great and noble lords, but none with such a fine sense of noblesse oblige as you." He lifted his head to jut his chin in that odd way of his; if the gorget bothered his neck, why did he persist in wearing it?

Though Tiana loved flattery the way a cat loves cream, there was something uncomfortable about this conversation. She changed the subject. "Do you really plan to wear all that heavy armor into a sea battle?"

"Oh Captain, I can easily swim in this bit of weight. I'm practically stripped. Only helmet and body armor left, with my arms and legs quite bare."

"Hardly," she corrected, giving him another narrow look. "Your arms are not bare at all. I'd think a long-sleeved woolen shirt like that would be . . . uncomfortable, Kathis."

He shrugged. "Really, there are more important things for us to discuss. First of all . . ."

Kathis proceeded to ask Tiana about a host of unimportant but seemingly necessary details. When at last he had finished, Bardon appeared. Tiana was kept busy and found no chance to think. And then it was time to sail.

The sun was setting behind the Kroll Isles, painting the waters and land a red gold. Now was the ideal time to approach the Isles. *Vixen* would be invisible coming out of darkness, while her crew could see where they were going. Even the breeze was strong and favorable. Tiana pored over Voomundo's chart.

The first lookout point they were able to pass at some distance. It was low on the horizon, nearly invisible in the dusk. Tiana was certain the watchmen could not have seen her ship. The second watch had to be passed at closer range, but the channel was wide and clear. By now twilight was a faint glow in the west and purple shadows had gone black. Tiana signaled for total silence and *Vixen* stole forward. Her black sails were full and did not flap. Every man sat motionless and silent through many tense minutes—until Tiana signaled normal running. No signal fire had appeared.

The third lookout point was some distance away and now it was a race against moonrise. Voomundo's chart showed every current. Tiana used them and every inch of sail to best advantage, but the moon won the race. This watch point was built on a cliff above two navigable channels. One was the normal channel, in plain view of the watch tower. With the moon up, even an aged scribe could see *Vixen* pass. The second channel flowed narrowly between a reef and great rocks, directly beneath the lookout cliff. Tiana steered into that track of danger and signaled silence. Bardon had taken his position in the ship's prow. Signal ropes had been rigged. Men held their breaths and hearts pounded. It was like sailing through a great mouth of gnashing teeth . . . and then they were clear.

The fourth shore-watch point would require the least skill and the most luck. The lookout was manned by a single watcher. If he were not keeping close watch, all would be well. Just when it seemed the plan was working perfectly, a man ran from the base of the watch tower, bearing a blazing torch. He raced toward a large pile of wood. Kathis's long bow sang and the man pitched over. His torch fell to the ground and died. In silence, Tiana squeezed Kathis's arm. He seemed to wince, but his teeth flashed in a smile.

They did not plan to sneak past the last lookout. This post must be surprised and stormed. It had been Tiana's intent to lead the attack party; now Kathis logically insisted that the task belonged to him. He picked six of his men, all that would fit in the small boat, and departed. Even for a small boat the path among the rocks was treacherous.

They managed.

Tiana wanted to stand and stare after those men going into the foggy dusk, crowded in mail into the little boat, bent on murder; ever-necessary murder. Instead she went to her cabin. Peeling off belt and blouse, she wriggled and strained into the breast-bracer she wore on Business. Sometimes it wasn't easy being a woman, she mused—and didn't the small-chested ones have it easier!

Once she had the blouse on again and tucked in, her vanity sent her hands up under her shorts to tug down the blouse-tails. She buckled on her Business belt: lockpicks, special clip, concealed stabber—tiny—special buckle; rapier sling on left, dagger sheath on right; whaleskin packet of thieves' tools behind. She added the lovely drop earrings—which were picklocks. Swinging her long black cloak about her, she went back on deck— to find Kathis and his men returning out of the early fog. Too soon, surely.

"What happened?" a frowning Tiana Highrider demanded.

Kathis shook his head encased in a round, fog-gleaming helm with a mail curtain on either side and behind. The ever-present gorget protected his throat.

"Don't know," he said, pulling off a boot to splash forth water. "When we arrived they were all dead. Chopped up in combat. Bodies were still warm."

"Dead!—were they all Kroll pirates, Kathis?"

He gave her a little smile; one knowing warrior to another. "No. One was a uniformed soldier. A Thesian marine. Dead as the rest. Chopped bad."

Tiana swore silently, staring off toward shore. Obviously that slimeball greasehead king of Thesia wanted Jiltha and had sent a raiding party! The dogs had got here first—barely. By themselves, the raiders might be no great problem. If there was one thing this game did not need, though, it was another player!

"Your lads are disappointed, Kathis. Why not give them a jack of ale."

And she turned to call orders. With the way to Storgavar's castle and all they sought clear, Tiana nevertheless ruddered cautiously toward the main island. Well offshore, she ordered the sails lowered. *Vixen* drifted slowly in, a dark specter on a quiet dark sea. Clouds like goblins were busily chewing the moon—no. They were not clouds.

A ship was afire in the harbor, pouring up smoke. At this distance in darkness, neither Tiana nor Kathis could make out individual human forms. They heard the screams of wounded and dying.

"It seems," Tiana murmured in a purr, "that the Thesian plaguls walked into a trap. It would be suicide for us to attack now." She reflected for a moment. "Force fails us, so we must use stealth. I'm a skilled thief; I'll go to Storgavar s castle. Alone. Bardon: take *Vixen* to this cove." She pointed it out on Voomundo's map. "If I'm successful, I'll rejoin you within three days. Otherwise you'd best go home." She looked into his eyes. "Three days, Bardon."

Bardon looked unhappy, but there was nothing unusual about that. He needed a haircut, Tiana noticed.

Kathis quietly said, "I am going with you," and his tone permitted no argument. Tiana looked at him in the darkness, and touched his sleeved arm. She saw his jaw tighten. That was twice. Well, she'd not touch the parky fellow again!

The small boat was lowered and the pair rowed off through the dark waters. Tiana's head buzzed with plans for her imminent theft. Yet she had left something undone. The white cat. Her train of thought had been interrupted just as she was about to solve that riddle. The deadly little beast was on her ship. For two weeks it had not attacked her, because she was taking it where it wanted to go. Last night, a ghastly lot of men vanished, presumably because the cat drained them of blood and threw the bodies overboard. Why? (Never mind how!) Because it needed blood to live—*no! To use its full power!* It guzzled all that in preparation for the raid, she realized. That was a logical stratagem: let her and Kathis's men do most of the fighting, then seize the treasure.

Now, however, she was rowing away, leaving the

white cat behind on the ship. *That hardly makes sense . . .
unless . . . unless the cat is here, with me in this cockle-
shell of a boat . . . well away from everyone else. . . .*

"Kathis? As a favor to me; would you just turn up your
sleeve, please?"

He complied without a word. As Tiana expected, the
arm was covered with fresh scratches. She swallowed.

"I see that Rarn hurt you, White Cat."

"You are a clever one, Tiana, but now it is too late."

At last Kathis removed his gorget—to reveal a diamond on his throat. It blazed white in the moonlight. Yet
Tiana saw that it was slowly turning a darker hue . . .
red. The armored Kathis rose and stepped toward her.

CHAPTER NINE

"Cat," Tiana Highrider sneered, "you're no sailor."

She leaned to one side, hard. The boat listed and Kathis, standing upright in armor, was instantly pitched overboard. For a moment the boat threatened to capsize, then righted. Tiana seized an oar and swung it like a club. The glow of that unnatural gem marked where Kathis would surface. His shining casque broke the surface and the oar smashed into it. The blow was solid though slightly off center, and Tiana was in haste to strike again. She knew her advantage was temporary; she was no match for this monster. The oar sped down—and *writhed*. In her hand it became a snake. Knowing it was an illusion did not prevent its spoiling her aim. The oar banged on Kathis's armored body, accomplishing little. As she raised the oar for another blow, Kathis . . . *multiplied*.

Now the water was alive with a dozen armored figures. A dozen glowing diamonds, eleven white and one blazing red. Tiana decided instantly; Tiana's oar crashed down on the wearer of the red diamond. The blow was true and hard. It would have killed an ox—or a helmeted man.

The red diamond shot out intense fire. It became a blazing red sun and the sky was split by lightning. Tiana was surrounded by soft sweet roses. Tiana was falling through endless space. Tiana was being kissed by a great frog. Illusions or not, Tiana swung the oar again and again. The boat rocked wildly. Sometimes she struck empty water, sometimes armored flesh. The important thing was to keep the pressure on. She knew she might be doing little physical harm but she was forcing the cat to spend its hoard of deadly power. She must give it no chance to think, lest it devise an illusion of deadly effect.

Through a wild tangle of delirium she struck and struck again. . . .

Then all was normal. Tiana was in the boat panting and the sea around her was empty. She knew the cat must still be here; was invisibility one of its tricks? She scanned the water for a false ripple pattern, any inconsistency. Nothing. If the cat was not on the surface, it must be swimming underwater. Hastily she seized the second oar and started to row. The small boat moved forward—and jolted. With a crash, a sword thrust up through the bottom of the boat. Boards snapped and water poured in.

"By the Back! Won't you ever give up, or just *die?*"

She swung her oar so that it struck the flat of the sword and snapped it. Drawing her dagger, she dived into the black water.

To her right a red star burned—in the center of a writhing octopus. It tried to flail away from her, and she swam at it. Eight tentacles reached toward her. Instinct told her one tentacle was in truth an arm; she stabbed it. Seven tentacles faded away. The last became Kathis's right arm, bleeding profusely. Should she try for a fatal thrust? No; with but a small illusion she would break her knife upon the armor. Better to wear her opponent down. Kathis turned, rose toward the surface in the eerie illumination of the diamond. He must need air, Tiana thought—as she stabbed his right leg. Again blood gushed into the sea, burgundy in the red-lit water.

Best finish this butcher's work before all this blood attracts sharks!

She saw the large dark form behind her and realized it was what she feared most. The shark arrowed rapidly at her. She kicked herself rightward and grabbed as it passed, a sleek awful thing of teeth and muscle. She stabbed again and again, but her knife would barely penetrate the shark's tough hide. The beast twisted, bent; its massive jaws snapped closer. Her lungs flamed. She had been too long underwater. Her grip slipped and fanged jaws tore at her right arm. Somehow she pulled it free and redoubled her efforts to slay the sea-tiger. Then, abruptly, she stopped.

Dung! The more fool I! She released her hold and rose toward the surface. The shark lunged at her bare legs. Its fearful jaws closed—and the illusion ended. As she had guessed, the "shark" was only the swamped small boat. The white cat had used its power of illusion to escape.

For a few moments Tiana did nothing but breathe. At last she began swimming for shore. Kathis/the cat was somewhere ahead of her. It would be good if she could overhaul him before he reached the foggy shore. Her enemy was at a great disadvantage in water. It was vital that she find him before he could trap new victims and drink their blood. The monster was hurt, its supernatural powers depleted. It must be slain, now or never.

Although Tiana was a fleet swimmer and her enemy wounded, she did not overtake him. Reaching shore, she searched among reeds and cattails for footprints. Well to her left she found them; the marks of a soldier's boots coming out of the water. During her underwater struggles Tiana had not lost the rapier slung from her belt. Now she drew it. If only she could sneak up on the white cat, one swift thrust in the back would settle the matter.

The tracks led to a small dirt road and there they ended. Beside the road lay a body. The position of the corpse was twisted and unnatural as if many bones were broken. Deep wounds marked the right leg and arm. Neither bled. Tiana stared down at Kathis. He was still alive, but only just, an extreme pallor bespeaking his heavy blood-loss; more than could be accounted for by the knife wounds. The diamond was gone from his throat. It had left a gaping red hole.

Tiana perceived a subtle but important change: despite the pain of coming death, Kathis's face was now ... warm. Human. His eyes opened.

"What—what happened?" His voice was an ugly rasp, very low and weak.

Was this another illusion, a clever trap? Perhaps; she did not think so. Her voice was neutral as she asked, "What do you last remember?"

"I was guarding the excavation in the Holy Grove of Syrodan when blackness came up out of the ground."

Tiana looked softly on the fallen warrior, and thought of what might have been. "Much has happened since then, Kathis."

"I'm dying?"

"I'm sorry; yes."

He smiled faintly. "At least the company is pleasant!" A slight tremor took him, and Kathis was dead. This victory Tiana regarded with mixed emotions. There was no reason to suppose a great mystery concerning the manner of his death. He had come ashore unarmed, grievously wounded, with his supernatural powers exhausted. He wore a very valuable diamond and he was a stranger on a pirate island. It was only natural that she find him robbed and murdered. The problem was that Tiana had fought a monster, but only a man had died. She felt no elation in her victory; indeed she was not sure she had won a victory.

And there was no time to worry about that. She set briskly off down the road. She still had a job to do, cat or no cat, and Tiana's will was forged on some preternatural anvil. Tonight, during the confusion after the battle with the Thesians, remained the best time to steal the Jewels of Ullatara, and rescue the Princess Jiltha. Surely both were within the keep of Storgavar. Since the pirate lord was known to believe in keeping all his eggs in one basket and watching the basket, it was likely that princess and gems were in the same place and well guarded. The question was where. In a tower? A dungeon, a hidden strong room? As Tiana walked, she came to two conclusions. As the first rule of successful theft was know the target, she must find an accomplice. Someone who knew the inside of Storgavar's castle. The second conclusion was that she was hungry. It had been a long day and it would be a longer night. Best she eat immediately, while she had a chance.

In the quest for food her nose proved a reliable guide. No lights burned in the large building she approached, but one window released a most pleasant aroma.

She entered a deserted kitchen; a recently and hastily deserted kitchen. The wood stove's fire was nearly out. On a table rested a nice burning candle, a large pile of clean dishes and a pot of thick fish stew. Redolent of leeks and basil, the stew was warm but not hot. *Someone was about to serve supper for several people, when cook and diners were called away.* Tiana put some more wood on the fire, and replaced the pot on the stove, chewing the inside of her lip.

While the stew heats up, she decided, *let's just explore the house and learn what happened.*

The kitchen door opened onto a medium-sized banquet room, lavishly decorated in abominable taste. The table was set, the wine was poured; the guests were gone. The rest of the house consisted chiefly of small bedrooms, all empty.

"A whorehouse," she muttered. "So where have the dear girls and their customers gone?" The next bedroom was larger and was furnished at much greater expense, if not in better taste. Assuming this to be the madam's room, Tiana searched it quickly. In a rather obvious hiding place she found a strongbox. A moment's work with her lockpick opened it. Inside lay several nice jewels and a considerable sum in gold, minted in several lands.

Tiana was not interested in petty theft. She hastened back to the kitchen. It was most puzzling that the House's proprietor had departed leaving her savings behind and unguarded! Indeed, nothing seemed to have been taken. . . .

"Wait!" A quick search of the kitchen larder uncovered only a few perishables. All the staples were gone.

The kitchen's second door proved to lead to a cellar. It stank. Tiana found it filled not with wine racks but with cages. Though she had expected this, the sight still made her angry. The madam used her cellar as a dungeon for conditioning freshly captured girls. Empty, the cages nevertheless showed signs of very recent use. One odd note; there were no chains anywhere to be seen.

A small noise brought Tiana's candle higher. She was wrong; in the very last cage huddled a small white figure. Approaching with care, she discovered the cage contained a naked young girl, so emaciated that one could count her ribs. Tiana could have picked the lock, but the cage was made of light metal. With a sudden violent motion she pulled, twisted, and the cage door sprang open.

"Come on, girl, I've food upstairs."

Not until the frightened, overawed girl was seated and spooning up chunky stew did Tiana begin to question her.

"What's your name, dear?"

"May it please your ladyship, I be Morna." Morna sniffed.

Tiana studied the russet-haired girl closely. Even if she had not been starved half to death the wench would have been no great beauty. "How come you here?"

"Pirates captured our ship and sold me to Vorgia. That

awful woman wanted to teach me to—to be a—but I wouldn't so they didn't feed me."

Tiana maintained a list of people she would murder at her earliest convenience. Since Morna wasn't even slightly pretty, it was probable that this Vorgia creature had bought her not to train at all, but to starve as an example to the other trainees. Tiana mentally added Vorgia's name to her list.

"What happened tonight, Morna?"

"The three-eyed bear came." Morna shuddered. Nothing jiggled, Tiana noted.

"What? Explain that, Morna dear. A *three*-eyed *bear?*"

"A large black bear with three red eyes, aye mum. It came down into the cellar. Vorgia and several men was with it. *It* told the men to collect all the chains. Then it looked at all the girls and said they would all do except me. They took all the others and left." Morna sniffed.

"The bear actually spoke?"

"Yes, and Vorgia called it by name."

"What name?"

"She called it Store-guhvar."

Storgavar. Tiana considered that a moment. "All right, Morna. I'll help you, but I don't have time to be a nursemaid." Quickly she explained how Morna could reach *Vixen*. "You'll find clothes in the bedrooms. Put together a sensible outfit. There's an open box of gold in Vorgia's room. Take one handful, now; you're too weak to carry more. And a nice necklace. If all goes well, I'll join you in three days. Well, don't just sit there, Morna—be about it!"

After the girl hurried off, Tiana sat watching the fire in the stove. She'd had her supper. There was no reason to sit idle and much reason to be about her business. Nevertheless she sat, and added wood to the fire till it burned to great height. There was an enchantment to the shifting patterns of a fire. One could imagine all sorts of pictures in flames. These seemed to contain a face; those two dancing spots of pale green were the eyes.

Tiana stared. Green flames! The image became clearer, more vivid. It *was* a face! The face of a man little known and much feared.

She was staring at the wizard Pyre.

The fire spoke. "I, Pyre who knows he is supreme,

once vowed by the World Fires to avenge you, Tiana. Presently there is nothing I can do save warn you, and that tries my powers to the utmost."

Even as he spoke, the fire weakened, the green going out of it, and Pyre's face contorted in pain. Tiana added more wood, blew on the fire, cursed a little. Nothing she could do would keep the unnatural flame alive. The fire died, and with it whatever warning the wizard intended.

Tiana departed the place in haste. An unknown danger existed and she'd best be at her work swiftly. She hurried along, pondering, and had covered about a mile when she came upon the corpses. One of them was a middle-aged woman; coarse features, too many rings, heavy makeup, and flamboyant attire.

"Hm! I think it's safe to remove Vorgia's name from my list."

She discovered that all the bodies had suffered considerable violence. Yet no spilled blood marked the ground, and horripilation made Tiana clench her teeth.

The white cat was dead, but something had made Kathis into that monster. And now—that faceless unknown was free and about its dark business.

CHAPTER TEN

Tiana stood thinking rapidly. It was now clear that this would be a three-cornered battle, and she was the weakest corner. Pyre's sending had been blocked by the . . . the three-eyed bear. Pyre! *Blocked!* If it could best the most dread of wizards, her foe was truly a Power. Judging by the actions of the white cat, the bear could logically be expected to . . . *ah*.

Tiana Highrider knew what she must do and knew she must be swift about it.

From the body of a dead pirate she took a heavy cutlass; a weapon far too massive for her, suitable only for a powerful warrior. Voomundo's map was clear in her memory, and several landmarks it showed were visible from where she stood. While this was her first visit to Kroll Isle, she was sure the place she wanted was not far. She hastened down the dirt road that wound inland, out of the fog. Presently she saw a faint trail leading back to the sea. She followed it, running. Ahead reared a small black hill overlooking a purplish bay. She was right. This must be Siren Bay, famed in evil legend.

Rather cautiously, she ascended the hill, drawing her silken rope from the small kit of thieves' tools at her belt's back. She tied one end of the rope to a thick copse of bushes at the top of the hill. It aided her descent of the seaward side of the hill.

In taverns around the world she had heard the grim tale of Siren Bay and Slippery Hill and now it appeared the tale was true. The seaward side of the hill was *steep*. Yet looking at it, one would think it could be climbed. It could not. The hillside was not earth, but smooth rock, covered with a rootless slime weed. It was extremely slippery. Were it not for the rope, Tiana's first slip would have sent her sliding down the hill to fall into the Bay. Using the rope, she went halfway down the slope. Carefully retaining her grip on slim, silken line, she tied one end of the rope to the cutlass and laid the weapon in the weeds. Moving well to the right, she climbed back to the top of the hill.

She surveyed her preparations and found them satisfactory. The cutlass was effectively hidden and the rope was laid so that it went halfway down the hill, then stretched across it. A group of acacias on the landward side of the hill seemed a good hiding place. Amid madderwort and wild petunias Tiana settled back to wait. If she had correctly guessed the course of events, she would not wait long.

The pregnant moon was full and high in a sky of lavender and cerulean and black jade, and now that Tiana was quiet she could hear the faint sounds coming from the sea. They were sweet, gentle clear sounds, laughter as might come from the quicksilver throats of women beautiful beyond credibility. The tale Tiana had heard also said that by moonlight one might catch tantalizing glimpses of those who laughed. Supposedly they were water women of great beauty, mermaids who came to the bay to sport in the moon-bright waters. How could one get a closer look? If one rowed a boat into the bay, the laughter ceased and one rowed back having seen nothing. If one swam the laughter continued. No doubt the swimmer obtained a closer look—and never returned. Through the years many men had vanished swimming in Siren Bay. Had they drowned in the passionate embrace of submarine lovers? Perhaps. The only certainty was that pirates of Kroll Isle used the Bay as a means of execution. They called it sending a man to "make love to the mermaids." It was effective and final.

Tiana was too guided by impulses to enjoy waiting, but when necessary she could sit silent and motionless. The moon was high and bright when her patience was rewarded. The advance scout glided up the hill, a soundless fleeting shadow. Though Tiana kept keen watch, she saw him only after he passed her position. She was impressed. Reaching the hilltop and finding no one, the scout shouted the All Clear and stood waiting for his comrades.

He did not wait long. Up the hill came eight men. Two

bore torches while six struggled with some heavy object. As they came closer, Tiana could see that they carried a man, bound hand and foot. At least the bound creature was presumably a man; the face was shaven and the head was bald. In general build he looked more like a gorilla; short, thick body, extremely powerful limbs. A huge man, powerful. Evidently he was in great rage. His black eyes were burning coals and despite a gag, a steady stream of blurred but astoundingly loud profanity came from his lips. The men who carried him were having a difficult time as he lunged, bucked and twisted in their grasp. Midway up the hill, they put down their captive and tried to kick him into submission. This was a mistake. The thick man paid no more heed to their blows than would a boulder. Arching his broad back, he applied his full strength to the rope linking his bound hands and his feet. With a sharp snap the rope parted. Tiana swallowed. With his hands still tied behind him and his feet still bound together the thick man had gained as much freedom of motion as an inchworm. His captors were in haste to retie the broken rope, and in the mad scramble one of them was careless. In an act of perfectly timed violence the thick man's bound legs shot forth to strike him at the base of the spine. With a loud *Snap,* the victim tumbled down the hill like a broken doll.

Moving more cautiously, the others succeeded in retying their prisoner. When they had hauled the thick man to the top of the hill, one of the torch bearers spoke.

"Impostor! For your crime of pretending to be Storgavar, lord leader of these Isles, you are sentenced to make love to the mermaids. Tradition gives you one last chance to speak."

"Blast your eyes, Urga," the big captive stormed. "Look at me. I *am* Storgavar. Why have you dogs suddenly gone mad?"

"You can not lie to us, impostor. All right, lads, let's to it."

While Storgavar raged at them, Urga and his men readjusted the ropes binding him. At last the knots were to their satisfaction.

"Ready," Urga called, "set—throw!" Several men shoved the pirate lord down the seaward side of the hill, while others held the ends of the ropes that bound him. When Storgavar was a few feet down Slippery Hill, past the point of no return, the rope holders pulled back, bringing him to a halt. Sharp jerks to the ropes flipped them loose. Storgavar's arms and legs were free—and he was slowly sliding down the hill.

Urga shouted, "My *lord leader*, I'm sorry we mistook you for an impostor, but now we've untied you. Step up here and we shall go back to your castle."

"Yes," another mocked, "*surely* if you're Storgavar, you can climb little old Slippery Hill."

"Bastards!" the pirate chief snarled. "I'll not beg." His hand reached to the top of his boot. Something bright flashed in his hand and he threw. Urga twisted to one side so that the knife struck him in the left arm rather than the heart. Unfortunately throwing the knife accelerated Storgavar's downward slide. While Urga cursed and the others laughed, the pirate lord plunged down the hill. His desperate hands tore at the slimy rock in vain quest of some hold—and of course he hit Tiana's rope.

In a moment he was on his feet. Climbing, armed with the heavy cutlass. In the flickering torchlight the slender silk rope was invisible. Urga and his comrades were astonished at the sight of a man climbing up Slippery Hill. Their surprise caused a brief but fatal delay. When Urga at last shouted, "He has a rope! Cut it!"— Storgavar was nearly up the hill.

One man was in position to cut the rope in time and his keen eyes spotted the thin silk. He stepped toward it, sword raised, and fell without a murmur when Tiana's rapier pierced his heart.

Then Storgavar was at the summit and dealing death with mighty blows of the cutlass. As a swordsman he lacked finesse, and it did not matter. The man's great strength made his thrusts impossible to parry. The torches fell and died. Since the moon had passed behind a cloud, the battle was a tangled clash in darkness. Urga shouted an order that was incoherent amid the ring of steel against steel. Tiana saw an opening and lunged, impaling Urga's throat. The press of battle shifted and combatants fell to slide downward. The fight had carried them over the edge of Slippery Hill. Now they were falling into Siren Bay.

Tiana was among them. She clawed frantically at the slick stone without slowing her descent a whit. Then a huge hand grasped her leg and she was lifted unceremoniously upward. Draping her across his shoulders like a sack of flour, Storgavar began climbing the rope back up Slippery Hill.

Reaching the summit once more, he put her down and laughed.

"Now I know the world's gone mad. My own men turn against me and I'm rescued by a beautiful girl." He paused. From below came screams and splashes, followed by peals of lyrical happy laughter. "I trust those lads will amuse the mermaids. Now who are you, girl, and why did you save me?"

"My questions first, and we had best walk back toward your castle while we talk. The Princess Jiltha; is she unharmed and still virgin?"

"Of course! There's little market for a used princess."

"What happened tonight, Storgavar?"

"We had warning that the King of Thesia and Ekron the wizard had sent a raiding party, so we fixed an ambush and . . ."

"Wait—who sent the warning?"

The pirate lord's massive features showed not exactly fear, but discomfort. "That warning was a strange thing. Should have known no good could come from it."

"What happened?"

"I held banquet for eleven of my captains. Since I aimed to honor them, I instructed my steward to begin serving with the man on my left, and thus around the table. Me last. The wine was rich and strong and the girls walked around the table whispering of delights to come and my steward brought out twelve platters of dam' good roast beef. He served as I instructed, but when he came around the table, he served the last platter to the captain on my right and stood before me empty-handed. I started to curse the fool but stopped. There were twelve platters on the table! Why wasn't there one for me? I counted and saw that including me there were thirteen men at table. Twice I looked round the table and saw only eleven familiar faces. The third time I noticed the fellow sitting on my left. A tall hawk-faced man, broad of shoulder, clad in black robes.

"His yellow eyes fixed upon me. 'Since I can not eat, you might as well take back this beef.'

"I sprang forward to seize the intruder, but my hands

passed through his body. 'Spectre,' I roared, 'who are you?'

"He said, 'Be not alarmed, Storgavar. I am Pyre and I come to give timely warning,' and I said 'Help from the most feared man in the world? I have heard the tales of your dark deeds!' and that damned apparition laughed at me! 'Do not speak to me of dark deeds, for I have Sight,' it said or he said. 'I can look at the ocean and see every drop of innocent blood you and your fellows have shed. If it were convenient, I would give you the destruction you deserve, but we have a common enemy. The wizard Ekron. He wants the Jewels of Ullatara and has conspired with the King of Thesia to steal them and the Princess Jiltha from you.'

"I told him that no raiding ship could pass *our* lookouts.

"'Tomorrow night,' this vision of Pyre said, 'they will land at Skull Point two hours after moonrise. You will have no warning of their coming, except my words.'

"As he spoke these words, he slowly faded. The last sounds came from empty air." —

Tiana had listened to this story with great interest. Now she asked, "You say Pyre's eyes were yellow?"

"Yes! Like topazes they were."

"I have seen these sendings of his twice. Once the eyes were gray; the second time green. When he appeared to King Hower, his eyes were black."

Storgavar laughed. "For all his powers, Pyre has his limits. There's an old saying: The eye sees not itself. That applies to him. He can send a perfect image of everything except his own eyes."

"Interesting . . . but tell me about the battle with the Thesians?"

"Hah! It wasn't much of a battle. We had the number on them and took them completely by surprise. If it hadn't been for that blond giant who led them, it would have been a simple massacre. As it was, he gave us some bad moments, but the outcome was never in much doubt. Being a giant his head stuck up above the rest of his men and made him an easy target for my slingers." Storgavar chuckled. "After we knocked him out, we killed most of the Thesians and took a few captive for later sport. I went back to the castle for a late supper and some wenching but I was scarcely started when word came that the world had gone mad. Several captains came and demanded to know why I had given such strange orders. According to them I had ordered our three largest ships made ready for a long voyage. They were to be emptied of all nonessentials and loaded with every bit of staple food on the island. Gangs of men were rounding up every man, woman and child and herding them onto the ships. I'd said no such, and went out to investigate and was promptly seized by Urga and his men. And that's it. Now it's my turn. Who are you? Why'd you save me?"

"I'm Tiana, captain of *Vixen*."

"No! I've heard of you!"

"Of course," Tiana said. "I saved you so that you can help me steal the Jewels of Ullatara and the Princess Jiltha."

"What! Rob myself?"

"Surely it is obvious that you have already been robbed. The question is, do you wish to recover part of what you had? I offer equal captain's shares."

"Why should I recover part when I can recover all?"

"Do you really want to fight black magic?"

Anger and fear waged war across the pirate lord's scarred face. Tiana watched fear win. "Who is this that has stolen my property, my position, my name and even my appearance?"

"A vampire, Storgavar. Right now it takes the shape of a three-eyed bear. It seeks either the jewels or the princess. Are they well hidden? Does anyone except you know where they are?"

"I have a strongroom only I know of. Since we were expecting a raid, I hid them in that room."

"Good! Then we have a chance to reach them ahead of the Bear."

"*We*," Storgavar muttered.

CHAPTER ELEVEN

Storgavar's castle bristled up against the moon. Squat, massive, a superbly strong fortress—and painfully ugly building. He looked proudly at it.

"A beauty, isn't she?"

"The castle looks like you," Tiana assured him. Before he could wonder whether or not that was a compliment, she asked, "Now where's this secret entrance?"

"Under your tail."

Tiana looked down at the boulder on which she sat. She sprang off. The pirate lord braced his shoulder against the massive stone, and slowly pushed it to one side. Revealed was a small dirty hole in the ground.

"This tunnel and all my other secret passages are doubly secure. Nobody but me knows where they are and the doors are all so heavy that only I can open them." With this boast, Storgavar lay down and crawled like a worm into the hole. Tiana followed. The tunnel proved to be what she had feared: a narrow dark hole in the earth. As she squirmed forward, she occasionally felt wooden support beams. Her fingers told her that they were rotten. She moved with some caution lest she dislodge a weak beam and bury them. *Well*, she mused, *the tunnel was built for escape under desperate circumstances. Not my place to grouse that it's unsafe and uncomfortable.*

"Storgavar," she called, "how is it only you know of this tunnel and the storage room? What of the workmen who built them?"

"I built them myself. My only helpers were half-wits and drunks."

"Very clever."

He snorted. "Huh! At the time I thought I was hiring capable workmen."

Now Tiana was crawling in mud, cold and revoltingly clammy. She wanted very badly to curse the fool who had built this tunnel, but she was silent. Storgavar crawled with little noise for so large a man and Tiana's ears picked up another sound. Behind the pirate lord and directly in front of her, *something* was alive.

"Are there water snakes on this island?" As she spoke, the thing moved. Something wet and slippery landed on the back of her head. Before she could move, it leapt off, landing in the middle of her back and hopping on down her legs. Gooseflesh ran over her on a million cold feet.

"No," Storgavar called back, "just frogs. Make you nervous?"

"Of course not." *My voice just quivers because of the chill.*

The next incident was harder on Tiana's nerves. The tunnel changed. A hole in loose earth became one carved out of solid granite. No more mud, and the danger of collapse was past. There was a little water on the tunnel floor. Apparently the tunnel sloped slightly downward, for as Tiana advanced the water level rose. Soon it was to her neck and she was swimming more than crawling. Then the tunnel turned sharply down. There was no choice: she must take a deep breath and go as far as she could. Storgavar was ahead. Either he had won past this obstacle or she would find his drowned body blocking her way. She filled her lungs and struggled forward. In the darkness there was no measure of time or distance save the slowly growing ache of her lungs. If she maintained a steady pace she could go a good distance, while a moment of panic would be her last. She discerned a faint gleam of light ahead. The temptation to rush was great, but she maintained her steady pace and in a few moments she rose into light and air.

She glanced around and saw that she was inside a well. The top was not far and she was quickly out. The room in which she emerged was small, dank, lighted only by a single smoky lamp. Clever of Storgavar to keep flint and steel here, in a whalehide pouch. The walls were featureless solid stone. Evidently the room had been carved out of bedrock.

"Where's the secret room?"

"In front of you." Storgavar's smirk showed his pleasure with himself.

Tiana's examinations of the wall proved it to be without joint or seal. There was no way a door could be concealed in it. "We've no time to play games. Show me."

"Gladly. There's a beam beside the well. Pick it up and stand close to me."

Puzzled, Tiana lifted the beam. She grunted; it was a hand-breadth thick and very strong. The pirate lord laughed and stepped forward. Two iron rings were set in the wall, about a foot apart and a foot above the floor. Stooping, he grasped the rings and heaved. With a grating noise, the entire wall grumbled upward!

"Well don't stand there with your mouth open, Tieannie. I can't hold this stone all night. Put the beam under it."

Tiana stared at the great bulk of stone her companion was holding. As she moved the wood into place, she asked, "Are you sure it's strong enough to hold such a weight?"

"Oh sure. This block of stone is volcanic rock, very light. Ten *ordinary* men could lift it, or rather ten men could lift this much weight. The way the door is built only one man can stand in the right place to lift it." He grinned and Tiana tried not to look impressed.

They entered a small room that resembled the treasure trove of a giant pack rat. Jeweled swords. Golden armor. A great pile of fine kascat furs, Norten candles, racks filled with bottles of superb wine, pots of the fragrant soap of Tashol; a great block of ivory, tall as a man and wide as a barrel; a set of glasses carved in jade and wide variety of objects that would have been junk had they not been wrought of silver or gold. In the far corner lay an ironbound chest.

Beside it, chained and gagged, was a dirty-haired blonde.

Tiana had seen the Princess Jiltha before; she'd been blond, beautiful, haughty, and elegantly dressed. Now Tiana saw a frightened small child, dirty, clad in torn rags. It would have been quicker to cut off the gag, but the sight of a knife in her hand would further terrify the girl. She knelt and began to untie the gag.

"My Princess, your father sent me to bring you home.

You may remember me—I'm Captain Tiana. You need no longer fear Storgavar. I've made a bargain with him." When the gag was removed, Jiltha did not scream, but burst into tears. Tiana held the child in her arms and comforted her.

"You told me nothing about taking her back to her father," Storgavar roared. "I imagined we should sell her to the highest bidder. After all—Storgavar and Tie-anna! We *belong* together."

"What you imagine is your problem," Tiana snapped. "A bargain is a bargain."

"True." The big pirate bent, picked up the chest. "I now have the Jewels of Ullatara. If you want to take this baggage home to her father, well and good, but you must undo her chains."

"I don't need your key." And Tiana reached to her ear for a picklock.

She saw that neither key nor pick would be of any use. The manacles that bound Jiltha were smooth metal cylinders without locks. Neither was there any trick to open them. The manacles could be opened only by great physical strength.

"What I close, none but me can open. In this castle there are no locks, but there are many doors that only I have the strength to open. That is why I am lord of these isles, *Captain* Tie-annie. My door is always open to any with the strength to challenge me." Storgavar delivered this boast in a roaring voice. He might have said more, but a black shadow fell across him.

The pirate dropped the chest and whirled to face an even huger creature—a bear.

In most respects it resembled a natural bear; black greasy fur, large yellow fangs, long sharp claws. In addition to two normal eyes, however, a larger red orb glowed in the center of its forehead. While the natural eyes were dull, there was no mistaking the malign intelligence behind the third eye.

For a moment man and beast maneuvered for position, the monster towering over the man. Then they were upon each other. Storgavar met his enemy with open arms. His calves braced, bulging, below thighs thick as Tiana's torso. His hands clasped behind the beast's back and his powerful arms contracted in a death hug. His head was buried in the bear's chest. Although it twisted and bent, it couldn't bite him. After clawing red lines across his back, the bear locked its paws and began to hug. Tiana stared at a simple contest of brute force. Gorilla and bear strained, and the weaker would die of a broken spine.

Tiana had little time to watch the fight. Her obligation was to free the princess. The manacles were designed to preclude use of a lever or pry bar. Although she was considerably stronger than one might expect a very womanly-looking woman to be, the iron bonds would not yield to her straining fingers. The manacles were welded to chains attached to a ring in the wall. She found no weak links, and the ring was strong and firmly set in the stone. How to free the princess? King and country depended on her solving the problem.

"Jiltha: I want you to do something."

"Yes, sir—I mean—"

"You may call me captain, just as everyone else does. What I want you to do is this: take a deep breath, shut your eyes, and slowly say out loud 'I trust you, Captain!' "

"It's magic?"

"In a way. Do it, Jiltha."

"I trust you, Captain. I trust you, Captain. I trust you, Captain." By the time Jiltha had finished speaking, Tiana had smashed open a bottle of rare wine, used the wine to moisten the tashol soap, and soaped Jiltha's wrists and hands.

"Now Jiltha, just let your hands go limp."

The small slippery hands easily pulled out of the manacles. Tiana looked up to see Storgavar rising from the dead body of the bear.

"By the Great Cow's Cud *that* was a fight." The mighty pirate seemed little injured by his ordeal, though he poured sweat and leaked blood. "Look at this. The thing's wearing a *huge* diamond in its forehead."

Tiana looked at the broken body of the bear. It was true. What had seemed a sighted eye now appeared to be a large diamond, the same stone she had seen on Kathis's throat. The sight triggered an avalanche of realization in Tiana's mind. There had been too many mysterious happenings; at last she understood them.

"Storgavar: you remember what I told you about Pyre's message?"

Tiana had said nothing about Pyre, but the pirate lord said, "Sure; what of it?"

"I think I now understand the attack he plans. I couldn't before because I didn't know who our enemy is. I've fought a faceless unknown. Now I know the enemy." As Tiana spoke, she rose and assisted Jiltha to her feet.

"I'm interested. Let's hear it." Storgavar's voice had lost its harsh tone. It had gone all smooth and soft. Nor did he remark on her freeing the captive.

"There were numerous clues. The strange events started when the second pit was opened, back in Reme. At that time the Right Eye of Sarsis disappeared. The steel egg that held it was found smashed. Also at that time Kathis became the white cat. Before he could gain his full powers, King Hower sent away the Jewels of Ullatara—including the Left Eye of Sarsis. Kathis strengthened. He sought the treasure, and killed rival seekers. When I fought Kathis, he used his power of illusion to produce several false images of himself. I had no trouble striking the real one because the diamond on his throat had turned red while the false images wore white diamonds."

As she spoke, Tiana straightened the rags that had been Jiltha's dress. In doing so she maneuvered them both closer to the door.

"Yes, yes," Storgavar said, "but what has this to do with Pyre?"

"I'm coming to that. Voomundo warned me that the Right Eye of Sarsis was free. Although it has the outward appearance of a diamond, it's alive. It possesses whoever wears it. It gives the wearer the power to change shapes and cast illusions. These powers come at great cost. I'm sure from the way the diamond turned red while Kathis and I fought that the thing was drinking his blood."

"An . . . eye. An *Eye*."

"Yes. In turn, of course, the wearer is a vampire." Tiana and Jiltha were now as close to the door as Storgavar.

"And this attack Pyre plans?"

"It's based on a weakness he and the Eye share. When he does a sending, he can get every detail of his appearance correct except his eye color. The Right Eye

has a similar problem, for it also cannot see itself."
Tiana and Jiltha were closer to the door than Storgavar.
The girl was still badly frightened and would run like a
rabbit if Tiana let go of her.

"I don't see how that's the basis for an attack."

"It's very simple. Jiltha, run!"

Tiana shoved the girl through the door. After her she
kicked the beam from under the stone block, which fell
with a resounding crash. The treasure room was in total
darkness. As the block fell, Tiana had a brief glimpse of
the chamber. What had seemed to be Storgavar was the
trinocular bear. The pirate lord's dead body lay on the
floor, throat open and blood gone. His arms were
clasped in a bear hug about the ivory block. He had
spent his power trying to break it while the bear feasted.

From the darkness came the soft sweet voice of the
Right Eye of Sarsis.

"That, Tiana, was only half clever. It was clever of
you to realize that I no longer look like a diamond, hence
the image on the floor must be false. But what you did
was foolish. You're as much trapped as I. More so. *I*
have the strength to open Storgavar's door. What would
you do, chisel your way out?"

If I have to, yes, Tiana thought. *That volcanic rock
should be fairly easy to cut. If I've trapped myself, I've
trapped you too. You must fight me on nearly even
terms.* She said nothing, nor did she make any sound.

The soft voice said, "Let us make a bargain. I want
only the Left Eye. We have been parted for ages. You
can see how cruel that was; long hungry ages, buried
underground with no red milk to drink, separated from
one's other half. You can have the rest of the treasure.
You can save Jiltha and go home fabulously wealthy."

You mean go home with my veins empty, Tiana
mused, and moved silently through the darkness. The
floor beneath her feet changed. First it became mud,
then quicksand. Her every motion seemed to sink her
deeper. Despite the sucking pull on her legs, she took
another step. Yes, now she was in the right position.
This was a blind fight. She could trust nothing she saw,
heard or felt, but her enemy could not see in the dark. It
had tried to trick her into speaking. While the buttery
voice seemed some distance away, she was sure it was

close, waiting for a sound to guide its paw in a death blow.

Suddenly the room was brightly lighted. A jar of oil had overturned and fire was spreading rapidly over the spill. The oil was about her feet and the fire was racing toward her. Tiana stood motionless and let the flames envelop her. She knew one moment of searing heat before the illusion ended.

Slowly, without the slightest sound, Tiana drew her sword. The critical moment was approaching fast. The Eye now knew it could neither trick nor frighten her into making noise. Now she was sure the were-bear lacked a natural animal's keen sense of smell. It could find her in the dark only by feeling its way. Tiana was sure it feared her rapier and would not risk blundering into her. She must gamble her life that she could guess the Eye's next move.

It could project an illusion of silence and darkness, and open the door. Tiana would stand silent and unseeing while the monster killed her. She had no defense against that move, but she knew the Right Eye had eagerly sought the Left Eye. Before going to the door it would open the chest and take the steel egg that held the Left Eye. From memory, Tiana had moved so that she was behind the chest.

She stood poised, slim sword ready to strike. In her imagination she could see the bear opening the chest. She knew where its head must be when it lifted the lid and her rapier was perfectly aimed to stab through the brain. She stopped breathing.

The problem was when to strike. A false thrust would make a betraying sound. Only her enemy knew the right time for her to strike and she was counting on it to tell her. Sweat slid down the center of her back. Her enemy, if not a coward, was clearly overly cautious. Back in Reme it could easily have slain her had it been willing to risk a direct frontal assault. Instead it chose the safety of indirect attacks, letting others do its work, even though such attacks failed repeatedly. Now this fault of over-caution would betray it. It was in darkness with an armed enemy. When it bent and put its paws on the chest, it would be especially vulnerable. Therefore at that moment it would send a major illusion to distract her. The illusion the monster sent to prevent attack would signal Tiana to attack!

At least that was her plan. Now as she stood in darkness, her racing brain began to find a host of faults in it. She had devised it in haste in the fever of battle. Too late now to revise or make another. Her hands were sweating and her last meal was uneasy in her stomach. Her heart was pounding hard and she needed to breathe. Hours seemed to have passed since she'd shut the door. Why didn't the Eye do something? Anything to end this waiting! Had she underestimated her opponent? Could it summon help?

From outside the room came voices.

With a loud grating, the stone block was lifted. In the doorway stood the three men who had lifted the door —and four archers, long bows drawn and aimed at Tiana.

"Drop your sword!" the bear shouted. "You refuse to surrender? *Archers, shoot* her!"

Four strings twanged. Four arrows sped at Tiana and her sword lunged forward into empty air to pierce something that was not there.

Two arrows drove into her right shoulder and two into her stomach. She couldn't help crying out. Although she saw the shafts projecting from her flesh, there was no pain, no blood. Her rapier stood in empty air, quivering as something writhed on it. The bowmen were blurring, along with the chamber itself. Tiana knew that her vision was sharp and clear, but everything in sight was becoming fuzzy and distorted. A sudden convulsion twisted her hilt from her grasp and there was total darkness.

Tiana knew she had won another limited victory. The Right Eye of Sarsis was still free and dangerous. All she had slain were the two who had worn it: first the man and now the three-eyed bear. She was trapped in darkness with a demon that would possess her if she touched it. Slowly and with utmost care she stepped back and moved to the far wall. Feeling her way along it, she found the door. Tiana drew her dagger and began trying to chisel at the stone block. Though she detested using a good weapon thus, she had no choice. The softness of the stone made her task possible, but it would be a long job.

After some minutes she missed a stroke; the wall was moving, upward. Suddenly she was facing the Princess

Jiltha and a great blond giant of a man in boots, tawny
leather leggings, and a bronze-bossed mailcoat of shining leather the color of mahogany. His eyes were sky and
his hair corn.

"Captain! I found this man and he agreed to help
us."

"Well," Tiana said, appraising the muscular warrior,
"that was a stroke of luck."

"Indeed," a voice said from behind her. "It is my
great fortune to find you three all at once. A virgin princess, a mighty warrior, and a beautiful woman. I shall
need each of you in the coming ceremony."

Tiana whirled to see the three-eyed bear. Two of
the eyes were blank in death—and the third central eye
blazed with preternatural life. *The dead bear,* Tiana saw,
had opened the chest; in its paw was a jeweled talisman,
caged in terrible claws. It flashed and glowed and became a great white void into which Tiana felt herself
falling.

*But this just isn't fair—I killed it! Is there no justice
at—*

No, nor consciousness, either.

CHAPTER TWELVE

Tiana had left Bardon with the difficult task of hiding a ship in the midst of an enemy stronghold. She had ordered him to wait in the only possible place of concealment: A graveyard. The pi laging of the Kroll Isle pirates had brought home to their lair many more ships than they had use for. These were stripped of everything useful, then towed to a deadwater inlet and left. Into this graveyard of rotting ships Bardon sailed the proud *Vixen*. Dawn was his enemy. For now, the pirates were busy celebrating a victory. *Vixen* must be hidden by sunrise.

Reaching the graveyard was easy, but not enough. The swift beautiful ship must be made to appear one more abandoned hulk. Sails must be lowered and replaced by frayed old canvas taken from the hulks. Slime and seaweed must be pulled up and plastered over the ship. A successful disguise required a seeming endless array of tasks, and Bardon drove the men without mercy. When the sun rose, he looked proudly at the mess he had made of the ship.

"Without Tiana," he muttered. "Without Caranga."

The day was spent in rest and quiet. The meals were cold, for Bardon dared not let Virakoka light a fire. At midmorning the lookout spotted three large ships leaving the pirate harbor. None approached *Vixen*. After that there was no activity to be seen. The silence that surrounded them cloyed and only made the waiting harder. So did the mosquitoes.

Bardon had had no sleep the previous night, and now his nerves would not let him catch up. Men had vanished yesterday. An unknown enemy lurked aboard *Vixen* and Bardon could imagine no way to find it. The second mate had daydreamed of his own command. Now he had it: command of a crew hiding in a graveyard in growing fear of an enemy they could neither fight nor give a name to!

With Kathis gone, Sergeant Berrock was in command of the Ilani soldiery. At dusk the red-faced, big-nosed man approached Bardon.

"We must talk. Kathis left me without no orders. Do you plan on obeying that Tiana's instructions?"

"Of course. She is Captain."

"Even if men keep on disappearing, you'll wait on her three full days?"

"Yes."

"And if she don't come back—you plan on sailing back to Reme and reporting everything to King Hower?'

"Forget it, Berrock. She is Tiana. She will return, bringing the princess with her."

Berrock spat. "Most likely her and Kathis are already dead. When she don't come back, will you sail home and report to old Hower? Tell him we didn't save his daughter or even find her? That we lost our ship's cap'n and the best soldier in his army—we don't know how—and that in doing all this not once did we draw blade and face an enemy? You're going to walk into the palace and tell him that? He's a kind old guy, but for that kinda report he'll have your head and mine too!"

"That's right!" Bardon snapped. "What would you suggest?"

"Attack." Berrock said it flatly, without passion.

"I see. You want to waste the lives of half our men in a futile attack, so that you can tell the king what a hero you were." Berrock's face clouded with rage and Bardon went on before the soldier could vent his anger. "Say what you will to me, but say it quietly, Sergeant. The others must not hear us arguing."

Berrock saw the wisdom of that. Despite sharp disagreement, both men kept their voices down. At last the soldier wearied of the debate and gave his head a jerk.

"What it comes to is this: neither of us have the wit to deal with this situation. That old black pirate, now. I hear he's a crafty ole dog . . . why don't we ask him?"

Bardon controlled his own temper. "He's still weak and I hate to wake him. But . . . all right. We *are* allies, you and I."

They went side by side, the casque-wearing royal

guardsman and the bareheaded pirate with his long hair drawn back and bound by a cloth-of-gold band. Stolen, of course.

They entered Caranga's cabin to find him awake and sitting up in bed. On the cabin floor lay several wine bottles. Empty.

"Where's Tiana? How did the battle go?"

"It would appear," Bardon replied, gesturing at the bottles, "that a mighty battle has been fought in this cabin."

"Bah, that was just Tiana's sweet trick to make me sleep through the battle. It's shameless the way that girl treats her poor old father. Now where is she and what happened?"

Bardon related the events of the previous evening while Berrock stared at the massive hair-matted black chest. As he listened, Caranga's face lined with worry, then grew hard. Bardon finished.

"Berrock," Caranga rumbled, "you were among the Ilani soldiers who arrested *Vixen*'s crew in Reme."

The sergeant looked somewhat discomfited. "Well, yes. No hard feelings, I hope. Just obeying orders."

"In fact, you were in command. Kathis made the plan and set the men in place, but then he made some excuse and left you to carry out his plan."

"Why, yes, how did you know?"

"It's obvious. Had I not been a blind fool I would have solved this riddle in time to save my daughter. Kathis could not be at Zolgis's pleasure house at the same time the white cat was at the Wayfarer!" Neither Berrock nor Bardon spoke; the one's eyes showed confusion and the other's growing horror. Caranga tried to keep his voice flat and hard, to conceal the weight of despair he felt. "You were right about one thing, Berrock. Tiana will not return. Either she's a helpless captive, or—more likely, dead."

"Drood grasp me!" Bardon breathed. "What shall we do?" He made no effort to hide his fear and confusion.

"Return to your regular duties. I am assuming command."

The responsibilities of command had made both men ill at ease but neither would willingly yield his authority.

"No," snapped Berrock. "We two was left in charge!"

"You're too weak," added Bardon.

Each man was so unwise as to place a restraining hand on Caranga's chest as he started to rise from bed. For Bardon the entire room seemed to rotate. Then he looked up from the floor at Caranga towering above him, his foot resting heavily on Bardon's chest.

Bardon spoke quietly. "Your orders, sir?"

Caranga gestured toward the unconscious Berrock. "Carry that out of here."

The black pirate stood erect and proudly naked until the second mate departed with the soldier. Then Caranga nearly collapsed onto his bed. He had flattened those two chiefly by the skill of his arm, not its strength. Yet even that mild exertion made him dizzy and feeble.

Well Susha's swinging paps, I've babied myself too much! He could have forced himself to be up and about before this. In fact if only he had been up last night, instead of sodden with wine, he might have . . .

Self-recriminations were useless. Tiana had rowed off with a deadly enemy. If she was dead, she was dead. If she lived, saving her would require all his wits. Caranga rose slowly and dressed carefully—and gaudily. The crew was frightened. To give them courage he must present an image of iron strength. None of his wounds had pulled open; none was infected. If he used his strength carefully he could manage.

He sauntered out on deck and surveyed Bardon's efforts at camouflage. There was no need to muster the crew; curiosity drew them.

"Hello lads. I got tired of resting. Last night you did a good job dirtying our *Vixen.* Tonight you'll do a better job cleaning her, for at dawn we sail into the stronghold of the 'pirates' of this middenheap island. King Hower sent us to take his daughter from the Krollers with our swords, and so by Susha we shall! But first we'll lie to them. Just a little. Our story is that I am an emmissary of His Kingship, come to arrange the payment ransom for the princess. Greed will force Storgavar to receive us. When we know what's about, we'll take . . . appropriate action."

Caranga looked about at them. Some were grinning. Nervousness was visibly evaporating.

"Berrock, choose ten of your soldiers and make sure every bit of their armor is polished and shining. Bardon, choose twenty of our sweet crew who might pass as honest seamen." Caranga winked. "Susha's armpits, what a task, eh! All the rest will remain below decks at all times. We hide our strength until it is time to strike. Now I've got to see to some charts. Move!"

Caranga retired to his cabin. Fortune favored him in one regard; to play his part he needed an elaborate dress uniform and this he had. The fit was good if not perfect. The tabard had been slightly damaged when Caranga impaled the previous owner, a Captain Zud, but Tiana had mended it that so it scarcely showed. After assembling everything he would need tomorrow morning, he eased himself onto his bunk. Bardon could supervise the preparations, and Caranga knew that tomorrow would demand much of him. He slept.

The dream began to form slowly. He knew he was in total darkness. He was not alone. There was movement in the dark, a vast slithering. The odor was of something huge and reptilian. Without wondering how he knew, he was sure that Tiana was somewhere in this darkness, in grave danger. He ran to find her, but his feet were turned in circles so that he rushed madly about going nowhere. With each passing moment the situation grew more desperate. Then, in the distance, he saw a light. To find Tiana he needed a guide in this darkness and he rushed toward the light. Nearing, he saw that he approached a block of ice, set ablaze and burning with a brilliant flame of aventurine green. By this light he could see into the darkness: a great snake was about to swallow an apple and that apple was the world.

Once Caranga saw this, all faded. For a moment he drifted in a limbo, then the dream was repeated. And then again.

Caranga awoke in a cold sweat. His thrice-experienced dream . . . was it a portent, a warning of what he must do? Or was it only indigestion? It had not been a dream as other dreams. A normal nightmare may be vivid, but the dreamer does not sense he is being forced to watch it. This dream had compulsion, as if some iron hand had held his head and made him watch.

Well, it didn't matter. If the thing had meaning it was not a meaning he could see. The night was best forgotten. Dawn was here.

He dressed in his finery, then stepped grinning out on deck. The sun was a ball of red gold in the east and the morning breeze was brisk and favorable. Soon men were staring at Caranga, pointing, calling out comments.

"All right, you baying hounds," he roared, "lift anchor and make sail. Today we will either save Captain Tiana and the princess, or we'll feed the sharks. I for one am dressed to meet a princess . . . or Theba Herself."

Caranga's tall boots and tight leggings were black, divided by the scarlet of the boots' rolled tops. His mailcoat gleamed a dark blue-gray in which gilded links flashed and winked. Over it hung the tabard, a sleeveless front-and-back cloak of scarlet emblazoned with a rampant dragon in gold thread. His helmet was a peaked casque surmounted by a gilded dragon. The huge buckle of his shining black belt was of solid gold, as big as his hand minus the fingers. Gold, too, was the hilt of his—Captain Zud's—sword.

He had left off poor old Zud's ridiculous jingly spurs.

As they neared the harbor, Caranga noted only small ships, several. Perhaps most of the enemy's fighting men were asea. How nice! If it were so, he must forget his plans and attack at once. He had after all captained this ship for years ere he had handed it over to his foster daughter, while he retired—and returned from that boredom to act as First Mate to a woman in love with command and competent at it as well.

Ships were not all that was missing from the harbor of the Krollers' keep. The docks were empty. From where he stood in his vessel's prow, the pirate could see six guardposts—all unmanned. Behind the docks lay the tangle of buildings that served these island-dwelling pirates as a town. The streets were empty.

Weird. And no one even comes to draw at the well! The hideous dark scars told him that part of the town had burned last night. Burned down. One low building still smoldered. The fire had spread, he saw, until it was stopped by that wide street. Since there had been no wind last night, the flames had spread only because no one had fought them.

"Oh, pox take it, why must this sweet world contain so many *mysteries?*"

He heard murmuring among the crew. They were prepared to carry out a dangerous imposture, but their audience had vanished. They were fighting shadows.

Caranga felt dismay—and, as leader, must put up a bold front anyhow.

"The cowards have fled!" he called, forcing a smile. "Helmsman! Steer for that dock to larboard."

As soon as *Vixen* docked, Caranga marched ashore with ten men. The small group was enough for a search while being easily controllable. Each wore a sword and carried a spear.

The first building they entered had been a tavern. Some of the tables and chairs were overturned. The big room stank of spilled ale and the floor was littered with mugs and broken crockery. Splotches here and there were easily identified as fresh blood. Hanging undisturbed above the door was a gold-embossed sword, definitely Thesian, apparently the trophy of some past success. The small but flawless ruby in the hilt made it valuable. While Caranga considered that, a man called up that the cellar was well stocked; Caranga ordered three kegs carried back to *Vixen*. A few mugs after supper would ease the crew's nerves and their griping. The kitchen yielded no food; every shelf was bare.

The next several buildings told the same story. The people had been taken, swiftly. If they fought, it had been brief and unsuccessful. Whoever seized them did not deign to take their valuables. Only food was missing. And bodies.

Caranga recognized the fulfillment of the first portion of his dream. This mystery was darkness, and Tiana was lost in it. Who had kidnapped the people of Kroll Isle? *What,* for sometimes it wore the shape of a man, the soldier Kathis; and sometimes the shape of a white cat. Of its true nature Caranga knew only that it was powerful, and evil. Why had the people been carried off? He had no doubt that the answer would be grim. Even the *how* of it was a problem. Three large ships had sailed yesterday. Yet even with people crowded in like slaves, there would hardly have been enough room.

He continued the search in that town of eerie silence. Soon they learned that some of the Krollers had remained. In a narrow alley they found a tangled pile of corpses, all drained of blood.

The pattern was clear, now. The Enemy planned a long sea voyage and loaded the ships accordingly. Large amounts of food for the islanders—and they themselves as food for the Enemy!

No doubt other heaps of bodies were scattered over the island. Did Tiana and Princess Jiltha lie in one of them? Caranga thought not, and did not intend to search. If his daughter still lived, he must pursue the three ships and rescue her. If not, he'd have vengeance.

As he made this vow to himself, he knew it was empty. The ocean was wide and trackless. His quarry had more than a full day's start. He had no idea of its course or destination. He had nothing at all, save for a dream. A dream!

Caranga, who prided himself on being a practical man, must choose: abandon all hope or base his actions on a dream. He knew Bardon thought him too old and weak to command *Vixen*. Well, perhaps he would prove that sad-faced white boy right, but he would take whatever fate gave him.

He led his men into the town's burned-out section. One building still burned a little, and it stank. There were many things that building might logically be; the least likely choice was an ice-house for ice was rare in this part of the world and mountains not close. The charred door opened at his touch and Caranga was not surprised when he stepped into cold.

He had found burning ice.

But where was the light that would find Tiana? Caranga asked himself the meaning of fire burning on ice and a most unpleasant answer suggested itself. To save his daughter he must follow the leadership of one more dread than all the demons in hell!

"You," he yelled at the nearest soldier; "Make a torch and light it from the fire on this building."

That was quickly done, and the black pirate grasped the torch. He passed the flame close to a block of ice. Most likely this was not needful, but he wanted to be certain the charm was complete. Caranga led his men back to *Vixen*. Placing the torch in the prow, he ordered the ship back to sea. There was nothing left to do on Kroll Isle; nothing at all.

The vessel was swiftly under weigh. "Captain, what course?"

Caranga stood silent. As he half expected—with a

crawling of his backbone—it was the torch that gave answer. The flame grew longer, brighter until it was a brilliant pale green finger of fire. It turned and pointed . . . *into the wind.*

Caranga said calmly, "That is our course, and though it leads to heaven or hell we shall follow it."

CHAPTER THIRTEEN

The light was so strong that it bleached all things and nothing could be seen. She was running through the blinding white void, yet she did not seem to be moving. Anger formed. How *dare* they do this to her? She was— who? It didn't matter: she was important to herself and she would make others treat her with respect!

As her rage mounted like roiling thunderheads, the void thickened. Glutinously, it resisted her motion. At first it merely seemed there were feeble cobwebs in her path. Then they were cobwebs. Then there were more and more of them, until she was wrapped in a tight cocoon. In a burst of fury she tore through the cocoon and Tiana awoke.

Her first vision was the face of Princess Jiltha. "Oh Captain, thanks be to Theba you're awake. We were so worried."

The girl began to weep hysterically. Tiana tried to reach her—and could not. She was chained, secured spread-eagle to the floor. The princess was chained similarly to a bed. Next to Tiana was the third captive—the blond giant Jiltha had *found*. Tiana noted that their captor did things in proportion. Gold bands were fastened about Jiltha's ankles and wrists, with light silver chains connecting them to the bedposts. Tiana's iron manacles were attached by short lengths of strong chain to bolts set in the flooring. For the giant, the oaken planks had not been reckoned strong enough. His massive chains were attached to steel beams. It was hard to imagine how a man so weighted with iron could move at all, but apparently the giant was something of a problem to their guards since someone had left several teeth on the floor.

The entire chamber was moving. They were at sea! From the pattern and degree of movement, they lay in a large ship under full sail amove through heavy seas. This cabin had once been lavishly decorated; now the velvet drapes were tattered rags. Where one would expect gold ornaments were only gaping holes. Of what was probably a lovely chandelier there remained only a few bits of broken glass. The waste vaguely annoyed Tiana. No doubt the Kroll pirates had worked hard to steal this ship and they had been foolish not to take better care of their property.

Still, that was their problem. Tiana had enough trouble of her own. Not that this was her first time chained down like a starfish! At least this time she wasn't naked. She spoke firmly.

"Jiltha, you are a princess. You must act with courage worthy of your high birth. We're in great danger and our only hope is to be brave."

The girl controlled herself with some difficulty. "I— I suppose I should make in-introductions. Captain Tiana Highrider, may I present Captain Bjaine. I believe you both came to rescue me from the Kroll pirates."

Tiana stared at the Northron in frank admiration. He was a magnificent physical specimen. His huge frame was in perfect balance and proportion. The hard, corded muscles of his arms and legs· bespoke not merely strength but speed and agility. Although his face showed the marks of a hard and violent life, it also showed a personality that loved life. Bjaine was a bronze giant crowned with golden hair and Tiana was immediately attracted to him.

She was well aware that his ice-colored eyes were roaming over her body, up the fine round curves of her bare legs, across her firm almost inexistent stomach and narrow waist, then onto her full breasts. He stared most intently at those last, and she guessed he was trying to make out her nipples through her green silk shirt. She pressed her shoulders down, pulling the shirt even tighter.

Well, she thought, *chained like this we certainly can't get anywhere just staring hungrily at each other! By the Cow's back—what a boy!* She spoke.

"I gather you were the leader of the Thesian raiding

party, Captain. I know you were captured but I don't understand how you escaped."

The Northron laughed. "That fool Storgavar thinks himself the only strong man in the world, but I can open his locks as well as he, that's how."

"Better, since he's dead now."

Bjaine frowned, for thought was not among his habits. Yet, in view of the mystery there was no avoiding it. "You say Storgavar's dead. Our guards talk like he's alive and in command of this ship. Can you explain what's going on here?"

"Partially." Beginning with the events of the Wayfarer Tavern, Tiana related her adventures. "When I killed the Bear," she concluded, "I thought I had disabled the Eye. Apparently it has some power to drive even the dead to its purpose. Once it opened the chest, it gained the magical powers of the Jewels of Ullatara. The crew sees him as their Storgavar."

The pale-haired, pale-eyed man smiled broadly. "Girl, I'll give you credit: you spin a tale passing well. Now tell Bjaine: what's your real name and what's happened to you?"

"My name, boy, is Tiana Highrider of Reme, Captain of *Vixen!*" She spat the words in anger. "A *pirate* ship. Crewed by *men*."

"Now now, we both know it's impossible for a girl to command fighting men. You southern people are soft and weak, but even here nothing so contrary to nature could happen. Now, really. What's your name?" His smile was beautiful. Teeth like snow. Dog!

"Tiana! Tie-anna, who's ridden the thunder. They sing my deeds in every pirate tavern."

"True enough, men sing of a fabulous fighting she-devil named Tiana. But everybody with his head on straight knows there's no such person."

"Bjaine," Jiltha interrupted, "have you any plan to get us out of danger?"

"Why certainly, little girl."

"What is it?"

"I'll wait till luck—Lord Fortune of the Snows—sets me free, then I'll kill our enemies. I'm bound to the serv-ice of the wizard Ekron, so I'll have to give you to King Hartes for his seraglio, Jiltha." He smiled broadly. "But Bjaine will keep you, Firetop . . . 'Tiana'—for myself."

Tiana couldn't decide which appalled her more, the arrogance of the man or his stupidity. She wished her shorts were baggy. And long.

"Oaf, you mean you're going to trust entirely to brute force and dumb luck!"

Bjaine decided it was fun to annoy Tiana. "Yes, that's what I mean." His chain rattled with his attempt to shrug. "It's worked fine for me all my life. Besides, neither of you have a better plan."

"*Has*," Tiana stiffly corrected. Jiltha said, "But I have a much nicer plan and we can carry it out right away." Seeing she had their attention, she continued, "The Bear said it wanted a mighty warrior, a beautiful woman, and a royal virgin for some Awful Ceremony. That's why it took us. Now I think I can take this bed to pieces and get free. Then Bjaine, Captain Tiana can marry us. Once I'm no longer a *virgin*, the Bear can't perform that terrible ceremony! So it will just have to let us go. You can take me home and Papa will make you Prince and Heir Apparent to the Throne of Ilan."

Tiana moaned inwardly. It was not enough that the Gods set her to fight a supernatural monster of hideous powers; now they sent her such . . . friends! Had she committed some sacrilege to merit such punishment? Let's see . . . back in Reme, she had killed a high priest on his own altar. Looking further back, she *had* robbed the Royal Tombs of Nevinia. But flooding it in the process was purely an accident. She had also burned down a chapel of nuns—with them in it, but they were *bad* . . . stolen the great ruby eye of the idol Horgarrav, and cut up the sacred bull of Injana for steaks. But all these actions were well justified by the circumstances! Nor had she ever killed anyone she didn't dislike. The ways of the Gods were hard to fathom; perhaps They were punishing her for some mischief she had committed as a child.

No matter, now the problem's this giddy Jiltha.

It would do no good to tell the silly child that her father would disapprove of such a marriage, for it was very clear that Jiltha wanted Bjaine. *How could she? That big homely musclebound dunce. I disliked him right off!* The girl must be given a strong motive for remaining a maiden. Tiana's voice was kind and soft.

"Jiltha dear, feel your neck. You'll find a small wound.

Bjaine and I both have them. That's where the bear tasted us. If the Bear sees you won't be useful in the ceremony . . ." It was plain from Jiltha's face that she followed this logic to its unpleasant conclusion. "But don't worry, dear. As soon as it's dark, we'll steal a small boat and escape." She writhed, twisted, grunted, hunched, tugged loose her picklock eardrop. Swiftly she unlocked her manacles. Before Jiltha could ask to be freed, Tiana sprang up.

"We'll need food and water. I'll be back as soon as I steal them." And she was gone.

The cabin door opened onto a narrow corridor. At its end the shadow of a guard was clearly visible. Right now Tiana didn't seek to escape, but to spy; to learn the situation on this ship. No doubt she could send that guard to Drood without raising an alarm, but it would be better tactics if she could sneak past him. Two other doors opened off this corridor. She stepped to one and listened. Silence. She slipped inside. This large cabin was well furnished and well maintained: the captain's cabin! Again: a real bed, rather than a seemly bunk. *Probably the lair of the Bear.* Her first impulse was to flee—and something caught her eye. The Jewels of Ullatara.

The chest was filled with a crystal rainbow. It was beauty, it was wealth; and above all it was power. Though she had no idea how to use that power against the Eye of Sarsis, here was an opportunity not to be missed. She stretched a hand toward the flashing gems, and frowning suddenly she snatched back her hand.

Her enemy's habit of caution dictated that this high prize must be guarded. She pulled a bit of broken crystal from the chandelier and tossed it into the chest. Nothing happened. She reached up and took a second piece of crystal. Calmly Tiana cut her finger and let a few drops of blood fall onto the crystal. She tossed the blood-smeared bit of glass into the chest. It fell with a *tink*— and instantly turned from red to completely clear. Every trace of blood was gone.

Yes. The chest is well guarded.

She heard sound in the hallway, and approaching footsteps. As the door opened, Tiana slipped under the bed. She saw only the massive hind-paws as the Bear strode into the cabin. Claws clicked. This was a foolish hiding place, a trap if her enemy had any hint of her presence. She bore a fresh wound, however tiny; would blood-scent betray her? The fell beast came to the bed, click-click. A black-furred paw was inches from her face. Tiana's face twisted. No, it would not scent her or anything else. Though the Bear walked, it was three days dead.

The uncanny power of the Eye of Sarsis did not prevent corruption.

Tiana tried to tell herself that things had worked out to her advantage. This ship was full of hostile eyes. Out on deck lay little hope that she could learn much without being seen, while here in the very lair of her mortal enemy she could spy nicely. Even as she told herself this, her stomach was cold and her throat dry. The Bear stood motionless, inches from her.

She was lightly dressed and it was growing chilly! These were southern waters, where cold north winds were most uncommon. Yet the wind howled outside and the temperature dropped rapidly. The sea was becoming rough.

The door opened. Tiana could see only bare feet and bony legs, but she knew it was Morna. Somehow that fool girl had gotten herself caught and carried onto this ship.

"My Lord Storgavar," the soft voice said, "is it your pleasure that I feed the prisoners?"

Apparently the Bear gestured; the dirty feet turned and left.

The violence of the storm increased apace. The ship staggered like a drunkard through the waves. Tiana could hear timbers moan in protest at the stress. From somewhere above came an awful scream, followed by a sickening crash. A man had fallen from the rigging. The Eye obviously knew nothing of the sea, else it would give order to heave to. No masts could long take this punishment; soon they must break and the ship founder. The rain was intense. Abruptly its vicious patter changed to a hard cracking noise: hail.

Tiana had heard Northers talk of such storms, unheard of in this part of the world. Occasionally a man's death scream could be heard above the rage of the storm. The Northrons could survive ice storms—in their warm clothing. Their ships were rigged with hand- and footholds so that crew could move even when the deck was a sheet of ice. The Kroll pirates were caught unprepared. Soon all of them would be frozen or swept overboard.

Tiana thought, *How very sad.*

Now came an explosion louder than thunder, followed by angry roaring. The ship was thrown violently about, a rat shaken in the jaws of a dog. Clinging tightly to the bottom of the bed, Captain Tiana knew what had happened. A sail, stretched by the wind beyond its strength, had blown. The roaring was the sail's fragments tearing in the wind.

A man entered the cabin: boots, to Tiana, and a voice without emotion or life. "My Lord Storgavar, the other two ships have hove to, contrary to your orders. What shall we do about such mutiny?"

"Nothing. Return to your post."

The Bear shuffled to the chest and stretched out its forepaws to the Jewels of Ullatara. The cabin began to shimmer; to fade. The bed above Tiana was fading, becoming transparent. She was trying to hide under a piece of glass. The Bear turned and looked toward her. It didn't see her. She looked and did not see herself. The cabin and all it contained, including Tiana, had become invisible. In place of the vanished cabin another scene appeared. Though the floor beneath her felt as it had before, it seemed to her that she lay on the ice-crusted deck of a ship. It had heaved to but was still in grave danger. The sheets were not properly trimmed and men worked desperately in the rigging to free ice-fouled lines. The ship was listing severely; a little more and it would capsize. A *snap,* and a spar fell straight at Tiana. It was a giant spear aimed at her, but she forced herself to remain motionless. It passed through her and struck the deck. She felt nothing.

The Bear changed; became Storgavar. "All right, boys, the storm abates. Make sail or the treasure we seek will escape us."

The storm did indeed seem to slacken . . . and the pirates paid no attention to this illusion. With screams of "Demon!" they attacked the Bear. Their swords passed through its body without effect. The whole scene began to fade. The forms of the pirates became misty blurs, but one figure remained clear and distinct; a tall lean ascetic man in black robes and a small salt-and-pepper beard.

The Bear stared at this figure in anger.

"Apeling! Foolish young apeling. You and your ancestors are but newly down from the trees, still wet from the womb of time. All your yesterdays are but a few grains of sand in my hourglass. I am old and I have seen mountain ranges rise from the bowels of the earth only to be worn down by the passing ages. Before my years you are a mayfly, a brief spark soon extinguished. Before my power you are an ant, to be crushed beneath my feet. Why do you so recklessly provoke my wrath?"

Pyre bowed very slightly. "Greetings, ancient snake. The why of it is simple. We both know there can be no peace between us. This storm I have summoned is the first act of my war against you."

"No, apeling! You do not have the power to summon this storm. You merely distorted the powers I had summoned."

"True," said he who dwelt in a keep called Ice, "but nonetheless I have saved two ships filled with people. Food you'll not enjoy."

"More likely this storm of yours will kill them."

"I have saved them from your belly," Pyre said calmly, very calmly; ascetic as a priest, this Pyre of Ice. "They are pirates and will survive or drown according to their seamanship."

The Bear laughed derisively. "So you think yourself a great wizard because you have snatched a bit of food from my plate. Fool, fool! Had I real need of them, I could easily end this storm and reestablish my control."

"Say rather, if you could spare the power. For eons you hoard power as a miser hoards gold. You saved much, but you need much and you have little to spare. Now tell me, ancient snake. Which will you do, order the ship that carries you to heave to, or sink with it?"

"I have power to take this ship to its destiny and then there shall be vengeance for thieves. You stole power from me. You stole food from me. You and your kind stole the world from my people. These things shall be paid for!"

"No, Sarsis," Pyre said, and he sounded tired. "You cannot turn the wheel back. Nor can you erase what has been written. Your people had their day and it is over. Your allotted years were as the sands of the sea but they have all run through the hourglass. You are banished from the world, Sarsis, and this effort to return will cost you both your eyes."

The Bear gestured angrily. Pyre vanished, and the cabin appeared again.

Tiana peered cautiously out from under the bed. The Bear paced about the cabin. After a moment it stepped decisively to the chest where lay the Jewels of Ullatara. She could not see what its forepaws were doing but suddenly the room was filled with dancing colored lights. The voice of the Bear filled the cabin with soft hissing words.

The Bear is but a shape it wears, Tiana realized. *The voice is the voice of the Eye of Sarsis, something far worse than a cat or bear.*

Aye, and the words that voice intoned, hissing, were not such as men had ever spoken. Every sound was like unto an obscene caress, the kiss of an enemy; the courtship by which a snake traps a bird.

The words ended. The dancing lights exploded in a blinding flash.

The cabin was completely black.

Slowly, slowly the dark melted, and Tiana noticed that the storm had somewhat abated. No—judging by the sound of the wind, the fury of the storm continued full strength, but the ship was riding much better. Though the hail continued, it sounded now as if it were striking a distant roof, high above the ship. Tiana swallowed. She tried to imagine what must have happened. Was the ship riding in a great bubble of force, protected from the elements by the magic of the Eye of Sarsis? The exact nature of the enchantment didn't matter; the important aspect was that while Pyre's storm continued, escape by small boat was impossible.

Tiana reflected ruefully that so far all she had accomplished was to miss her lunch. Nor was there aught she could do, now. She must lie silent and motionless, hiding scant feet from this monster from the dim past.

CHAPTER FOURTEEN

"Lord Storgavar, the lookout reports sighting the island, even as you foretold. We shall reach it within the hour."

The Bear gestured dismissal and began to choose certain of the Jewels of Ullatara. Under the bed, Tiana was nearly desperate with frustration. She had blundered. She had lain helpless while precious hours trickled away. If this island was the site of the fearsome ceremony planned by the Bear, all hope of escape was lost. If this was an intermediate stop, it was an opportunity to be seized at all risks.

Opportunity to do what, run home like a whipped dog?

It was maddening that she could not slay the Eye of Sarsis; at least she would sabotage its plans before she escaped with Jiltha. But what did it plan? Why had it come to this island? The force controlling the Bear, seen by the Krollers as their leader, was the Right Eye of Sarsis. Its twin was still locked in the steel egg. Clearly the Right Eye would seek to free the Left Eye as a matter of first priority. So it came here.

Why? What was special about this island? If the wind was from the north, then the ship's course was southwest. South and west of the Kroll Isles the Ocean was uncharted, unknown.

Wait—Voomundo's map had shown something, a small island southwest of the Krolls. It bore no name, only a tiny symbol. For moments she racked her brain, then it came to her. The symbol was a lightning stroke.

The Bear had completed its preparations, had chosen the enchanted gems that would serve it on . . . Lightning Island.

When it was gone, Tiana move rapidly but with stealth

back to the prisoner's cabin. On seeing her, Jiltha stifled her exclamation in time. Bjaine mumbled something; it was unintelligible because his mouth was full of food. Morna looked up, said, "Hello, Tiana," and continued to feed the bound giant.

Under the Bear's control, Tiana thought. *She does what she's bade, and takes note of nothing else.*

Tiana swiftly picked the locks on Jiltha's manacles while relating what had happened. She turned to the chained warrior, started to free him, then stopped. "Bjaine, if I release you, will you follow my orders?"

Credit Bjaine with a brief attempt to keep a straight face. He failed and burst into roaring laughter. At last he controlled himself.

"Girl who calls herself Tiana, you need my strength to save your life. You have to free Bjaine or we'll all die. Naturally, when I'm free I'll make you mine, but once you get used to being my slave you'll enjoy it. Bjaine won't beat you unless you need it."

She looked at him coldly. "If you can't take orders, you're useless. Come, Jiltha."

Bjaine stared after them. "That foolish girl can't understand what's good for her," he mumbled. "Come Morna, let's have some more roast pork." The Nor'man had said that chance would free him and let him fight his enemies. In the meantime it was wise to eat and maintain his strength. "Morna my girl, you say they let you have the run of this ship. Do you suppose you could find some wine?" Bjaine knew he faced two singularly horrible deaths. The Bear's ceremony and the devil on his stomach. Still, he believed there was no point in letting tomorrow's problems spoil his enjoyment of today. "Ale would be fine."

Outside Tiana gestured for Jiltha to stand motionless. The corridor was dark, but the doorway at its end was occasionally illuminated by lightning flashes. The accompanying thunder was strangely muted. Tiana slipped forward through the darkness, her belt in her hands. From the shadows it was clear that a guard still stood just beyond the doorway. The man had as much warning as if he were attacked by a shadow. A flicker of motion, and he was lying still upon the floor, her belt tied tight about his throat.

In an awestruck voice Jiltha whispered, "Is—is he dead?"

Tiana loosened her belt and started slapping her victim's face. "No. At the last moment I held back. I don't understand why but this wight fought as much as a statue."

After a moment the man revived. His eyes looked at neither Jiltha nor Tiana. Indeed they did not move but focused blankly on infinity. Without a word or gesture the guard rose and stepped back toward his former position. Tiana stopped him.

"I nearly killed you. Why didn't you fight back?"

A brief spark of intelligence flickered in the man's eyes, then died. "When my Lord Storgavar went ashore he took half the crew with him and ordered the other half to stand at their posts and do nothing."

"Oh," Tiana said pleasantly, "how nice."

The princess and the pirate queen stepped out on the deck. The world was suddenly emblazoned with a blinding flash of color. A myriad-hued splendor reverberated across the sky, accompanied by muffled thunder.

"It's only lightning," Tiana said, peeling Jiltha's fingers from her arm.

"But why the colors?" The princess was torn between fear and wonder.

"The Bear set a spell to protect this ship from the storm. It used an enchanted gem and now if you look closely at the sky, you'll see it's faceted. We're somehow inside a great jewel."

Jiltha looked at this strange wonder, then smiled as if she had a very happy thought. "Captain Tiana, why don't we sail away in this ship and leave the Bear marooned? The crew won't try to stop us and I'm sure I can persuade Bjaine to help us."

Tiana moaned inwardly. Jiltha seemed a storehouse of plans, all of which called for pressing her virginity on the Northman. She had framed an angry reply when she realized the plan had some merit. To a fighter such as Tiana it was galling to run away from an enemy. Yet where was the choice? The Eye of Sarsis was a Power and could not be harmed by mortal means.

"We've two problems, Jiltha. First it takes many hands to sail such a ship as this. Second the Bear has Powers and can draw us back before we get far. The

first problem is yours. The crew has been so long under
the Bear's illusions that their wills are nearly dead. Perhaps you can rouse a few of them. Search the ship. The
Bear didn't bother to delude Morna and there may be
others like her." The tone of command in Tiana's voice
softened. "I'm trusting you with this task, Jiltha. Do it
well and you will save all our lives. You're a princess of
a great royal line, bred to high courage. I know you'll
prove yourself worthy of the king your father, and your
heritage."

"You're going to leave me alone?" Jiltha was trying
hard not to show fear.

"Yes. I'm going ashore. The Bear can't be slain but
I hope to do something that will distract it long enough
for us to escape."

As Tiana spoke, she moved to the side of the ship. Before Jiltha could reply, she dived into the water and was
swimming for shore with smooth easy strokes.

Tiana was uneasy about leaving Jiltha, but she had set
her to an important task she hoped would keep the girl
out of mischief. She was approaching the edge of the
gem shield. Beyond the shield roiled five or so yards of
violent surf, then the beach. Taking a deep breath, Tiana
plunged downward. She was a strong swimmer and
moved rapidly forward despite powerful currents.

The danger lay in the shallows; large sharp rocks like
the teeth of a giant with the surf smashing against them.
There was a moment when she thought she was being
chewed by enormous jaws, then she was wading up the
beach, bruised but not seriously injured.

Three long boats had been drawn up on the strand.
Three hard pushes sent them sliding into the surf, where
they were pounded to fragments.

After this small act of sabotage, Tiana set off on the
trail of her enemy. The tracks in the sand were half
erased by the cold rain. Despite that and the darkness
they were clear enough for her to follow. Thirty yards up
from the beach the sand gave way to bare rock. She saw
no sign that marked the passing of the Bear and his men,
but the rocks were nearly impassable except in one direction. What was this island? Because of the rain and
the night she had never had a clear look at anything
beyond a few feet distant.

Is this only a mass of naked rock, with a fringe of sand

at its edges like a bald man's head? She had seen many
such dead pieces of stone, but the Bear had come here
for a purpose. What was there on this desolate isle that
would aid in opening the steel egg?

She hurried on. The path went steadily upward. Perhaps half a mile from the beach she found the first evidence that something dwelt on this island. The path was
partially blocked by thin, bright silvery lines. They were
as fine as the strands of a spider web, although the pattern was not such as any spider would weave. It was a
fragile thing, easily brushed aside. Tiana did not; she
bent and examined it closely. The strands were not
merely silvery, they were fine silver wire! After a moment's consideration she lay down and began crawling
under the web. There was one certainty about this web:
someone or something had been to great trouble to build
it. Was it a barrier or a trap? She had one fearsome enemy
and wasn't anxious to make another.

She went on, carefully and hardly comfortably. Most
of the gleaming network was behind her when an even
more discomforting thought came: the Bear and its men
must have passed through here too, causing considerable
damage in the process. Therefore the web had been repaired recently. She licked her lips. The spinner of silver
had to be close by. It probably watched her at this moment.

Telling herself firmly not to hurry, Tiana hurried. And
then she was out of it, and moving on over good old hard,
normally dangerous rock and—

The second web was smashed and not yet repaired.
That prompted nervousness. So did the corpses: Kroll
pirates, four. They had shed no blood and the only
wounds they bore were hand-breadth, round *burns*. The
men had seen whatever slew them and had tried to use
their swords. They had not drawn blood. One nice Sin-
chorish saber was still intact—save that in three places
the edge was melted. The other weapons were fused blobs
of steel. Tiana swallowed.

Some of the silvery network remained intact and she
advanced, taking care to cause no further damage.
Maybe if she—

Abruptly the darkness was broken by a dull glow. She
turned and saw the source: a shining ball of blue radiance. It sat at one edge of the web, pulsing. And growing.

At first sight of it, it was no wider than her thumb. Already it had swelled to the size of the wounds on the dead men. *Hello,* she thought inanely; *I was just out for a walk and saw your light. . . .*

The pulsing blob of radiance rose and slowly approached her—*floating.*

Wishing she were engaged in a nice pleasant sea-battle with a few attacking ships, Tiana saw no point in retreat. She was in its web. She continued, with care. *See? I haven't damaged your lovely artwork one little bit.* Her skin crawled. Breathing became a voluntary act. The blue *thing,* which she recognized as ball lightning, hovered above her. It lighted her path while making no aggressive move.

She made it. Only when she was clear of its web did the thing of light begin to buzz about, lifting strands of silver, heat-fusing them into place. Tiana released a long breath and concentrated on standing up.

She continued to climb that eerie trail. The rain turned warm. It stopped. Pyre's storm had ended. No, wait: that most powerful of wizards had admitted that he had only distorted forces summoned by the Eye of Sarsis. The air was calm now—a dangerous, unstable calm. The forces of Storm were gathering, gathering for a purpose. She was sure of it, and—the egg! The Eye of Sarsis had summoned the rage of the elements to open the steel egg!

All this was clear to Tiana now. What she did not understand was how the Eye would use such force—or how she could spoil its plans.

Now the moon broke from behind emptied clouds so that for the first time she was able to see more than a few paces in front of her. To her left rose a sheer wall of living stone. It was nearly featureless, though ten or so feet above her head ran a narrow ledge, like a shelf. To her right massive boulders towered, and from beyond them came the sound of the sea. She must continue straight ahead. There, of course, lay the problem.

Ten paces ahead glittered a large intricate structure of silver wire and ribbon. Its center was marred by a mass of broken crystal fragments. Much of the web was torn and shredded and fully a score of the ball-lightning creatures bobbed bluely about, repairing it. Krollite corpses lay scattered about in front of the web, within it, and on the far side. The rock wall showed strange burn marks and jagged, freshly blasted pits.

Tiana put it together and knew that the Eye had fought a pitched battle here for passage. By ruthlessly spending the pirates' lives—if those zombie-like slaves still lived—it had won through.

- She could hardly be expected to read the mood of a shining ball, but from the vigor they displayed in speeding about their repairs, Tiana felt it clear that they would tolerate no interference. Nor could she hope to make her way through without interfering. And the web completely blocked her path.

She looked up at the shelf-like ledge again, and let her gaze roam the rocky face separating her from it. Scars of the recent battle should serve her as foot- and hand-holds, she thought. With a last glance at the busy, busy balls of living—sentient?—lightning, she began to ascend.

She gained the ledge that formed a walkway, worming over it and on her thoroughly wet stomach. The projecting shelf formed a path that went up rather steeply. So did Tiana. By the time she was past the web, she was too high above the trail to drop back. Her only choice was to continue along the ledge. It was wet, and slippery, and—*Oh, wonderful! It's getting steadily narrower. This must be my night to pay for someone else's sins!*

She kept moving. Too soon, she had to walk sidewise, her back pressed against the rock face. The moon hid its face and she was glad. She was not interested in seeing how far she was above air floored with jagged and very hard rock. She kept moving, sidewise step at a time. The shelf was only slightly wider than the length of her feet. Her legs trembled. She advanced, holding her breath. Almost abruptly the ledge widened. Just as she let her breath out in a sigh, the precarious walkway ended even more abruptly.

Oh damn. She stood still for a while, just breathing, trying to relax tense muscles.

The moon reappeared. Tiana looked ahead in the quicksilver glow. About an arm's length beyond the edge of the ledge there *appeared* to be a hole in the cliff face. Perhaps it was a dead-end cave. Perhaps it went somewhere. Perhaps it was her imagination; just a shadow. Clutching what handholds she could on the smooth stone, Tiana leaned forward. To discern that it was a cave and to look in required her to stretch to her limit. And a little more. . . . Now if she could just swing one leg over and sort of hurl herself . . .

The loud crack sounded directly beneath her feet. Even as her heart pounced straight up into her throat, she *moved*.

The stone ledge broke off and tumbled crashing into the valley below. For Tiana there was a moment of mad scrambling, followed by weightlessness and impact. Then she was crawling into the hole, on hands and knees. And then she lay down, and for a long while she concentrated only on *being*, and on how nice it was not to be straining one single muscle.

She began to crawl. The cave was not large enough for her to walk and yet not quite so small that she must wiggle in the manner of a worm.

Far too soon she discovered that she was not alone.

Something was coming out of the darkness toward her. It did not breathe; sound was amplified in this tight horizontal shaft and all she heard was a harsh, metallic grating. The thing's hard body was obviously wide enough to scrape the cave walls on both sides. Tiana's was not. As sword and knife were useless against the Eye, she had brought only a dagger. She reached for it only to discover that it had departed the sheath, probably in her mad scramble off the collapsing ledge.

Something about three feet wide and *hard* was coming at her, and she was unarmed. Retreat meant a most unpleasant backward scrabbling followed by a considerably less pleasant fall, hundred of feet onto solid rock.

A bit of groping in the darkness discovered a stone twice the size of her fist. It was a poor weapon, but better than none at all. Now she became aware of heightened light, between her and the approaching menace. Of it she could see only that its bulk was great. It had stopped. Seeming scores of futile plans raced through Tiana's mind, and then the light began to retreat, slowly. It seemed . . . a beacon? Beckoning? Tiana followed.

Presently the cafe or tunnel forked. Her unseen guide took the rightward passage, and paused to wait. Tiana chewed at her lower lip. Should she trust this total unknown or take her chances on roaming blindly? The light-thing seemed polite enough—and she knew some cannibals were most polite in asking a person to dinner.

I came here to fight the Right Eye of Sarsis. I need whatever help I can find. Even . . . even a guide that might be a cannibal.

Hauling her stone, she turned down the cavern the light-thing had taken.

Through a labyrinthine system of caves that eerie bluish glow led her. Her knees suffered and the chunk of rock she dragged along grew heavier and heavier, more and more a bother. She abandoned it. Still the light retreated, just at her pace. Weaponless, alone, Tiana followed.

At long, long last they emerged onto a broad plain, and Tiana saw her guide. Almost she forgot to rise and stretch and flex her legs; the light emanted from the thing itself: a crystal worm many times her length!

Worm? Well, it was vermiform, and the five-score segments of its length were sharp-edged blocks of crystal, water-clear. The thousand legs appeared to be . . . silver! Though it was all beyond her experience and knowledge even of the impossible, she was sure the liquid she could see coursing through that incredible body was some liquid metal.

Even so, the wonder of the city before her distracted her from her strange guide-companion.

Perhaps to call it "city" was not right; the wrong descriptive term. Was an anthill a city of many creatures or was it a whole; a single vast entity? Whatever one called it, this great lacework was filled with a steady hum lit by small bright flashes; lightning in blue and white played over all. She mused: *Buildings?* No; but complex vast shapes of fine crystal; lucid and all sparkly. That spire's twisting angles were such that they showed the moon many times; flashing images in silver, crimson, amber and azure, cerulean and slate. All gleamed and leapt about its curving surface. Leftward stretched a lake of what seemed molten glass. To her right lofted a many-pointed star twice her height. The impossible continued; the star was a single enormous ruby—burning at its highest point with a flame of intense cobalt blue. Tiana was horrified that such a fabulous treasure was being burned as a candle—until she saw that the blue flame licked *downward,* and that sand was being fed into it. The fire's heat was *creating* the many-pronged ruby!

She was aware of a pattern in all this; metal and stone; heat and glass.

Throughout the crystalline complex moved strange beings in their numbers; she saw the ball-lightning creatures, and more of the crystal worms, and beings that flew on wings of fire. And she saw other *things*. Apparently sentient and certainly living, they were beyond her powers to describe even to herself.

Even while she stared, marveling, Tiana reminded herself not to let wonder dull the caution she thought of as her natural trait—as she denied impetuosity. All this fabulous beauty was manifestly and completely inhuman; nothing she saw was even normally animalistic or belonging to the kingdom of plants. She had merely followed, and could be in great danger indeed. She doubted that having her sword would have afforded her a whit of protection, though it might have increased her confidence —somewhat. As to the dagger: it was well lost. If something here tempted her to use arms, she was far better off not having them.

Slowly, trying to be casual and slow, she worked the kinks of long crawling out of her athletic body.

A second worm approached her, seemingly without hostility. On its back rested two small black cubes. Had it brought them to her? She reached out—and it backed away with a crystalline shimmer and flash. She wondered what she'd done wrong. The creature had moved slowly and cautiously; perhaps it wanted to be sure she handled the cubes with care? Again she reached, slowly, gently, and this time she was permitted to take them.

Both black cubes were of a size to fit in one of her hands, and she could close her fingers over them.

One of the silver-spinning lightning balls appeared, hovered, and moved slowly away. Feeling that she was being invited to follow, Tiana did. None of these beings, she mused, must be able to speak. Well, little matter. Surely their message was plain enough: We mean *you* no harm. The black dice are fragile, so . . . throw them and give someone an unpleasant fate! The question was, why didn't they use such a weapon themselves?

Maybe it's so dangerous they prefer giving it to an expendable . . . friend, she thought without delight. And she followed the thing of ball lightning.

The blue-glow led her to the edge of a cliff—and rose, to speed away. Tiana gave it a look askance. *Oh, thanks a lot,* she thought. Yet from this elevation she could clearly see Lightning Island at last: a single great mountain rising from the ocean like a great shiny beast arching its back to shake off the water. The summit rose to a towering height, and flashed. At first she thought that was an illusion of the moonlight, but she realized that the mountain was indeed veined with silver.

Why, she wondered, with no scientific principles to guide her. Did a silver mountain somehow attract lightning? Was that the basis for the island's weird life that was so alien to anything she knew—including sorcerous demons?

Her cogitation was cut short. Lights flashed from near the mountain's top and thunder roared. A flight of the winged flame-creatures dived at the mountainside. *They look like giant attacking fireflies, converging on a specific point—oh! They must* be attacking! *Ohhh . . .* Lights played and flickered over her face and Tiana had to blink and squint. She watched some of the firewings rise to strike again, while others fell like dying sparks. She jerked at the sound of a ringing crash that might have been the smashing of one of the crystal worms.

It is an attack—a battle!

The Eye had come here to perform its fell sorcery atop the mountain—and the island dwellers were fighting with all their ability to defend the source of their very existence! Suddenly Tiana was cursing by the Cud and by the Back. Why had her allies trusted her so, given her what she took to be a weapon and then led her here, where she was only a helpless spectator to their battle for life?

While the sky was alive with flitting flashing fire and ringing crashes and eerie humming, Tiana glanced down. Her anger dissipated.

Beneath the cliff on which she stood, a trail led up toward the summit of the mountain. She realized that these creatures of light and lightning, though they put their all into the battle, knew they would lose and trusted her to avenge them. Soon her enemy, their enemy—*our enemy* —would be flush with victory and weakened by its efforts. Then it would return, to pass beneath her and her black dice.

The flashing battle reached its climax: a crescendo of thunder and lightning, followed by an eerie, total silence. One way or another, it was over. The air was calm, though it smelled strange and she was aware of an unstable feeling. A cloud, massive and black as a smith's anvil, was moving slowly toward the mountain. Tiana watched tensely.

"Well, hello."

She jerked nearly enough to go over the cliff at sound of that voice, and turned to see the speaker.

"Bjaine! What are you doing here?"

The big handsome Norther shrugged. "I don't know. A strange thingawhichy led me here and ah, gave me these black dice. Got no idea what I'm supposed to do with the things." Casually he tossed one of the dice from left hand to right.

"Stop! Treat those cubes with care!"

Bjaine blinked, nigh-invisible blond lashes briefly shuttering eyes like the sky of day. "Why? What do they do? You mean they're dangerous? How do you know? You still claim to be Tiana, by the way?"

Tiana had no idea what the dice did, and she was not about to admit it to this . . . barbarian. "You'll soon see! That fell Bear is about to pass this way and we will throw the black cubes on him."

"We will?" Bjaine continued to look maddeningly cool, almost smiling.

"Yes! Didn't your guide tell you?" Before he entered into that potentially embarrassing subject, she asked, "How did you get free?"

"Jiltha found the key. You see? Simplicity itself. I vow, 'Tiana,' it's not only a terrible liar you are, but plain foolhardy. Fighting is a man's work! Best you get along back to the ship and cook up something nice. I'll be hungry once I've settled that Bear for good and all."

"Bjaine, you are without doubt the—"

She was interrupted. The black cloud had reached the silver-flashing mountain, where it poised—and discharged all its gathered fury in a single lightning stroke. Such was the force of that bolt that the pirate and the Northron heard only the beginning crackle. After that they saw and heard nothing. Though neither was looking directly at the mountain, both felt searing pain in their eyes. Then they went blind, and the blast struck them and they fell down, their brains as blank as their eyes.

Tiana regained consciousness first. Brightly-colored spots danced before her eyes and her ears rang. Staggering, she slapped Bjaine.

"Awake, oaf!"

"What happened?"

It was clear to Tina. The Right Eye of Sarsis had summoned all the fury of the elements. All the rage of a hundred storms had been in that single strike. That blast had smashed the steel egg, freeing the Left Eye of Sarsis. In the process it had greatly damaged Lightning Island. The cliff on which Tiana and Bjaine stood was fractured, unstable. Elsewhere she could see signs of several rock slides. No doubt the fairyland city of the lightning beasts had been grievously injured if not destroyed. She had no time for sadness—or patience to explain anything to the Nor'man.

"It's time for us to fight, that's what happened. Stand ready with your cubes. The Bear should be below us soon." As she spoke, an uneasy doubt came to mind: *perhaps the Eyes of Sarsis passed while we were unconscious.*

"Girl, would you look at this die? I think something's wrong with it." The cube the giant held up was no longer uniformly jet black. One corner was gray. A pure white crack flashed on the surface.

It occurred to Tiana that the dice, on being thrown, were meant to release something they contained. The blast of thunder must have shaken them about. It was lucky the cubes had not been shattered. Bjaine's gave off another white flash.

"Bjaine, I think you'd better get rid of that thing."

"But the Bear is coming."

He pointed. Tiana fought to clear her vision. Yes, the enemy approached. Throwing the unstable die would warn it. The die flashed again. The time between flashes was definitely decreasing.

Tiana spoke in a calm commanding voice. "We'll throw as soon as the enemy is in range. You must use a gentle underhand toss, no wrist snap." While she was speaking his cube flashed three times more.

The Northman laughed at her. "This little toy really

frightens you, doesn't it? Bjaine told you fighting is man's work." He tossed the die in the air and caught it. The flashes were now scant seconds apart.

It was all Tiana could do not to throw one of her cubes at Bjaine. The Bear came steadily closer and the flashes grew more rapid. The die was beating pulses of light like the heart of a storm god—and Tiana yelled.

"Now!"

The four dice flew through the air. Tiana shut her eyes and covered her ears. Even so she saw the brilliant white flashes of lightning and was shaken by the nearby blast of thunder. Her nose recognized the clean scent of fried oxygen, then the odor of burnt meat. She opened her eyes and saw the Bear. She was not sure whether its body was charred, but it moved and she saw the two blazing red eyes in its forehead.

"Bjaine, help me push this boulder. We've got to start a rockslide."

The massive rock did not budge for Tiana, but when the giant placed his shoulder to it there came a crunching, and the boulder pitched over the edge. The rockslide was larger than Tiana planned. The ground beneath their feet twitched and shivered. They raced back as the cliff face fell away. A network of cracks opened beneath Tiana's feet. The ground she ran on was sliding down. Firm rock was but a few paces away. One more stride, and she leaped with all her strength. It was close, but she saw she wouldn't make it—and then Bjaine's long arm swept out to catch her outstretched hand.

He swept her up and cradled her in his arms. The trail up the mountain had become a vast jumbled mound of broken rock. "Well girl, you claimed that monster couldn't be killed, but I've buried it! Let's get back to the ship—mine. There must be wine on board somewhere and I'm thirsty."

Tiana was too drained to snap at him. She even let him hold her hand in his big strong blond-furred paw. The strength of him!

When they at last reached the ship, they found Jiltha in command.

"It's really quite easy," the princess declared. "At home when I wanted something I told the guards that my father, the King commanded it. Here I tried saying,

'Lord Storgavar commands' and the crew obeyed perfectly."

The anchor was soon raised and the ship set sail.

For Tiana this cruise was her first chance to relax in a long, long while. She boasted that she knew no fear but the strain of this conflict had worn her more than she would admit even to herself. Perhaps her foe was not destroyed, but no matter. The Eyes of Sarsis would stay buried for a thousand years. Let Pyre worry about the problem.

Daily she revelled in the sun, basking in its golden rays, listening to the wind in the sails and the murmur of the sea. By night she roamed the deck, watched the phosphorescence of the waters as the ship knifed through them. For all its size this ship made good speed. The night air was crisp and clean as only sea air can be. The stars above were as jewels set on black velvet.

The North Star lay astern and slightly to port. Tiana was sure the ship headed northwest to Reme and if the favorable winds continued, they should reach home port soon. She was coming home in triumph. Probably Caranga and *Vixen* waited for her there.

All was well and she was very content. It was gratifying that Bjaine now recognized her as the famous sea warrior she was. He had been awed at first, then had begun a very polite and appealing courtship. Yes, Bjaine; handsome, brave and strong Bjaine. Of course he'd never learned to use his brain but that was a habit she could easily teach him. In the meantime he took orders very well. Probably now was a good time for her to marry and settle down. If she made Bjaine first mate of *Vixen,* Caranga could retire in peace. *Bjaine, Bjaine, what a magnificent man; what a lover he'll be!* The future was filled with delightful prospects and there was only one small annoyance. She liked to run a clean ship. From time to time she caught an unpleasant odor: something rotten. No doubt it was a dead rat, its decaying body hidden in some dark corner, but her best efforts did not find it. It was annoying that there was something rotten on this ship.

The Northman was also relaxed and happy. That foolish girl Tiana had apologized for all her silly lies. Even better, after very little beating she had acknowledged herself his slave. How lovely she was on her knees.

She served him and catered to his whims as a proper slave should. Of course with that devil on his stomach he could not properly enjoy this lovely slave. Well, this little delay would but increase the satisfaction he'd take from her luscious body. Soon this ship would sail into Port Thark. He would deliver Jiltha to King Hartes and the wizard Ekron would remove the devil. Bjaine was happy and looked to the future with bright lust. The only small annoyance was that sharks were following the ship. Even though the cook wasn't throwing waste food overboard, still they followed. Well, that was a small matter.

The day the ship reached port began for Tiana as a day of triumph should begin.

She ordered the crew to run up her colors: the black flag with a red fox's head. At sight of that banner the men in Reme harbor hoisted every flag. Men and women shouted and danced for joy. A band hastily formed and began to play. Children threw flowers. The royal barge appeared and King Hower came on board. As her pride reached its height, Tiana again smelled something dead and decayed. It was awful; what must the king think?

He did not seem to notice. In a mellow voice he said, "Tiana, you have earned this gold bracelet of victory. Step forward that I may put it on your hand."

She stepped toward the king and the rotten odor grew much stronger. Hower snapped the gold bracelet first about her left wrist, then about her right. "Thank you, Tiana, for your seamanship. You brought this ship swiftly and safely to its destination."

As he spoke, the port of Reme shimmered and vanished. The new scene was a jungle-surrounded bay. The gold bracelet became a set of iron manacles. King Hower was the skeleton of a Bear, still partially covered with fur and hung with tatters of decaying flesh. The natural eyes were gone, but twin red fires blazed in its forehead. The sweet smooth voice of Sarsis spoke.

"Now it is best that you sleep. When it is time for the Ceremony of Return you shall be brought to me in the Temple of Cignas."

Tiana recognized the jeweled talisman in its paw, but a white void rushed at her. She was aware of endless falling, then nothing.

BOOK III

Pyre:
FLAMING ICE

CHAPTER FIFTEEN

Bardon spoke with carefully measured politeness: "Caranga, I recognize your authority as acting captain. I apologize for my past failure to respect that authority, but now I feel I must ask certain questions."

The first mate looked sternly at the second, then relaxed. This Bemaran was a good sailor he'd probably been too harsh with. "Very well, Bardon. Tap that alekeg and sit down. You have a right to know what's happening. I'd have told you sooner but the answers to your questions are not pleasant."

Bardon drank and breathed a little easier. After the humiliation of being forcibly removed from command, he had not dared question Caranga's orders even though they appeared mad.

"We've been sailing south into unchartered waters for days and days, with only that . . . unearthly *torch* as guide. We're lost, Caranga. Are we going to follow this phantom until the food and water run out?"

"We're not quite lost. I'm an old sailor, Bardon. I know a bit more about the world than the men who sit home and draw maps. Our present course should bring us to land in another day or two."

"What? Where? Why didn't you tell us? The crew is so frightened they're murmuring against you."

"Well, it won't make them happy to learn our next port will be Sonul."

"Sonul? That's only a myth, a horror story to frighten the credulous."

"Hardly." Caranga refilled his big two-handled mug. "I've been there."

"Then . . . surely the city's not as the tales describe it —monsters walking the streets devouring people?"

"That's true. Oh, Susha's Scar, it's true! Sonul is an

enjoyable port if one doesn't look beneath the surface. Do look, and you'll find Sonul is a much worse place than the tales describe. Bardon, that place—"

"Iceberg!" The lookout's bellow came from high above. "Iceberg dead ahead."

Bardon had just filled his mouth with ale. He sputtered, spat. "The fool is drunk on watch. By the Cud and Ar's Staff, I'll have him flogged!"

Caranga reached the deck ahead of his second. "Helmsman, hold your course. Step lively, you wharf rats! Prepare to drop anchor. Make ready the grappling hooks."

Bardon felt the chill and stared. It *was!* A mountain of *ice!*

Vixen swiftly came abreast the looming iceberg, dropped anchor and, with some difficulty, grappled to the frozen mass. The wind that blew across the massive chunk of floating ice struck *Vixen* as the breath of a frost giant. Dressed for the warmth of southern waters, some crewmen scurried to find warm clothing. Most stood in cold discomfort, fearful of missing some weird occurrence. Bardon was beginning to understand. The cold air biting his skin was small discomfort compared to the coldness in his spine. Though his apprehension was great, he forced his dry mouth to speak calmly.

"I . . . gather we are waiting for someone?"

"Yes," Caranga nodded. "The new master of *Vixen*. I told you we were sailing into hell. Now we must meet the devil who will be our captain."

Sunlight struck the ice and broke into thousands of dazzling rays. The intense white glare baffled every blinking eye. Eventually some spied the small darkish ape that moved through the blinding whiteness. With a curse, Bardon shaded his eyes. His straining gaze resolved the shape into the figure of a lean man in black robes. It was a tiny man—no, it was a tall man a great distance away. He paced toward them through a long glittering corridor of ice, greenish ice like a prodigious aventurine. Bardon jerked his head and blinked, for he could not believe his eyes. When he looked again, he saw the man's features: sharp-planed face like a bird of prey with dark eyes, bright as a hawk's under predatory brows. The beard was very close-cut and on the chin only. Now the robed man was walking to the ship on one of the grappling lines. A Sarchese tightrope walker could not have balanced on that line, for it was slack. This mattered little to the approaching man; he did not deign to balance, but strode as if he descended a wide staircase. When he reached the deck of *Vixen,* Caranga bowed.

"My Lord Pyre, let me show you to your cabin."

The wizard shook his head with a jerk. "Just call me Pyre; I have no need or time for polite ceremonies. Order your men to raise anchor and make full speed for Sonul."

Supper that night was a gloomy business, a last meal of the condemned. No man, save Caranga, had any idea what awaited them in Sonul, but all knew the city had earned its grim reputation. There was no question of mutiny; indeed no man dared whisper to his neighbor, for fear of the wizard. *Pyre!* Pyre of Ice!

Pyre spent the night in what had been Tiana's cabin. Bardon, who had the first watch of the night, observed the wizard go alone into the empty cabin; yet throughout the night Pyre's voice could be heard. The words, in no language Bardon understood, were in the tone of an argument, haggling over price. The second mate wondered what the wizard was selling. The . . . sounds that answered Pyre's voice were never human. Bardon heard a birdlike chirping. Bardon heard a hollow weary moaning as from one long dead recalled unwillingly to life. A light girlish laughter that changed into an obscene aged cackle; a humming as from a great bee. Toward midnight the wizard had a night guest who did not speak. Its heavy breathing could be heard and the floor groaned when it shifted its weight. There were other guests, other sounds. Bardon could not describe them and he would gladly not have heard them. Then came the speaking silence. The sounds of the sea and the wind intermittently faded and vanished. When, startled, he shouted, he found he could not hear his own voice part of the time. For the moment his curiosity was stronger than his fear. When he whistled a steady note, part of the sound vanished. As he listened, he realized that the silences formed a pattern; they were strange, inside-out words. He could almost understand them. He recognized Tiana's name, then Jiltha's.

Sarsis, something, something, *ceremony of return*, something, *sacrifice of a royal virgin* (!), much he could not discern, then *"We—terms. Since we love destruction for —we vow to burn you—fire."*

Abruptly Bardon realized that he was eavesdropping, a most unhealthy practice. Had he heard the mighty wizard make a bargain for his own destruction by fire? That made no more sense than this voyage filled with insane events. The second mate was glad when his watch ended and Caranga relieved him.

Bardon's sleep that night was most uneasy. He was brave enough to live with fear, but more than fear assaulted his mind. He had commanded a ship for a few hours and managed it badly. Events were dark riddles he could not solve. He could not cope. Why had he become a pirate in the first place? Born of a very minor noble house of Bemar, he could have had a place at court, in Aradot. No, his was a great noble line, no less long and glorious than the King's; it was just that none of his ancestors had done anything notable in more than a century. Worse, his father and grandfather had been poor. To be honest, Bardon ca-Lionheight was a pirate for the sake of greed. It was his hope to win a share of a fabulous treasure and restore the family fortune. More than that, Bardon wanted to do great deeds, to prove himself. Marrin hound, his childhood playmates had called him, after a breed of dog once very popular. The Marrin blood-line was long since played out. Bardon's greatest fear was that it was true. Bardon. Marrin. He hadn't gone to court because there he knew he'd be one more fop; Nothing. Bardon. Marrin. Instead he became a pirate, and because he was loyal and efficient and intelligent, Tiana and Caranga had trusted him with every routine task. He was still young; yet wasn't the pattern of his life already clear? Wouldn't he always be a would-be, an errand boy for others who did great deeds?

There were the self-doubts that plagued Bardon's sleep, and he awoke stiff and depressed. Marrin hound.

"My lady," the sad-faced young man said to an imaginary damsel in distress, "I, your hero, am come to your succor." And he cursed and bashed a fist into his cabin wall.

At dawn the lookout sighted land. The sun was a ball of molten gold, still low on the horizon when they entered the harbor of Sonul.

The appearance of the city of fearful legend was a relief and a disappointment. It was extraordinary only in that it was completely ordinary. The buildings were of the type normal to the tropics: single-story thatched huts. All were in good repair, and of similar size and design. Their appearance was rather bleak, for they were simple functional structures without the slightest decoration. At first glance Bardon thought that since all the houses were nearly the same, the city of Sonul must have neither rich nor poor. Yet that would not explain the lack of ornamentation. . . .

The streets, he noted, were only hard-packed dirt—yet for a wonder they were clean. The overall impression was one of clean, uniform drabness. Bardon found it hard to believe that so mundane a place was the object of such grim legend. Well; Caranga, for all his dark hints, had admitted that the legends were false.

Vixen docked smoothly. Pyre stalked out on deck. Most of the crew was waiting for breakfast. The wizard walked among them black-caped, black-robed, a grim raven among lesser birds, and they did not seem to notice him they feared. To the watching Bardon it was more like seeing a tiger walk unheeded in a flock of sheep. Pyre tapped an Ilani guardsman on the shoulder. The man started, looked in terror into the wizard's eyes. Pyre touched two more men with the same effect. Bardon noted with discomfort that the mage had chosen three men with bodies much like his; tall, angular men with very little flesh on their bones. From within his robes Pyre produced a money pouch and tossed it to Bardon.

"You will take these three men ashore and do some shopping. We need ten mules, provisions for a week and a hundred picks and spades." The wizard handed him a scroll of extraordinary size, its ends capped. "Also, you will deliver this message to the House of Rulers. Be sure that none save he that sits upon the throne breaks the seals."

Reflecting uncomfortably that Pyre had chosen four men who together would not provide a cannibal with a good meal, Bardon turned to go about the wizard's business. As he turned, Pyre clapped him on the back.

"Good luck, boy."

Bardon knew he didn't look much like a pirate, for all

that he wore a ring in his left ear. The wizard's departing fingers brushed quickly against the golden loop. Bardon and company went ashore.

Odd; no one had been sufficiently curious about the visitors to come down to the quay. Only when the pirates stepped out onto a thoroughfare did they see the people of Sonul. Without exception, they were completely naked.

Bardon had traveled the world enough not to show surprise. What did surprise him was that all these folk looked good, unclothed. In any normal collection of people, most would look better dressed. Certainly Bardon's own scarecrow body was better covered. Not so here! He looked carefully without discovering anyone with a withered limp or scar or mark or blemish. All were clearly in perfect health, their bodies young, firm, strong. The city people seemed almost members of a huge family; all strongly resembled each other. The adults were nearly the same height and all on the well-fed side. Oddly, the sight of many naked females did not arouse him. Their skins were a rich deep brown, their legs were shapely, and their breasts full—but their faces were completely bovine, entirely devoid of feeling or expression. All were plump.

Seeing that his little squad did not share his distaste for cow-faced women, he harangued them: "Come on, you rogues, we didn't come here for sightseeing."

Bardon and his men were more than a head taller than the Sonulites. With their clothing and fair skins they could not have been more conspicuous, yet no one paid them any heed. He stopped one man.

"Please direct me to the House of Rulers."

The fortyish fellow looked at him blankly, then walked off. Several similar efforts went the same way: no one understood any language the four visitors could speak and no one was interested in trying. Bardon pondered the problem. He could put off finding the House of Rulers and go buy the mules. He could find a stable with his nose. Still, he wanted to deliver the scroll as soon as possible. It was an awkward thing, more than an arm's length long, and rather heavy. Moreover he was a ship's officer and the men looked to him to plot their course under all circumstances.

That hill inside the city should afford a commanding

view; from there he should be able to espy the House of Rulers. Out of the edge of his eye Bardon noticed something. His sword flashed out and with the flat of the blade he struck the backside of one of his men.

"Alpheg, we're looking for the House of Rulers; we can find the whorehouse later! Now march!"

The hike through the city gave him no new information about the people of Sonul. Instead Bardon reflected on what he saw. The myths called this place a fearful hell, while it seemed a paradise. He saw neither wealth nor want. The rule appeared to be equality; everyone with what he needed and no more. There were dreamers who would call that the ideal kingdom. To such dreamers it would seem natural the women be content with the beauty nature gave them and give up the vanities of cosmetics and coiffure, but the city women were content to be nearly identical. Was it natural for women to cut their hair a practical length and do nothing with it?

Halfway up the hill Bardon called a brief halt. From here he could see most of the city. There were several larger buildings within the city and, on the outskirts, numerous stables. Beyond, neatly plowed fields stretched as far as the eye could see. Two things he did not see; any building that might reasonably be a palace or walls. The city of Sonul had no walls, no fortification; no defenses of any kind. Bardon could have understood old walls, crumbled with disuse, but the total absence implied that war was unknown. Far too good to be true, surely!

Largumdurga interrupted his thoughts. "Sir, I believe I've figured this place out. See how these people are all young. They must have found the secret of eternal youth! They spread frightening stories about the city so the whole world won't crowd in on them."

"No," Bardon told the Bashanese, slowly and very quietly. "It's true we've seen no aged, Durgy, but we have seen a lot of children. If these people lived forever they wouldn't breed rapidly."

The two men looked at each other, uncomfortably. The more Bardon thought about it, the more uneasy the physical perfection of these people made him. The city of Sonul could not be exempt from age, disease and accident! Yet he had walked a long way through crowded streets without seeing anyone who wasn't physically perfect. Did the aged and infirm stay inside?

*Perhaps, but there's a far less pleasant explanation:
the imperfect are somehow . . . removed.*

On impulse he stopped, handed his sword and scroll to
Largumdurga of Bashan, and bent to shake off his mailshirt. Unarmed and unarmored he walked toward the
man he had chosen as his victim. Though Bardon was
taller, the Sonulite was heavier and much better muscled.
The pirate drew back his hand in an obvious motion and
slapped the man's face with all his strength. The blow
staggered the fellow. Challenge and insult were plain. . . .
And the Sonulite looked at Bardon without anger, indeed
with no expression other than vague puzzlement. Then he
simply walked away. Bardon picked up his mailshirt, a
little bundle of linked chain. Should he try the experiment
again? No, best to dress and be about his business. No
matter how incredible, the men here clearly had no fight
in them. How could they exist? If nothing else their women
were portable wealth, attractive to sea raiders. Their rich
farm lands should be the envy of hostile tribes.

Had his mind not been occupied Bardon would have
noticed it sooner: his earring was too heavy.

He touched it. The gold hoop was gone!

In its place he wore a pentagram of very cold metal
—Pyre had switched rings! What dark scheme was the
wizard plotting? No matter; Bardon did not care to be an
expendable pawn. As he walked, he tried to be casual
in his fumbling to remove the earring—only to discover
that it was a continuous, seamless piece of metal. He
could remove it from his pierced lobe only by tearing his
flesh!

This was absurd. The wizard had put the thing in his
ear in an instant, by an effortless sleight of hand. It
must be easy to remove, if only he could see the cursed
thing.

"Sir, you're a living wonder."

He looked up. "What do you mean, Durgy?"

"Here we are strangers in a large city and you march
us straight to where we want to go."

It was true. Directly in front of them stood a squat
graystone building. Low, windowless, it was somehow
faintly repellent. It was also the only building in the city
that was more than a simple functional structure. This
had to be the House of Rulers.

Should he tear the pentagram from his ear or wait till

he could find a tool to cut the metal? He'd look a pretty fool, standing before the masters of Sonul with his ear bleeding.

"All right, boys, let's see if anyone here can speak our language."

The door to the House of Rulers was bronze, carved with a pattern imitating the scales of a fish or snake. Bardon banged on it, demanding admission in every language he knew. He was answered in his native Bemarish.

"Remove your armor and lay aside your weapons."

When the four visitors had done so, the door slid silently back to reveal guards who were clearly not of the same race as the city people. Indeed they scarcely appeared to be men. Small black eyes seemed to glint with a bestial ferocity. Wide and powerful jaws opened to reveal canine fangs above short bodies that were thick with muscles positively bulgy.

Bardon was ashamed to show fear. With a front as calm as he could manage, the dolorous-looking man stepped in among those . . . creatures. When his men sought to follow, the guards stepped forward to block their way. Largumdurga looked at the bared fangs of the snarling beast-man.

"By your leave, sir, we'll wait outside," he said, and the brazen door slid shut before Bardon could reply.

He submitted to a rather rough search, after which the guards' attention fixed upon the scroll. One started to undo the seals. Bardon slapped his hand away.

"No, for the master only, masters only."

The beast-man's eyes blazed with rage for a moment, and Bardon saw death there. Then he . . . *it* seemed to understand.

They led him through a labyrinth of passageways, most of which led downward. Apparently the House of Rulers was an extensive set of underground tunnels. At last they pushed him through a door and locked it behind him. He was alone in a narrow room lighted by a single small lamp that flickered weakly. The door at the far end of the chamber turned out also to be locked. Bardon had an intense sensation of being watched. He wondered if it could be illusion. The thought, or concept, of weapons kept coming into his mind, again and again. He had no weapons. He had only his bare hands. The pressure of the hidden eyes grew more intense. It was a question, a demand.

Suddenly Bardon was moved to shout. "Look, I'm unarmed."

The pressure vanished and he heard a click. The door at the far end of the room was slightly ajar. Just as he started toward it, his earring whispered. The voice was Pyre's.

"Not yet. First you must open the scroll."

Bardon stopped in shocked surprise. Then anger filled him and he quivered with it. Controlling himself with some effort, he whispered, "Why should I play your dark game, wizard?"

"Two good reasons. First Caranga gave me command of Vixen because I am the only hope of saving Tiana and Jiltha. You are oath-bound to their rescue and hence bound to my service. The second reason is even better. The scroll contains a sword. If you do not remove and hide it immediately the rulers of Sonul will decide you're an assassin and kill you out of hand."

"Damn your evil soul, what do you want me to do?"

"Break the main seal."

The main seal was a blob of red in the shape of a flame. When Bardon broke it, it burned his fingers. The scroll rapidly unrolled like a living thing. It dropped a strange sword in his hand—and immediately rerolled itself. The flame seal was whole, unbroken. The sword was the same cold metal as his earring, a sword of ice; an enchanted sword. It had the feel of a living thing in his hand.

"Hurry, man, hide the sword."

Bardon stared about the empty room. "Where?"

"Use that height of yours—put it in the ceiling."

Bardon imbedded the fell sword's point in one of the beams. A poor hiding place, he thought, but it would go unseen unless someone happened to look directly up at it.

"Now go to the Rulers swiftly; this delay may make them suspicious."

Bardon stepped through the door into a large audience hall of paneled wood walls and stone floor. The chamber smelled . . . earthy. The area where he stood was well lighted while the far end was in darkness. A throne squatted darkly in the center of that dark. Little could be seen of the man who sat in the high-backed seat, for he wore dark, dark robes and the wall behind him was curtained in forest green velvet that might as well have been black.

A smooth, sibilant voice hissed from the throne.

"It is our policy to encourage trade with the outside world and ordinary merchant ships are welcome in our harbor. You, however, come in a ship of war. Who are you and why do you intrude upon our realm?"

"I am Bardon, second officer of the ship *Vixen*. As for why we come here, I really cannot say but Pyre sent this scroll to you." He scarcely noticed the servant who took the scroll from him. He was again overwhelmed by the sensation of being watched. The question "who am I?" kept coming into his mind. The searching was intense but brief.

"Well, marrin hound," the voice hissed from the throne, "your master chose you well. We can learn nothing from you because you know nothing. The scroll you delivered is passing strange for its uses much paper and ink to say very little: only that Pyre believes there need not be war between himself and us, and to this end he requests an audience tonight. We grant this request. We grant his further request that you, Caranga and six others may be his honor guard. However, no weapons may be brought into the House of Rulers. You may go."

"May" was not the appropriate word. Though Bardon was eager to leave, the guards were even more eager to be rid of him. He was rapidly propelled through the passageways and flung out past the bronze door. He landed on his backside in full view of his men. So glad was he to see the sun again that the loss of dignity was a secondary annoyance.

Standing among his men was one of the city people, a man whose eyes showed a slight spark of intelligence. "Rulers send help get mules and shovels," he said in the Narokan tongue that Bardon could just handle.

Though Bardon had told no one what he wanted, he was not surprised. This was but a further proof that the Rulers had read his mind. He still resented Pyre's use of him as a cat's-paw but now he saw why it had been necessary. As his body had been searched for weapons, so had his *mind*. Only after the Rulers had searched and found nothing had Pyre revealed the sword to him.

Bardon examined the Sonulite, who seemed a bit older than the others. "What's your name?"

"Name?"

After a few tries Bardon concluded that the problem lay not in his knowledge of the Narokan language or the man's ignorance. The wretch had no name.

The bargaining for the mules and picks and shovels was a most unusual experience. The man simply named a price. While such a take it or leave it "offer" seemed grossly unfair to Bardon, the Sonulite had orders from which he dared not depart—and every mule's price was the same. Bardon carefully chose the best, and decided he was getting the best of the bargain.

Supplies were a problem. Grain and dried fruit were available at a reasonable price, but the man looked blank at all references to meat, pigs, cattle or sheep. Bardon had met vegetarians before but never people who did not understand that meat was food. If *Vixen*'s crew was to march any great distance overland, they would need meat. Reluctantly and yet ingeniously, he bought five extra mules.

Pyre's money pouch was full of gold. People who had mules must possess horses. Why should Bardon and his shipmates march when they could ride? Following this logic the second mate asked about horses and was promptly shown a stable of plow horses. As work animals these massive, powerful beasts were superb, but a man would be better off walking then riding one of their slow and huge-footed number. The man was blank when Bardon asked for riding horses. When he mounted a plow horse in demonstration, the Sonulite watched in vague puzzlement. Bardon realized these people had horses and mules and no concept of riding and Bardon was getting a headache.

When he returned to *Vixen* with his purchases, the second mate saw that his ship was no longer alone in port. The newcomer was a long canoe, equipped with a single outrigger. The tribesmen of some nearby village had apparently come to trade. He counted twelve of the black warriors, carrying spears and dressed in loincloth, amulet, and shells.

Piled on the side of the dock were their trade goods: Ivory, tiger skins, and gold nuggets. On the other side stood their purchases: some thirty of the city women. At first glance nothing about this scene disturbed Bardon: bride purchase was hardly an uncommon custom. Then he saw that the warriors' teeth were filed to points. The horrible suspicion grew in his mind. He turned to his guide.

"What are those men doing?"

"Buy girls."

"Yes, but for what?"

The guide thought for a moment, then smiled, his eyes bright. "Now understand. Not understand before. Now understand what is meat. Men buy girls for meat."

Bardon swallowed, shocked to hear his suspicions confirmed. He looked at *Vixen;* his shipmates were on deck and watching the black warriors warily. Standing procedure was that weapons were kept ready in a strange port. Bardon knew that bows were strung and close to hand. If he but shouted one order the cannibals would find their stomachs filled not with human flesh but with arrows.

Should he kill a dozen men over what might be an error in translation? If the girls were going to the cook pot, why weren't they chained or caged? Why weren't they crying? If they were brides, why weren't they giggling? Whatever their fate, they were leaving their homes. Why did they show no emotion?

Think as he would Bardon could not resolve the dilemma. Again he was enraged with himself for his inability to act decisively. He was the paralyzed witness to events rather than a leader. Still the offspring of a played-out bloodline: marrin hound.

While he whipped himself for not making a decision, the chance to decide was taken from him. He saw Caranga striding along the quay toward the black warriors. He could not understand what the old man shouted at them, but it was clear they did for they shouted back and raised their spears. The black pirate raised his sword and charged the black warriors. He was lost in a tangle of bodies.

"Archers!" Bardon bawled. "Hold your shafts. Swords: Attack!"

His own sword was out and he rushed into the battle. Two spearmen came at him and he recognized clumsiness. They were badly out of practice. He sidestepped the first and split the second man's belly. The dying man fell against his comrade and before the latter could recover Bardon's sword clove him. Peripheral vision showed Bardon a spearman coming at his back. He couldn't turn in time, but it didn't matter. It was only the falling corpse of a man Alpheg had slain. A spear came at his head and he parried easily. His sword's sharp edge bit through the wood and the warrior was looking foolishly at his broken spear when Bardon slashed his throat.

Abruptly it was over. *Vixen's* crew came running to a battle, and arrived at a tangled pile of corpses. Caranga, who had slain most of the cannibals, stood in triumph upon the dead. His gaze fell on Bardon, and his eyes were angry.

"I'm an old lion, but I'm still a match for twelve jackals."

The reprimand angered Bardon. "Sir, I grant these men were so unskilled you could have dealt with all of them, but how was I to know? They could have been twelve skilled warriors."

"Their bearing and stance should have told you," snapped Caranga. "Besides it's plain reason that if they were fighting men they wouldn't need to *buy* meat." His eyes softened. "Well, you meant well, and probably you saved me from being shot by my own men."

Watching Caranga walk away, Bardon fingered his moustache and weighed that faint praise from a reformed cannibal. Slowly a dangerous resolve grew in the mind of the second mate of *Vixen*. Captain Tiana was gone: dead or in the hands of Sarsis. She had left Bardon in command, and Caranga had come off his sickbed to relieve him of that fleeting importance. Now Pyre had supplanted them both. Pyre!

I am through being errand boy for Caranga and cat's-paw for the "wizard of wizards!" Sink the risk! I will face this arrogant lord of dark enchantment and force the truth from him. Cud of the cow—my ancestors cry out from their barrows for me to do something!

The resolve was strong when Bardon started toward the wizard's cabin. When he reached its door, it occurred to him that Pyre might not be alone. For a moment he hesitated. He had no desire to meet the owners of those awful voices he had heard. With a hand on the latch, he re-encouraged himself, and thus self-supported, jerked open the door and swung into the cabin.

He found Pyre alone. The wizard sat bolt upright in a chair, and he did not move. His eyes were droplets of onyx fixed on infinity. In short mauve cape and floor-length robe of dull black that clung to his lean frame, he was obviously not breathing. Bardon touched the hand on the curling arm of the straight chair, and found those long lean fingers hard and cold. A shudder ran through him.

But wait—surely the mightiest of wizards was not dead. His soul must have departed his body, sent forth.

Last night he talked to others, *who visited him,* Bardon mused. *Now he has gone to visit others.* Tugging up his mailcoat's skirt behind, Bardon sat down to wait. It was not easy to sit in the domain of a sorcerer and await the reanimation of a lifeless body. Far from comfortable, Bardon shifted with a jingle and clink of metal links. He rearranged the position and hang of his belt three several times. His headache returned, running up his back and into the left side of his head.

The wait was not so long as it felt. Without any sort of preamble Pyre's bird-of-prey eyes focused on the younger man.

"Why do you trespass here?"

Bardon's anger proved stronger than his fear. "I come to make two demands," he said, and his head pounded. "First that you remove this accursed ring from my ear. Second, you shall explain the mystery of this evil city."

"Your first demand I refuse," Pyre said, sitting spear-straight and moveless—but breathing again. "I gave you the Star of Avan and it is not my custom to take back a gift."

"Then I'll have the ship's carpenter cut the metal."

"The Star of Avan is forged of ice metal, young sir. It cannot be cut. The carpenter would only spoil his tools and his equanimity."

Bardon slapped his thigh in frustration and anger. "I don't care if the ship's cook has to cut off my ear to remove this thing!"

"Bardon, Bardon. They are your ears and certainly you may do with them what you please. To remove the Star of Avan, however, you will require the services of a headsman's ax. Surely you agree that is a bit . . . drastic. After tonight I can take back the Star, but you will be happier if you accept my generous gift. As to your second demand, already you know too much. I shall tell you a little more anyhow." It was godlike condescension, and Bardon seethed even as Pyre rose. "I have, however, been long in the position. A moment."

The wizard sucked in a deep breath and turned his head leftward, farther than any man should have been able to do. Slowly he returned it to the fore, nodded deeply, and nodded backward, so that his crown pointed at his heels. Then he slowly turned his head far, far to the right. And back, and nod and nod. He looked at the seated man, bristly black brows mildly arched above supercilious eyes that were bright as garnets in sunlight.

"Now. Sonul seems a strange city to you, naturally—because it is not truly a city. More accurately it is a people ranch. The—"

"A what?"

The wizard made a vaguely impatient gesture and continued. "The strange customs here, the lack of either wealth or poverty, the unusual psychology . . . all are explained by the fact that the people of Sonul are domestic animals, bred for docility. There are no walls around the city because in the event of war the Rulers of Sonul would defend themselves, not their herd. There are, among the people of Sonul, no sick or aged because—"

"Merciful Theba!" Bardon exploded, his eyes wider than normal. "The inhabitants here are slaughtered while they're still young and healthy!" Even as he spoke the ghastly words he knew them for truth—and could not quite believe them. "But . . . but the Rulers of Sonul . . . what manner of monsters are they?"

"Not monsters, Bardon. Merely our enemies. I brought *Vixen* to this port that we might fight a battle in an age-long combat, the Shadow War."

"The Shad—I don't understand. Are not wars by definition always open and public?"

The mage shook his head slightly, replied blandly. "On the contrary," he said, with the faintest hint of mockery in his voice. "Wars are always as secret as possible! It is merely that the means commonly used are clumsy and conspicuous." His beard, only a patch of salted pepper under his mouth, twitched as he spoke. "Often I have looked in my glass and laughed to see ten thousand stomping oafs in clanging armor trying to surprise another such army, which in turn is trying to surprise the first army. Often the blind fools wander for days in search of each other. The Shadow War is fought by subtle means and so is a secret to common man. You, Bardon, are a fine example of a weapon in the Shadow War. You hold yourself in contempt, you see, and I have arranged for the enemy to accept you at your own valuation. No no; don't interrupt just yet. Such a proven fighting man as Caranga they would watch with great care. He could do little against their defenses. Against you they will not even guard. Tonight then, when you and I and Caranga go to the House of Rulers with seven others, you—"

"Wait! Did you say seven others? The Rulers gave permission for only six—"

"True, but the beastmen who guard their door cannot count that high. No one thinks of everything, you see —almost no one. Tonight, when we go to the House of Rulers, it will be you who takes the Sword of Avan and by mighty deeds prove yourself a great warrior."

Bardon swallowed, stared. What the wizard promised was what he desired more than life itself. For a moment his suspicions waned. Still, he was Bardon, and uttered first his favorite word:

"But how? I suppose you can shield your mighty mind, and the others don't know your plan, but the Rulers will know everything as soon as they look into my mind."

Bardon had not noticed until now how large the wizard's eyes were. "That's no great problem. From now until well after we enter the House of Rulers, you will do no thinking."

Bardon blinked his mild, troubled eyes for what seemed a rather long moment—and he was standing again in the narrow room with the two doors. The voice spoke in his ear.

"Hurry man, get the sword."

At first glance the dark ceiling seemed to be empty. "But what if it's not there?"

"Then the Rulers have outwitted me, and we are all dead men."

Fear gripped Bardon, not fear of death, but fear that his life might end with a disastrous failure. He had failed too often already. His head tightened.

The sword was still in place. He felt a strange thrill when his fingers grasped the hilt. He was aware of a sensation of rapidly increasing skill and coordination. More than that, it was as if long-dead instincts were awakening. Because it *felt* the right thing to do, Bardon strode to the first door and touched the knob with the point of his sword. There was a click and the door was open. In his ear the voice of Pyre whispered, bidding him do all the things he had just done. Faster than Pyre could give instructions he was racing through the labyrinth of tunnels that was the House of Rulers. Locked doors opened at the touch of his enchanted blade. When he met guards, they died swiftly.

While Bardon fought, Pyre negotiated. Though Bardon paid little heed, he could hear most of what was said. The wizard stood in the audience room and spoke not to the figure on the throne but to the black velvet curtains behind the throne.

"It is true that I am on one side of the Shadow War and you the other, but in the past there has been peace between us. The Rulers of Sonul have wisely been content to defend what was theirs and have not joined with others in attacks of human kingdoms. I have punished the others when they went too far, but I have never caused the cold wind to blow upon Sonul. I recognize the greatness and nobility of your ancient race and I have no wish to harm you."

From behind the black curtain a hissing voice asked, "You do not resent that we keep humans as food animals?"

"Of course not," Pyre replied. "You manage your herd very well. The people here live longer and much more comfortable lives than in most human kingdoms. There is no reason for war between us. Sarsis seeks to return and thus disturb the balance. I must deal harshly with him but this need not concern you."

The hissing voice said, "We are a dying race. You and your kind have stolen the world from us. Others have fought to regain what was stolen, but we of Sonul have not fought for we wish our last years to be peaceful."

"Time, not man, stole the world from you," Pyre said in a calming tone. "Even here in the tropics it is not warm enough for your race."

The hissing voice was louder, angry. "Ssarssiss can change that. Ssarssiss can make the world warm again."

"Nay, but I will not permit it. I will destroy the Eyes

of Sarsis and send him back into the gulf of outer night to wander blindly forever. There is no need for the Rulers of Sonul to perish in this battle."

The hissing voice lost its anger, became calm and sweet. "So these are the terms you offer us: that the Rulers of Ssonul may march peaceful to their graves. There were those among us who thought we should act without hearing your offer, but it is well that we saw how far your arrogance could carry you. Now you shall hear our terms."

(Bardon heard Pyre order him to take the left hand passageway, but he was already speeding down the rightward way.)

"We, the Rulers of Ssonul, promised that you could come—but not that you could go. You came into our midst bearing no talisman of power, your men unarmed. The House of Rulers is well protected. No spirit or demon may be summoned to aid you here. Therefore our terms are simple: Death. This was decided upon when your ship came to Ssonul."

Bardon came to the end of the passageway, a blank stone wall.

Pyre sighed. "I regret your attitude but I am not surprised by it. I offer you one last chance to reconsider before I use this." He drew a massive candelabrum from under his robes. The center large candle burned with a bright golden flame. Around it a host of small candles burned with silver flames.

Bardon raised his sword against the stone wall and it slid back to reveal darkness beyond. Now he heard contempt in the hissing voice and perhaps a slight hint of fear:

"Do you think us children, to be frightened by such mummery? That spell can only be effective against those already weak with fear."

"I have often lied, but I tell you truly: I regret that I must do this."

Pyre's hand moved toward the center candle. His fingers were blackness moving against the light. As if the gold flame were a solid object, his dark fingers began to squeeze the bright flame.

Bardon plunged into the darkness, knowing it held the enemy he sought. The change he felt when he first grasped the Sword of Avan rushed to completion. He

stood in a sunbaked desert. In front of him coiled a viper
of great and terrible size. Venom drooled from its huge
fangs. It seemed right and natural that he should be a
small bird with a sharp beak. He hopped toward the
scintillant green snake. Closer, closer till he was inches
from those viciously curving fangs. The instant before
the serpent struck, a quick flap of his wings pulled him
back. Gleaming fangs brushed his feathers. In and out;
they danced the ancient rite of death. Bardon's backsteps
always left him within the snake's reach, while the snake
always kept part of its body coiled. The trick, he knew,
was to judge when the enemy's patience would fail. The
dance continued and the moment came. The fanged
mouth shot toward him and the thrust of his wings pulled
him back. For an instant the snake lay uncoiled before
him and his sharp beak sped down. It pierced the brain.

As the serpent writhed and died, the scene changed
and Bardon was a man in darkness—with something
evil dying on his sword.

Pyre's fingers extinguished the golden flame. "Farewell, Old One." From behind the black curtain sounded
a brief cry of pain, then the gurgle of death. There was
no sound in the audience hall, yet the chamber seemed
filled with a chorus of screaming voices, begging for
mercy, offering wealth, power, anything if he would but
spare them. With deft strokes he snuffed out the small silver flames. As each candle died, the chorus lost a voice
until all the candles were out and the soundless voices
gone.

Bardon stepped back from his victim and its stench.
He was glad of the darkness for he had no wish to see
what he had slain. He tripped and fell through black
curtains. He saw he was in the audience room but before
he could check himself he stumbled against the throne.
The figure that sat there pitched forward, crashed to the
floor. He was only half surprised to see a wooden
dummy. A sense of pride and achievement filled Bardon,
for he knew it was his sword that had made the wizard's
spell effective.

"My Lord Pyre, this night we have done a great and
noble work, to slay these monsters."

The wizard's cold bright eyes fixed upon him. "It was
a great work, but an evil one. Once these were the lords

of all the earth. Now we have robbed them even of their lives."

Bardon protested, "But they were treacherous. They asked us to come and talk, planning to kill us. They were evil monsters, keeping people as cattle."

The wizard shrugged. "As for the first, we were successful in these negotiations because we brought more bad faith to the bargaining. They planned to slay us only after hearing what I had to say. While I was still speaking, you were working their death. As for the other, perhaps you and I are monsters for we eat beef while we could live on vegetables. The Rulers of Sonul ate only what nature appointed for them to eat."

"By all the mud on the Great Turtle's back," swore Bardon, "your conscience is too nice by half. Your name is a synonym for evil the world over, but this day we have saved a great city of people from vile slavery and obscene death. We have given them their freedom."

Pyre sighed with the weariness of the world.

"And with that freedom comes the right to mismanage their agriculture so that they starve; the right to die of a host of diseases from which the Rulers protected them; and the right to defend themselves as best they can against their neighbors. I've no doubt the cannibals will use Sonul as a pantry." Pyre shook his head. "You are a young man and may tell yourself that freedom is worth any price. For myself I know I have again earned the infamy of my name. It does not matter. The only certain philosophy is that the gods look with favor on those who reach the battlefield first. We fought the Rulers of Sonul that our backs might be safe when we fight Sarsis. Now we must hasten to the place of that battle. The real battle, Bardon. Ancient Sarsis."

CHAPTER SIXTEEN

Caranga set his fists behind his hips and arched his back in with a grunt. He dashed sweat from his brow so that it pattered on the ground. Wearing only a very dirty white tunic that bared his brawny arms and legs like the knotty boles of oaks, he surveyed the hillside.

At the edge of a rich grassland, this once featureless, arid landscape was pocked now with the thousands of holes dug by him and his men. These past days of toil had demanded more of both crewmen and Ilani soldiers than would a fierce battle. Every man must be pounds lighter in lost sweat, and not all of it from the warmth of working in bright sun. Even gallons of wine would not wash away memories of this ugly task. Caranga knew that what they had done was necessary—and it still made him feel unclean. Raising a sweat-gleaming arm the color of basalt and darkest amethyst, he shouted.

"All right, cease digging! We have raised enough. Put aside your picks and shovels, lads. You have done what men may do, and done it well. All you can do now is await the outcome of a battle we can't help in. Back to Sonul with you, and abide there. If Susha favors us, and your Theba too, we shall return to you with Captain Tiana and Princess Jiltha."

He broke off, gnawing his lip. There was more he wished to say. Especially he wished to give his rogues his blessing, for he feared he would never see them again. He'd have been speaking to empty air. Despite their labors, the pirates needed no second order to speed back into Sonul. A sudden thought struck Caranga then, and he laughed.

"With my sweet sea rovers loose on the city," he mut-

tered, "the next generation of Sonul will have some fight
in their spirits!"

His smile faded when he glanced over to the wizard's
tent, some yards away. It had been a normal enough
large, dun-hued tent they'd raised. Now, depending on
how the sun struck it, Pyre's field abode might appear a
great block of ice or a raging fire. He wondered if the
illusion had some purpose or if that damned arrogant "wizard of wizards" just loved his drama almost as
much as he loved himself. Caranga paced over to it—
ice, just now, though it emitted no cold—while he
scratched one muscled ham. Bardon stood waiting for
him, just outside the tent, wearing dirty white tunic and
the quilted, leather-faced jack normally worn under his
good coat of linked chain. Just now the mail was nowhere
in view and the half-sleeved undercoat hung open, laces
dangling as if defeated by the sun.

It's well he's here, Caranga thought. *There are things
a man says to his friends before the final silence, and
that's never seemed more nigh.*

"Bardon . . . there are two things I want to say to you
and the first is an apology. Drood knows how many
times I was short o' temper over something that had nothing to do with you, but I spoke harshly to you because
you were handy. Wait a moment; the second is to thank
you, Bardon. You've been a loyal friend through many a
stormy voyage. By Susha's circumcision, you are as goodly
a white man as ever I sailed with."

The second mate looked surprised, then emotionally
affected. Slowly his long lean arm came out so that his
hand lay on the great round of Caranga's shoulder, and
Bardon's fingers tightened a bit.

"Thanks, Caranga. I hear you. I understand. But—I
doubt the time for last farewells is to hand." He looked
solemn a moment, then grinned. "Shall we?"

They entered the tent, with Caranga reflecting on this
new Bardon. These last days the skinny fellow had
acted with a strength and confidence Caranga had never
seen in him before. He even looked cheery—not just un-
mopey, but cheery, which made him seem bigger. *When
a list of all my faults is drawn up it shall include the fact
that I sheltered that whelp too much! Just a skinny white
boy with good blood and a brain worth protecting from
combat I thought. Dung and cess! Pyre, for all he used*

*him so ruthlessly, gave him something important to do—
and by the Back and Susha's backside, he did it!*

Thus thinking, Caranga entered the tent and faced the wizard.

Pyre stood staring, brows coolly arched and tiny close-mowed beard at rest. Arms behind his back. Looking longer if not quite so thin without his black robe. This one was just as long, so that only his toes showed, but it was white, and it showed no wrinkle or sign of soil. On his chest, at the end of a slim chain of dark base metal, hung a strange sigil. In two halves. A coiled, nasty-looking serpent of green jade, broken.

There was shock for Caranga in seeing signs of strain on the face of the mightiest of wizards. The brooding sorcerer so far from his keep called Ice was able to see their future, and evidently what he saw was not cheering.

Nevertheless he spoke crisply—and with his usual arrogance. "I called you here to apprise you of our situation. The information will likely be of small value to you, true. But it would be a useless vanity for me to withhold it and Pyre is without vanity."

Oh, of course, Bardon mused. *Just as Caranga is without fear. And just as I am twelve feet tall and have wings.*

"For good or ill," Pyre went on, "we are about to wage the last battle of the ancient Shadow War. If we succeed, there will be nothing left of the enemy save a few outposts of the slowly dying, places such as Sonul *was.* If we fail here and Sarsis returns, then he shall indeed have the power to make all the world warmer. Tropical! The children of the Snake shall again be masters of the earth."

"Your pardon," Bardon interrupted, "but—we three? We seem a slender peg to hang the world on. Are there no others to aid us? This Voomundo Caranga speaks of, perhaps. Or the good Sulun Mighty, or even your enemy Ekron? In view of the grave danger to all humankind, surely you and he can agree to a truce as fellow men interested in our survival—even if the truce is but temporary."

Pyre shook his head wearily. "The answer to all your so hopeful questions is . . . no. True, I helped Voomundo's soul to return to his body, but it had been away too long. It is not a viable separation, you see. He has the peace of death. As for Sulun Tha, we are fortunate he has decided to remain neutral, rather than help Sarsis who has much right on his side. Ekron . . . Ekron is a mystery. He is a man only in outer shape. His soul is that of a toad and the victory of Sarsis would be to his advantage. I have arranged for him to be busy elsewhere, but I read in the stars that some magicking of his is a danger to Sarsis. I dare not probe this mystery lest I warn Sarsis of the danger."

"But Sulun Tha is a man," Caranga rumbled. "Even if Sarsis has some ancient claim to the world, why does not Sulun Tha see that his means are evil?"

"Sarsis drinks blood and he has allies who relish the eating of men's souls and delight in the sacrifice of virgins. In contrast to these mundane character faults, I have committed a truly cosmic evil. The Eyes of Sarsis are considered indestructible, for no creature, man, demon, or god may harm them. There exists no power, spell or means to destroy them. Therefore I did the unspeakable. I bargained with the *non-beings*. You and I and Sarsis and they that dwell in the gulf of night and the demons in the lower bowels of Hell all share a common property; existence. The *non-beings* do not exist but are nonetheless very effective for the working of evil.

"A being may cause destruction to fill his belly or to satisfy a thirst of vengeance; to display arrogant power, or any of a host of reasons. The *non-beings,* the *others* . . . these love destruction for its own sake. They are the essence of evil. To traffic with them is dangerous to all that live, yet through them I have gained the means to destroy the Eyes of Sarsis. Unfortunately this means can only be used when the Eyes are helpless, drained of blood and power until they are exhausted. Certain aspects of that power may not be renewed by drinking blood. Much has happened to force the Eyes to spend their power, so that now they are weaker than at any time since they gained the Jewels of Ullatara. I have gathered all the strength I could. There were many who owed me debts and are paying by service in this fight. It will be a close thing. At the end of the battle either I or Sarsis will be close to exhaustion and the other entirely spent."

Pyre paced two steps, turned back.

"If I prevail, well and good. If I fail, there is yet some faint hope: the danger to Sarsis from Ekron's magic. Caranga, I have told you what you must do. Bardon, you are now Commander of the Star and Sword of Avan. Back in Sonul you proved your instincts were more accurate than my instructions. Therefore I can give you no instructions, only tell you your limits. Attend me.

"Avoid any direct attack upon the Eyes of Sarsis. *No creature with blood can stand against them, do you understand?* The minions of the Eyes are deadly foes, but you have some hope against them. I have made such preparations for defeat as I may. Now we shall test my plans for victory."

Pyre turned and with a robed rustle moved to a large table covered with sand. "This is the field of our battle." His left hand swept over the sand and it rose beneath his hand to form a mound in the shape of a coiled snake.

"This is the Mound of the Great Snake. It is some two hundred feet high—and several miles in total length. If all goes well, it shall remain merely a pile of earth. At the head of the mound is the Altar of Sacrifice." He put in place a small block of smooth black stone. Then from under his robes—which had been hanging perfectly straight —he produced a model of a lovely buiding whose walls were a lacework of marble and ivory. This he placed close to the black stone.

"The Temple of Cignas. It is filled with the bodies of men Cignas turned to stone by eating their souls." He placed a many-headed snake beside the temple: "Cignas." Next Pyre added the figure of a snake, green, a foot long with sparkling topaz eyes. "Sarsis is yet some distance from the temple, approximately here." A dozen smaller snakes, less than an inch: "The minions of Sarsis."

Now Pyre produced three small human shapes: a male and female figure, each in armor and a female figure wearing a chaplet. These he placed close to the Sarsis figure.

"In addition to Tiana and Jiltha, the Eyes have captured a Northish barbarian, one Bjaine. The Ceremony of Return requires a matched pair of warriors, male and female, and a royal virgin. If all goes as the Eyes plan, tonight at moonrise Jiltha will be borne to the altar. At the same time Tiana and Bjaine will be taken to the Temple of Cignas. In the Temple they will be made Bearers of the Eyes, vampires whose blood is in turn drunk by the Eyes. Then Tiana and Bjaine will go to the altar, where . . . But there is no need to detail this uncleanness!" Pyre looked at the other two men with his hawkish dark eyes under setose brows.

"At the end, all three will have died horribly and Sarsis will have returned to the world." He continued to stare for a time before turning back to his sprawling model. "We are here, just above an ancient tribal burial grounds." Pyre placed a replica of the tent.

"Well we know," Caranga said. "My lads have unearthed many and many of those long dead these past few days."

"Aye," the wizard said. "Let this represent them all."

Pyre placed a single figure flat on its back on the sand. Caranga looked with revulsion at the figure. He knew it was only carved wood but the resemblance was uncanny. Most of the corpses they had exhumed were not decayed but *dried:* the flesh shriveled and hardened until it was like wood.

"These are the other pieces with which I shall wage this war." From within his robes the wizard drew a set of symbols and images. These he placed beside the table of sand rather than on it. A tiny likeness of a hawk; a bird of crystal; a miniature chariot. Another snake identical to the twelve minions of Sarsis. Three long blocks of ice, and an ugly little stone. A little white wisp of cotton. Caranga had often seen the final figure, pictured on charts; it was the head of a frost giant blowing a cold wind.

The wizard lifted the tiny hawk, pushed it onto the table of sand.

"The game begins. Attack on a minor piece."

Game? Bardon thoght. *What sort of silly—oh, Ap's Beard!*

The hawk-figure came to life! It flew across the table, passing over the model of the tent. As it did, Caranga heard a thunder of flapping wings and a mighty chorus of strident cawing. If he could believe his ears, thousand of hawks had passed above their heads, screaming their war cries. The tiny hawk approached the snake figures. Singling out the one farthest from the Sarsis effigy, it attacked. Its prey was suddenly alive, fighting viciously. The fight was brief. The hawk swiftly gained the advantage—and then Sarsis struck. Nothing remained of the hawk but a few scattered feathers, barely large enough to see. Had there been doubt in the minds of the two pirates, none remained now; this "game" was real; this *was* the battle!

"Ahhh," murmured Pyre. "Sarsis spends his power recklessly. He should have sacrificed that minion. Either he is trying to bluff me or his reserves are greater than I calculated. We shall see." Pyre placed the frost giant figurehead on the table. "The minions of Sarsis cannot long endure the Cold Wind, for their blood has no warmth."

Caranga was suddenly aware of a freezing blowing without. The cold permeated the walls of the tent. At first the table of sand had appeared an ominous children's game. Now he realized that fearsome forces were being invoked. Everything here had its counterpart in reality. When a figure here was moved, it came alive and guided its living original, forced it into action.

"Wizard—could this not destroy Tiana and Jiltha, rather than save them?"

Pyre did not seem to hear. He placed the cotton on the board. It changed, rose, becoming a floating cloud. The cloud grew, spread, and moved slowly toward Sarsis. It was clear that there were complex figures moving in the cloud but they changed too fast, baffling Caranga's eye.

"They that dwell above the earth aid us," Pyre said, and lifted the ugly stone.

Bardon saw the subtle change: while before the darkish stone had borne a blurred resemblance to a living thing, now it was clearly a horror unlike any creature that had ever walked the earth. He did not place the stone on the surface, but pushed it into the sand from the side of the table.

"They that dwell beneath the earth also join the battle."

He laid the three long narrow blocks of ice on the table. They began to crawl like worms . . . no, Caranga saw; not *quite* like worms. For as they traveled, they grew longer and they plowed up the sand. They *slid,* huge and ponderous. Outside the tent distant rumblings sounded and the ground trembled continually. Sorcerous glaciers bore down upon Sarsis!

"The first and second ice worms attack Sarsis on right and left flank," Pyre said, almost whispering. "The cloud holds the center while the third glacier attacks the Mound of the Snake. Sarsis will not enjoy having several miles of *ice* plow through his ancient body."

The pieces were moving as Pyre described. The large snake struck at one of the ice worms, partially smashing it. The damage was obviously trivial. The worms continued to advance. Lashing, striking, the snake rained blows to right and left, breaking ice without halting the worm's advance. The cloud swept forward. Caranga knew it was easy to imagine the figure of a brave romance in a shapeless cloud, but here was no imagination. The cloud was a mighty host of armed chivalry, charging to battle. It struck the snake, and tiny bleeding pin pricks appeared on the coiled body.

The earth beneath the serpent trembled. The Temple of Cignas quivered, its foundations undermined. A hole appeared beside the black stone altar and hideous hands reached out to pull the altar down. The snake smote the ground as a smith pounds upon his anvil. The earth beneath it proved unstable and it was being pulled down. Another charge of the cloud dotted the green body with more scarlet. Unhalted, the ice worms were closing in from right and left and the third worm was nearing the mound.

Pyre lifted the crystal bird. "The immortal phoenix, eternal enemy of the Snake." He opened his hands. The glittering figurine did not fall.

It flew low across the table. Its shining wings were an incandescent rainbow and where they touched, the sand was melted to glass. "Sarsis will expect a rescue attempt and I shall not disappoint him." He placed the tiny chariot on the table and Caranga watched it speed across the sand. The earth opened beneath two of the minions and they vanished.

"A turncoat is always useful." Pyre lifted his own tiny snake to place it among the minions. It was impossible to discern which was which. The crystal bird approached from the snake's rear. It struck, sinking its talons deep into the back of that reptilian neck. There it clung, beating the snake's body with its burning wings. The third ice worm was slowly grinding through the mound.

The frost giant's head had moved closer. Its breath was spraying everything with glittering ice. The serpent's attempt to sweep the burning wings through that cloud failed; the cloud had shifted its attack to the snake's tail and was cutting pieces out of it. Meanwhile the snake's midsection had been pulled under the ground.

The chariot, wheels a flashing blur, was nearing the prisoners. One of the minions stood close by and for an instant it appeared to be helping the prisoners. The snake struck, smashing the chariot to fragments and devouring the minion in a single gulp.

The searing wings had touched much of the green body, darkening it. Caranga's nostrils twitched. Could he be smelling burning flesh? The emerald serpent beat the back of its head against the ground in a futile effort to dislodge its crystal attacker. Coils heaved and rolled and dust puffed. Then the beating wings came too close to the fanged jaws.

The snake bit into the burning wing and held. Smoke issued from its mouth and, distinctly strong now, the odor of burning flesh. Despite what must have been agony, the serpent tightened its grip as it strove to pull the phoenix from its perch. The bird's claws did not relax their grip. A twisting pitch of the serpentine body slammed the bird against the earth, and again. When it was at last wrenched loose, its talons tore loose gobbets of the snake's flesh.

The fanged jaws flashed and sank into the bird's body.

"Uh!" Caranga squinted against a burst of flame and light and—nothing remained of the crystal bird save a minute diamond, egg-shaped.

The reptilian victory was achieved at considerable cost. Sections of the tail attacked by the cloud were bleeding profusely and scarcely moved, as if hamstrung. More of the snake's body had been dragged into the ground. The first and second ice worms were much closer, with plain intent to crush the serpent between them. Already the third of their number was making a ruin of the mound. The frost giant's breath struck the snake so that the blood of its wounds visibly froze.

Pyre surveyed the scene thoughtfully.

"If there is a time," he said, and his voice rasped throatily, "it is now. The warriors of my army have slept long and long, resting for this their greatest battle. Now my soul goes forth to them, that the long dead may rise and fight. I leave you."

The wizard's eyes went blank. His limbs stiffened, hardened, became cold. On the table, the wooden figure of a mummified corpse rose and began marching, lurching a bit, toward the besieged snake. Caranga *heard* that advance; the tread of thousands of marching feet, outside the tent. He hated his gooseflesh and was glad he could not see beyond the walls of Pyre's tent. He stared down at a puppet corpse that walked without strings, an unnerving sight. Seeing a vast army of the dead marching into combat might be more than his sanity would bear.

The horrid outré forces were converging on the snake. Did this mean his beloved daughter would be saved or given the doubtful blessing of a clean death? If she lived, might not rescue by such weird and truly ghastly powers blast her reason? *I myself am without fear, but Tiana—Tiana is only a girl, still, no matter how she . . . ah, if only I'd burned that accursed map unopened! She'd never have been drawn into this nighted intrigue.*

More than half the snake's body had been pulled underground. Such success had been accomplished at the expense of abandoning the assaults on temple and altar. The cloud had split the tail wide open, and it oozed. Mighty ice worms were crushing the snake's foreportion between them, while the wooden corpse held the head down and pounded upon it. Having moved in close, the frost giant froze the split tail solid. All Pyre's forces except the third ice worm were close to the enemy, and defeating him.

The watching Caranga frowned. This seemed a tactical error to the pirate with long experience at assault. It were wiser, surely, to hold some forces in reserve. He could not see what happened next on the table of sand, for the ground beneath him twisted and lunged. The earth shook like a bucking horse and he was thrown from his feet. That restless earth opened beneath him and he fell backward.

For an instant Caranga thought he was falling into the open mouth of hell; then he landed on his backside. Quickly he scrambled out of a shallow crack in the ground. Bardon, too, was rising to his feet.

Both pirates stared at the greatly altered table.

Of the cloud, the frost giant's head, and the first and second ice worms there remained no trace. The third worm was rapidly melting. Wounded and bleeding, the snake reared triumphant beside a red glowing pool of molten sand. In that awful lake floundered the last traces of the corpse-figure that represented so many resurrected warriors—animated by the soul and brain of Pyre. The puppet's hand was valiantly raised above the surface like that of a drowning swimmer.

It burned as it sank.

"*Lost*," Caranga whispered.

"But how?" Bardon demanded. "How could such an array of might be whelmed this way?"

They stepped out of the tent and into stinking, smoking horror. Scant hours before the earth had been undisturbed. Now three broad tracks rent it, marking the passage of three mighty rivers of ice. While other signs indicated that the table of sand had showed a true presentment, the pirates' attention was fixed on what sprawled out before them. Where once a grassland had stretched in fertile beauty, now a proud mountain rose to towering height. Smoke and fire belched from the mountaintop and molten rock poured in rivers down its flanks.

The two men of *Vixen* stood stunned. At last Caranga swallowed and spoke.

"Lava. We knew Sarsis could make the world hot. Now we see the means."

They reentered the tent. Pyre's empty body still sat stiffly before the table of sand. The eyes were merely chips of agate, utterly void. There was no hint that his lost soul might ever return. He had imbued an army of corpses with the seemingly indomitable force of that soul, and the army had been returned to corpses. All Caranga saw here was evidence that Pyre's soul was trapped on the far side of mortality. How long would the wizard's empty husk of body last?

Caranga was spurred to curse the Gods and Fates for laying such burdens on him, but that would not help. A terrible defeat had been suffered, and perhaps it was final, terminal for humankind. Yet some small measure of life and power remained. There remained yet one blow to be struck. A man ought not to lie down and die until the last measure of his strength was spent. He turned to his aide.

"Come, Bardon," he said, quietly. "Let us to our tasks."

Bardon did not move and Caranga stared at him, expecting the younger man to say something. After an awkward silence, the second mate shook his head and that strange pentacular earring swung and flashed beneath his lobe.

"No, sir. I said before that the time for last farewells had not come. I still believe it."

CHAPTER SEVENTEEN

Caranga stood with his back to the Mound of the Great Snake. About his feet lay those he had slain. After carrying out Pyre's instructions, the black pirate had wandered about looking for some way to hinder the plans of the Eyes of Sarsis. Thus he had come upon the large work gang. They were shoveling dirt, repairing the damage inflicted on the Mound by the third glacier. When he charged, bellowing his war cry, the slaves had scattered like sheep before a lion. Only then did he see their beastmen guards. At first glance those armed and armored creatures appeared formidable foes, but as he expected, they fought only as highly trained animals. Caranga's broad blade slew them by ones and twos as they attempted maneuvers that failed because they were performed by rote without understanding.

At last they broke their training. Throwing aside their weapons, they had attacked like a wolf pack. The slaughter had been rapid and brief.

The victor leaned back against the mound and began to bind his wounds as best he could. Soon the moon would rise. That might mean his daughter's death; indeed the death of all he knew and valued. Yet Pyre had promised some faint hope, a last chance to snatch the world out of the jaws of the Snake. Caranga had carried out his part without understanding it. It felt very good to have wielded weapon without sorcery.

As instructed, he had carried the wizard's cold empty body to the Temple of Cignas, arriving well ahead of the Eyes of Sarsis. The model had not done justice to the temple's beauty.

Its walls were a complex lacy tapestry, as if someone had woven the pink-white marble rather than carved it.

The tiny flowers that nearly covered the building had not grown there. They were glass, perfect replicas of natural flowers. Inside stood hundreds of statues of men and women. Each figure was nude and posed with great dignity and beauty. Here three strong men were moving a great rock, there a dozen maidens spun in a gay dance of spring. Lovers ranged in pose from the first tender kiss of young love to intense passionate embrace.

Caranga had no time for more than brief inspection but it was clear that whoever had arranged these statues believed the human form was a thing of grace and elegance and had built this temple to celebrate that beauty. Yet Pyre had said that these statues had been made from living men and women by eating their souls. It seemed impossible to reconcile this accusation of hideous evil with what he saw.

Still, Duke Holonbad did have a lovely collection of stuffed wild birds, and the duke loved to eat fowl.

Caranga's instructions were to conceal Pyre's body among the statues, but it seemed unlikely the wizard wished to be stripped naked. Therefore Caranga left the body in a dark corner, and departed unseen.

That was all the wizard had bidden him to do. It seemed a useless task, like placing a legless, armless cripple to wait in ambush for a mounted warrior in helm and mail. Even if Pyre's lost and shattered soul could somehow reassemble and find its way out of the cosmic night into his body, was the wizard not powerless, his last resource spent?

Neither did Caranga expect that his preventing the repair of the mound would do more than inconvenience the Eyes of Sarsis.

He had finished binding his wounds when, over to his right, he heard digging sounds. *That makes no sense; that sweet glacier caused no damage there!*

He moved toward the sound, to discover another slave work-gang rapidly digging a hole through the Mound. They were adding to the damage caused by the glacier. Had the slaves rebelled? No; the beastmen guards were still among them. But this was clearly sabotage. Caranga was more deeply sunk in despair than he realized. For a moment his brain refused to function, for hope can be most painful.

Then it became clear. The slaves were ruining the

Mound because they had been given false orders. There was a traitor among the minions of Sarsis! A host of confused questions raced through his mind. There was only one certainty: this dark game was not yet over. With mixed fear and hope, Caranga waited for moonrise.

For long and long Jiltha had rested in the soft womb of darkness. Only slowly did the nightmares come, tiny pinpricks of terror. Steadily they grew worse. Formless horrors attacked her. She tried to grasp the darkness, to bury herself in unconsciousness. The assault of fear only grew more intense and deafening screams filled her ears. Only when her breath ran out did Jiltha realize that it was she who was screaming.

No kindly nurse came murmuring in response to this royal nightmare.

Awake and frightened, Jiltha tried to take stock of the situation. She was outside but could see little by the dim starlight. She lay on her back on cold hard stone. A chilly wind puffed across her naked body. How dare anyone treat a princess thus? For a moment anger and embarrassed modesty displaced her fears, then the royal adolescent found she could not move her arms and legs. She was bound in all four limbs; secured upon an altar of sacrifice.

Again she was not aware of screaming nor could she stop until her lungs ached.

Only exhaustion calmed her—or quieted her, at any rate. Her eyes focused on a shape standing a few feet from the altar. At first glance she thought it a tall man clad in robes of dark, dark green, but it stepped toward her moving with more than human suppleness. The cowl was the wrong shape to hide a human head. A soft sweet voice emerged from the darkness within the cowl.

"Calm yourself, Princess. You need fear no evil. You are here to help in a great and noble work. I am Cignas. You need not fear that I shall harm you. I have come to celebrate your beauty, to enhance it and preserve it forever. Behold what a delicacy you are."

The glass appeared before her eyes. She still lay in darkness but in the glass she saw a brightly illuminated image of herself. The altar beneath her supine form was a dull black stone that reflected no light but was flecked with bits of sparkling quartz. Thus she appeared to be floating on the vault of night, the stars beneath her. Jeweled gold bracelets and anklets decorated the wrists and ankles they also prisoned. A chaplet of silver and blazing blood-red rubies circled her golden head. Otherwise her beauty was unadorned and unconcealed. And what beauty!

She knew a brief conflict between shame and exhibitionism—and then Jiltha was proud to be so lovely, glad that any should look upon her, Never before had her skin been such a perfect creamy hue and texture, without blemish. Her hair was a shining spun gold. The last trace of baby fat was gone and even her tummy was tiny and taut. She was superbly shaped, her limbs exquisitely formed as a dancer's. She had long fretted that her breasts were only buds that were never going to bloom. Now all such worries vanished. She gazed with pride and wonder at twinned round grandeur, and she smiled in delight. Her fear was replaced by wonder and gratitude.

"Cignas, you did all this for me?" Her voice remained high and most girlish. "Thank you, oh thank you. But how?"

"It is my art. One of the minions of Sarsis worked with you during your journey here, but mine was the final shaping. Nor am I finished enhancing you. Raise your leg a little."

That did seem an order, and improprietous . . . but under the circumstances, Jiltha did so, and watched in the glass. The figure of Cignas did not appear. Roses did, white roses, to be pushed partly under her legs. She watched with fascination as Cignas bade her raise her arms, lift her golden head, roll slightly to the left, to the right. As she did so the unseen hands placed more fragrant white roses around her. Now she saw herself resting nude on an island of snowy roses, floating across the star-spent night sky. The sight pleased her vanity so greatly that she did not notice until the last blossom was placed:

"Cignas . . . I hate to complain, but . . . you forgot to remove the thorns."

"No, Jiltha. You need a touch of color. Look, see how lovely the crimson of your blood looks against your creamy skin and the white roses."

The pain was small and the voice of Cignas was soothing, lulling. She saw that the red on white contrast was indeed lovely. The urge to submit, to let this artist make of her what he would, was a sweet persuasion. Still, Jiltha was a spoiled aristocrat who had not learned to suffer without complaint.

"But it hurts," she whined. "What do you think I am, a pheasant you're preparing for a banquet?"

"That is an apt comparison."

That statement was too unpleasant to be assimilated quickly, but Jiltha began to realize she was here to sacrifice more than her virginity. She wanted very badly to scream. That would be useless and she knew it. Bribery and threat, too, were out of the question. Perhaps a cunning lie would save her? Her only hope was to think calmly, but the base of her spine felt cold and interfered with thinking. Her fear grew stronger as she tried to devise a good lie and could not. The knowledge that yielding to fear would be fatal merely increased the terror that clouded her mind. Her mouth was dry. Her tiny stomach twisted in a tight knot and she was about to go into screaming convulsions—and she saw the approaching figure.

He was a tall gaunt man, armored and carrying a shining sword. A scarlet cloak flapped and fluttered about him.

Cignas also sensed the approaching warrior and turned to meet him. The dark robed figure grew, changed, became a vast coiled serpent. Raising its head, the snake hissed at a sky gone bright blue. It slithered whippily through the sand, tightening coils thick as Jiltha's arms. She looked with horror at that wriggling instrument of death, a hairtrigger spring with venomed fangs. The reptilian head shifted while the beady eyes watched something in the sky. Jiltha saw it. A tiny speck floating across the blue, coming closer to the bright sun . . .

Abruptly it was dropping. She had one clear glance at it: a hawk diving out of the sky to attack the snake! And then the hawk had vanished in the blinding sunlight. For several heartbeats there was only the bright sun, then a blur partly obscured it. An ear-splitting caw resounded and the sand was blown about by mighty wings. The snake struck at the blur and hit nothing. A frenzy of shining claws and beating wings was followed by quiet. The hawk dropped the snake's dead body and the desert scene dissolved and night returned.

Cignas, in his somber robes, lay motionless on the ground. The warrior was pulling his strange sword out of the body. Jiltha saw no blood. For an instant she was curious. She wondered at the face of this master chef who prepared human beings. Her second thought was that she'd be happier not seeing it.

The warrior strode to the altar with a chiming jingle of good mail. His sword darted forth and Jiltha flinched. Only its point touched the bracelets and anklets which prisoned her; only touched them. They clicked open. She was free.

Jiltha gazed in awe upon this victor in enchanted combat—her savior. Her sigh heaved her new attributes.

"Who—who are you?" Her voice was high and tiny in the darkness.

"I am Bardon, Commander of the Star and Sword of Avan. I am come to your rescue, Princess."

"Oh! You talk just the way a hero *should* talk, my hero!"

Aye, Bardon thought, who had said the words a hundred times in his wishful dreams. Heroes, he had long thought, should both behave and talk as heroes. He did, using his best voice: "Natheless we are in grave danger still, for even my powers cannot prevail against the Eyes of Sarsis. We must leave this evil place, and with great haste. Come."

He had already removed his cloak, which he now wrapped around her. Jiltha only just had time to snatch the ruby-studded silver chaplet as her hero drew her away from the altar. He hastened her toward a dark hole in the ground. At its mouth she hung back; burrows in the earth hardly seemed fitting places for princesses and their heroic saviors!

"Have no fear, lady Princess. They that dwell beneath the earth are my allies." He lifted her and descended into the ground. "Since Your Highness has no shoes, I shall carry you."

He certainly did, the thrilled Jiltha noted, and with seeming ease! What a man! Commander of the Star and Sword of Something! What a noble, perfect hero! The hole became a tunnel, and Bardon hastened down it, his way guided by the pearly light of his enchanted sword.

Jiltha was aware that shoes were not the only clothing she lacked. In addition to a crown she had a long narrow cloak that wouldn't close in front. He was lean and spare of chest; she no longer was. Still, nestled in her hero's saving arms she felt quite comfortable; more than comfortable!

"My lord Bardon, shall we be pursued?"

"Yes, Your Highness. The Eyes of Sarsis need you to complete an evil ceremony and will go to any length to recapture you. If we are fortunate this tunnel will lead to the field of battle where the immortal Phoenix was slain. It is not due to be reborn for a thousand years, but I hope my sword may revive it."

Jiltha reflected in depth on that strange news. What romance and glamor but . . . if all went not well, her fate was one best not thought about. If all did go well, she would be flown gloriously back to the palace. Daddy would take one look at her new maturity and arrange her marriage to one of the princes of the neighboring realms. She visualized them: Fisheyes, Dragonbreath, and Whatsisname, the fat boy with all those pimples. More likely, Daddy would choose His Exalted Highness and Defender of the Realm, Prince Argarf—Froggy. Jiltha had found occasion to remind her father of Froggy's unconscionable ugliness. King Hower had replied that if she married *Prince Argarf,* she would grow to love him, in which case he would be handsome to her. Jiltha didn't believe it. Going to bed with Froggy would not make him into a handsome prince; more likely she'd get warts.

In Bardon's arms, she looked up to study his face. He was not truly *handsome,* her savior and hero, but . . . there was an austere nobility about his angular features, and it stirred her. She sighed.

My savior! My hero! Only now did she notice the ring —pentacle, really—in his ear. It seemed a wonderfully romantic touch. Jiltha snuggled. When Bardon paused to rest—which delighted her, really; it did after all prove that he was a *man*—she attained her feet and spoke softly.

"My good lord, our situation is desperate, but we may do that which will make pursuit futile. The Eyes desire me only because I am a virgin princess."

Bardon remembered Jiltha as a spoiled child, less to his taste than the cow-faced women of Sonul. "Your

Highness, were I to take base disadvantage of your fears, it would dishonor us both."

Jiltha decided that either her hero was very very noble indeed or because of the darkness he hadn't got a good look while she lay on the black altar. She could solve both problems.

"My heroic lord, marriage by Sword Oath is a little used but ancient and honorable custom. I give myself to you not from fear, my savior and hero, but because I love you with all my heart." With her hands clasped behind her she lowered her eyes and stepped back from him, wishing the sword gave off more light.

To her delight it suddenly flamed brightly. Thus she was well displayed as she dropped the cloak. She preened in the light, turning slowly so that he would see every intoxicatingly sweeping curve of her. Then she stepped close and pressed her body against Bardon, noticing his large eyes and positively gaping mouth. *Ouch! Dratted mail . . . but O, the male!*

For a moment Bardon stood dazed while he was kissed by a very beautiful and very naked girl. Young woman, even. Drat this mailcoat! This situation involved a most complex decision. He could foresee many problems, whatever he did. Then he remembered that Pyre had bidden him follow his instincts.

CHAPTER EIGHTEEN

Tiana awakened suddenly from dreamless sleep. Her mind was clear. Indeed, it was well rested and functioning at peak capacity. She remembered the past events and understood them. The Eyes of Sarsis had outwitted her. She had dropped an avalanche on an illusion, then served illusions, sailing the ship to the Bear's chosen destination.

She could not see, for something covered her eyes. She felt she was resting on a soft bed, tightly bound by many ropes. The bed was moving; was she still at sea? No; this was not the roll of the restless waves. Tiana was lying on something soft, large and *alive*. Her bonds, too, were alive. Twisting slightly, she was able to uncover her right eye. It was night. Perhaps she was in a garden, for the air was filled with a delicate sweet scent.

"You are awake. It is well."

The voice came from her left. It was a sibilant voice of sweet softness, much like the voice of the Eyes of Sarsis. When she tried to turn toward the sound, she succeeded only in covering her eye.

"Be still a moment."

Tiana felt something sharp close to her neck. She felt warm liquid spill on her, then her head was free. The figure on her left was concealed in black shapeless robes but was clearly not human. With a pointless short-bladed knife it cut the worm-like things that held her left arm. The rope worms were a living part of the bed on which she lay. As soon as her arm was free, the black figure placed the twin of its knife in her hand.

"Time is short, so you must help yourself. The tendrils have little feeling. Cut them with swift clean strokes, without pulling at the main body. Above all do not cut or injure the main body."

He or it began to free her left leg. Once its skin brushed against her bare flesh. It was cold, and scaled. Tiana regarded the dark figure with suspicion. It had given her a knife that was not a weapon, and nothing in the appearance of this creature of darkness prompted trust.

"Who are you?" she demanded.

"My name was forfeited long ago. I am an ally of *Pyre*."

"That's small recommendation. Why do you free me?"

"So that you can—" It stopped speaking and glided away from her. Though Tiana had heard nothing, she concealed her knife and pretended to be unconscious.

Watching through eyes that were slits she saw stone walls and two more black-robed figures approaching. They came close to her. One reached down toward her leg and there was sudden burning pain. Tiana let the leg twitch, and sighed. The black forms turned away from her, apparently satisfied that she was still senseless. Now they saw the ally of Pyre. No words passed between them, nor did the two move toward the one. The three figures stood in frozen silence, while tension gathered until the air seemed laden with it. A single word registered in her brain, as though whispered there almost silently but with much force: *Traitor.*

Though Tiana could feel no breeze, the robes of the two dark figures fluttered as if a wind blew from Pyre's nameless ally. Its robes moved slightly, a ripple as if an occasional gust came toward it from the two. The robe of one of the dark pair was flapping violently, an unrestrained motion as if there was nothing under the fabric.

That robe flopped and collapsed like a sail cut from the rigging. Of whatever had worn it there was no trace. Now the unnatural wind blew strongly in both directions. The robes of the two remaining figures flapped more and more intensely. Abruptly all motion ceased. The robes of the ally fell to the floor, empty. The last dark figure turned briefly toward Tiana, then hurried away.

Swiftly but cautiously Tiana cut her way free. She set off to find Bjaine and Jiltha. A few paces from the live bed that had held her, she found a second: a pallet of soft gold fur with long silk hairs that slowly moved. Jiltha's clothes lay beside it. It was empty.

An unconscious Bjaine stood beside it, chained to a steel form. His yellow hair dangled. Like Tiana, he was fully dressed, though his leather mail coat was gone. His shirt was torn. Dark red flowers had been twined about his neck so that he must continually breathe their narcotic perfume.

The world and I are probably better off with this Nor'man just as he is! Still . . . Tiana cut the stem of the flowers and, using Jiltha's clothes to protect her hands, pulled the flowers away. Almost at once Bjaine began to mumble groggily. Tiana had a feeling that she needed no picklock—and too she had a deliciously wicked thought. Stepping back, she aimed a hard kick at Bjaine's backside.

With a roar the giant pulled the steel frame to pieces, wrenching his chains loose. Tiana watched with admiration. Small wonder that this magnificent brute trusted to luck and brute force. His strength was so great that his enemies perpetually underestimated him.

His eyes cleared, became flecks of sky, and he saw her. "What madness is this? Why aren't we in Thesia?"

"There's no time to explain, Bjaine. The Bear is not dead. We must find Jiltha and flee."

"Where's the Bear?"

"I don't know. From what it said, probably in the temple."

"Good," grunted Bjaine. "You find Jiltha and I will go slay our enemy."

Tiana was shocked by the way the man calmly proposed suicide. "Bjaine you—idiot! Your brawn is useless against that unnatural monster."

He looked at her with unhappy surprise. "Suddenly your tongue has grown sharp and you try to give Bjaine orders. Mayhap you need a good beating and then the binding cord."

"Don't you d—oh!"

The giant blond seized Tiana, and calmly began beating her. In his mind, beating a woman was like spanking a child. He wished to cause pain and humiliation, without serious injury. With his right arm he shook Tiana back and forth while leisurely slapping her face with his left hand. Unfortunately for the Northman, Tiana was fighting in earnest. His iron physique could absorb great punishment but just as he pulled Tiana violently toward him, she threw an elbow smash at his neck. The giant wavered for a heartbeat, then crashed to the earth.

In some small horror Tiana realized she could have killed this deluded Northman. To her (some, small) relief he was still breathing, albeit with some difficulty.

Tiana considered her dilemma. Blast and bedevil the man! Even if she could find Jiltha, which did not seem likely, she just couldn't abandon this oaf, so despicable and so lovely. Certainly he was too big to carry! If she couldn't run, she must fight. That seemed hopeless, for mighty weapons had failed and now she had only a little knife without even a point.

Still, Pyre had arranged to free her, and she was sure it was not from the goodness of his heart. No. The wizard wanted her to do something.

The knowledge of what she must do had died with the nameless ally. She could not solve this riddle; indeed she found that she could not concentrate on it. There was the distraction of a strong feeling that she was being *watched.* Ah! She had looked at it before; now she saw it. Bjaine's shirt had torn more, and gaped slightly open. From his magnificently muscled belly, a red eye was staring at her.

One tug revealed the demon confined by the pentagram. So this was how the wizard Ekron had bound the Northman to his service!

Suddenly Tiana was smiling. *Everything fun is dangerous,* she'd been known to say. Well, this would be dangerous—and fun. Tiana knew what she must do and knew that she must do it swiftly.

When the moon rose, she had just finished her task and was leaving the garden, moving silently through the shadows. Hearing a slight sound from around the corner she approached, she dodged behind a large flowering bush. Several black robed figures passed the bush, *gliding* eerily. Then Tiana was racing away. She reached the steps of the Temple of Cignas before she saw another of the minions of Sarsis. This one stood in the doorway of the temple.

"I have business with your master!" she shouted urgently. "Stand aside."

It moved out of her way without the faintest sign of surprise. Tiana hurried past. The Bear stood in the center of the temple, a piece of ugly rottenness in a shrine of beauty.

The stench was terrible. Tiana's stomach lurched and turned at this mass of slime-covered bones. Bits of rotted skin hung like tattered ribbons. And still it stood, and walked. Its awful eyes no longer blazed, but burned with a dull red glow. Those eyes focused on her and it spoke.

"You are wise to submit. The battle is over and we have won. Further resistance is futile."

"Battle?" Tiana blinked. "Yes, you do appear . . . weakened."

"True, but it does not matter. While you slept, Pyre and we fought. Ours was a battle such as the world has not known since time's dawn. We have won, for our power is slightly greater. Pyre fought with skill and apish cunning. His most clever move was the winged chariot he sent, apparently to rescue you. By that trick he caused us to destroy one of our own minions. Thus he substituted a traitor in our ranks, unsuspected. But despite his cunning and the forces he rallied against us, we have prevailed. Nothing can prevent my return now! In the Ceremony of Return you shall be my servant, and my meal."

Tiana bore something in her hand. She moved closer to the Bear. "As a matter of fact," she replied equably, "I came here to kill you."

The obscene gurgling that emanated from the Bear might have been laughter. She sprang forward and slapped that which she held over the Right Eye of Sarsis. The Bear's clumsy paw scratched at it: a sticky piece of human skin. Thus it broke the pentagram inscribed on that skin. The Bear howled as it began to disappear into a mouth of night.

Hmp, Tiana observed. *That demon off Bjaine's belly has no shape and no form, but it certainly has great hunger!*

There was a flash of complete darkness and Tiana smiled.

"Farewe—Fare *not* well, Sarsis," she murmured.

Her smile faded when she beheld the Bear erect before her, throwing the piece of skin from itself. *Oh, Theba—won't it ever just die?* Its bright green eyes blazed as it shouted its contempt.

"Silly stupid trull . . . you think such a petty trick could harm us?"

The room spun and the figure of the Bear was no

longer in front of Tiana. Dizzily she whirled to see the Bear behind her, barring her path to the door. Raising hideous, rotted paws, it stepped toward her. Weirdly, its stench was gone.

"Now we shall take you."

The sound of its voice did not completely cover the background sounds: the crunch of bones and the sound of great teeth chewing with gusto.

Green eyes and no stink, eh? Tiana knew that again she saw illusion; a trick to make her feed herself to the devil and permit the Eyes of Sarsis to escape. The demon's mouth was but a step away—and she knew not in which direction. She knew only that she dared not flee the advancing Bear, that she must not move. The sickeningly decayed beast was close, reaching out to take her in its revolting embrace.

The paws closed about her . . . and the scene faded, became blurry; and dissolved.

No trace remained of the Bear. On the floor two large diamonds clattered, flashing as they danced up and down. Pools of red seemed to swim in their depths. She saw no sign of the demon, but she heard the intense sucking noise. Blood spurted out of the big gems to disappear into empty air.

This no illusion, she thought. *The demon has devoured the Bear and is draining Sarsis's store of blood. It can't consume the diamond—the Eyes. But—*

The red tinge in the gemstones faded to a pallid pink, to a spot. Slowly it diminished still more. And then it was entirely gone. The sucking noise ceased and the diamonds lay still, clear as faceted crystal. Beautiful. Tiana gazed upon two eminently desirable stones, the seizing of which would produce a life of ease. Except that she knew better. She looked at the dread gems with dismay. Was there no way to destroy the accursed things? For the moment the Eyes were without blood and power. Yet she knew very well that if she touched them, they would drink her. Tiana did not fancy herself as the Bear's replacement; the next host-body for Sarsis.

At a loss, she was pondering when something moved behind her. She whirled to face a slim long column of white.

It said, "So Ekron's magicks *did* defeat the Eyes."

"Pyre!"

"Brought here by Caranga, yes, as an empty body. Able to reunite soul with this clay on the death of a minion and Sarsis's present weakness. Well done, Tiana; I had feared that only your death would bring my soul and body together again."

"You said . . . defeated?" Tiana glanced hopefully at the diamonds.

"Aye—and just as dangerous as they were back in Ilan when some idiot dug them up," Pyre assured her. "Now then. Tiana: at the far end of the temple you will find a large jar of oil. Fetch it."

In a delight that was almost a delirium of relief, Tiana ran to obey. She was halfway back to the wizard, lugging the oil, when she stopped. She stared, as if unable to understand how he had accomplished her obedience.

"Sacred Udders—I'm no slave! I have been used enough by our enemy. Why should I be commanded to fetch and carry for you? If you want my help, Wizard, ask politely, as one equal to the other."

The deep cold eyes fixed on her, the eyes of Pyre of Ice. "If you were my equal, Tiana High-and-mightyrider, you might do and suffer what I am about to do and suffer. *Now pour that oil over my body.* All over me, Tiana, and hurry! All, *all* hangs in the balance!"

As she poured, Tiana said, "Whether the world falls or not, Pyre of Ice, you will say 'Please' if you want your next command obeyed!"

The diamonds clattered restlessly on the temple's flagging. Drenched and dripping, bedraggled and decidedly unimposing, Pyre turned from her without acknowledgment.

"Sarsis," he said, and he sounded sad. "We have come to a final parting. I am victor, for the Sons of the Ape are more subtle and deceitful than the Children of the Snake. I can say no benediction for now I work your damnation. Let it be remembered that I did not seek this day, that I fairly warned you that there was no return for those whose time is past."

"You—you sound *sad!*" Tiana's voice accused.

Pyre turned to her, his robes plastered to him with oil so that he could not have concealed a twig. Nevertheless from within that once-white robe he drew forth an unlighted torch. As he handed it to her, its greased head burst into flames. Tiana jerked, and gave him a satirically reproachful look. She held onto the flaming brand.

I am not sure I am longer capable of surprise, she mused.

"Your part in this plan is simple, Tiana Highrider of Reme. I am going to place the Eyes of Sarsis on my own eyes. They will —"

"Pyre! No!"

"They will possess me and—"

"Pyre! Wait! Stop and listen. Please!"

He gazed serenely at her. *How could he?!* "Very well, Tiana, I am listening. But the Eyes are peril so long as they exist, no matter how harmless they appear."

"Yes but you can't just—Pyre, listen! Once, in an inn, you sought to scare me to death—most literally! When that failed—because I don't know fear, of course—we talked; rather, I and a *sending* of yours talked, Wizard. We came to an agreement, once you explained a few matters. You said words to me, and I have not forgot a single one:

" 'Tiana, your magnificent beauty is a flame and your brilliant wit is as sharp as your rapier. You have been a thorn in the side of many of the great and powerful. Were I not so far down the lonely path of black arts, I myself would naturally desire you. The world will be a poorer place when you leave it. I, Pyre, who knows he is supreme, vow by the fires which shall destroy the earth that I shall avenge your death.' "

"You remember well, Tiana, though I did not preface 'beauty' with 'magnificent' or 'wit' with 'brilliant' and I said 'might desire you', not 'would naturally.' "

"Well, you should have said it my way. Do you know what I thought, then?"

"Tiana, the Eyes—"

"I thought: *And I, Tiana, who knows she is supreme, Pyre, vow that we'd be a marvelous couple indeed!* Pyre . . . I . . . don't want you to do this thing."

"Sentiment," he said, and his voice was almost soft. It firmed. "My alternative does not exist. Now attend, woman, and do what you must. I shall place the Eyes of Sarsis on my own eyes. They will possess me, drink my blood, and make me their vampire slave."

"Pyre! No!"

"You selfish damned hero, will you shut up! Think of the world, not of one willful *girl* named Tiana. When that has happened, if you love the world and me—and if *my lady* would be so kind—you will *please* set me afire!"

"Pyre—no, wait. There are things I would tell y—"

Too late. He stooped, snatched up the awful diamonds, and pressed them to his closed eyes. Just as he did he said hoarsely, scratchily, with effort and as if from a distance, *"Fire. . . ."*

And the crystalline gems began to sparkle with liquid red.

He had succeeded in angering Tiana enough so that she did his last bidding. Her torch touched his oil-soaked robe. Immediately the fire raced upward, red and hot. It enveloped the wizard's robe and the wizard so that all in an instant he was a thing of leaping tongues of flame. Flame red as blood. He stood erect, his limbs rigid and emotionless. No scream of pain, not even a groan, escaped his compressed lips. The crimson diamonds became eyes and those eyes held not mere pain, but a horror beyond all pain. Then the little chin-beard of peppered salt sizzled and leapt up in yellow that swiftly became red flame.

This much Tiana saw, before all was wrapped in leaping devouring scarlet flames that crackled and danced and ate. She stepped back a pace from mounting heat.

Oh, Pyre. Did you really have to?

The fire grew even more intense, and began to swirl. It roared. It was a great spinning whooshing pillar of flame, searing the marble floor, turning white, forcing Tiana to back away, raging up to ravage the high ceiling. Tiana fled that unnatural and ferocious heat and even so she feared that her back might well burst into—

As she reached the arched doorway into the cooler night, cold struck her back like a hundred hurled needles. She turned back to stare at the pillar of flame—which had turned green. Whatever it touched was covered on the instant with frost. The cold radiated by that uncanny aventurine flame was as fierce as the heat had been, though not all Tiana's shuddering came from her chill.

The new phenomenon was short-lived. As she watched, the green fire waned and died. This time it was not replaced by aught else, other than the bright flame of a wizard's life. Pyre stood there whole, unscathed. His robe was the color of freshest milk.

An awestruck pirate moved warily toward the wizard.

A trace of the fire lingered still, green flames that burned frighteningly in his eyes. Trying to be ready for anything, Tiana watched those eyes. If they turned clear, or red . . .

The last of the green fire flickered and was gone, leaving melting rime, and Pyre's eyes. Yes, Pyre's eyes: deep, dark, hawk-bright. Not diamonds. Not rubies. Jaspers, perhaps, or more nearly chips of walnut-stained glass. Pyre's eyes. They stared past Tiana, those eyes, and their gaze appeared to be focused. Once again, she turned.

Standing in the temple's arched doorway were eight figures enveloped in black robes. Pyre raised his hand, extended it, opened it. Within his open palm lay twelve effigies: tiny snakes. Four were broken into pieces. He commenced to close his hand as if to crush the remaining eight.

"Do you accept my terms?" he asked, and Tiana, caught up in the silent drama, jumped at his voice. The black figures went prostrate. "Good," Pyre said. "Then go."

Without sound or sign they slipped out into the night and were gone. After a moment of staring, Tiana's awe gave way to anger.

"What folly is this? Those fiends are utterly without mercy, and you have granted them quarter!"

Pyre said, "Yes, I have. Quarter was mine to grant or deny. I gave it."

Tiana gritted her teeth, closed her eyes for a moment, sighed. "Why?" she asked, in a voice slightly less loud and accusing.

He gazed coolly at her, brows only slightly arched, his mien seemingly imperturbable, he who had just been enveloped in roaring flame. And he shrugged.

"I had two reasons, Tiana. These are the last remnant of a great and noble race that was once lord of all the earth. Their ability to love and create beauty far surpassed ours—humankind's. Look about at this temple. See the beauty he found in the human form. The time of the Children of the Snake is past and it is meet that I permit them to die in peace."

Tiana looked closely at the statues. "By the Cud! No artist could make such perfect detail," she said, and it was a snarl. "These were once living people! You speak of letting those monsters die in peace! I'll wager that

means thousands of years granted them to work such uncleanness."

"True, but there is my second reason. My powers are
at low ebb. Had I forced a fight, you and I would be join-
ing this collection of statues."

As she did hate to lose an argument, Tiana changed the
subject. "Will you be all right? I have to go find Jiltha."
She wanted away from this man to whom she had made
more admission than ever she had to any other.

Pyre's eyes went blank for a moment. He smiled and
refocused. "Jiltha is with Bardon. In fact at this moment
she is conceiving his child."

"No! I mean you're lying! Bardon would never rape
such a—a child."

"You no longer know Bardon. We changed him, he
and I. Moreover, Cignas prepared Jiltha for the Altar
of Sacrifice. She is no longer a child, but a most desirable
woman, in form. As for rape, it is more the other way
around. Jiltha has long been more than willing to rid herself of the troublesome commodity you and her father
sought to preserve. Oh, Tiana! Not so long a face! They
are *married*, by sword-oath."

"Cess and dung, I'm not worried about their *morals!*
Jiltha is a throne princess. Her husband must one day be
King over Ilan. Bardon had trouble being a good second
mate to two such strong leaders as Caranga and me. Oh,
he was entirely efficient at handling details, but I could
never trust poor mope-face Bardon with an important
decision. Give him a choice between two clear alternatives
and he'll find a muddled compromise with the disadvan-
tages of both and the advantages of neither."

"He is no longer mope-faced and has found a bit of
confidence and self-respect. Besides Tiana—you have just
described the way Hower rules Ilan. Bardon should make
a fine successor."

Tiana sighed, almost smiling. "Pyre—are you weary?"

"Come. You no more expect me to make such an
admission than I do you. We share the world's confidence
and ego, Tiana Highrider!"

"Hmp. Well, as to Jiltha . . . there's small profit in
arguing over an accomplished fact. Unless . . Pyre? How
great is your magic?"

"You would have Jiltha's virginity restored? A trifle."
He snapped his fingers. "It is done."

Tiana's face brightened.

"Now," Pyre told her equably, "Jiltha is losing her virginity a second time and will bear twins. If you like, I'll restore her again, and she will have triplets."

"Don't bother. I'm sure Bardon must be growing tired. You know—I *saw* that snippy little beard of yours blaze up. How is it you are alive? Or are you?"

"I assure you that I am, Tiana. The fire that at last consumed the Eyes of Sarsis was one of purest sorcery. While there is some magic in every common flame, this entirely sorcerous fire was like a maze. I, having made . . . certain arrangements, was able to pass through unscathed but the Eyes, caught unprepared, were undone."

Still annoyed that the arrogant devil in his spotless robe had made sport of her in the matter of Jiltha and her "commodity," Tiana was happy to glance around and see the chest from the ship of the Bear-Sarsis. *Ah.* The battle was over. She had set forth on a mission, and been . . . distracted. That distraction was now disposed of, by a demon of Ekron's and by Pyre's flames. Like it or not, she had failed in one aspect: preserving Jiltha's status. There remained the chest; the spoils.

Let's see . . . how can I cheat dear Pyre out of the Jewels of Ullatara?

"You cannot, dear Tiana," Pyre told her, and he too almost smiled. "However, I shall merely take those of the Jewels that possess powers sorcerous. You may have the rest, which is considerably more than half. Being a wizard and certain of my Self, I am indifferent to worldly gain; baubles. Here, you may have these four diamonds. They are badly flawed and so their power is gone, for me. Not their buying power! The same is true of the emeralds in this crown. What need have I with six cracked discolored emeralds the size of eyeballs, set in beaten gold, when none is useful in magicking? Baubles. Ah. Now these, however, are talismans of great power."

"You—you are taking gems that would ransom emperors and giving me the *dregs!*"

"Hardly, and besides no emperor is presently in need of ransoming. The normal mundane value of these trinkets, as I said, is a matter of indifference to me." Pyre picked up a fabulously valuable necklace in which rubies glowed like clots of blood. "This piece is useful only in a spell to cure the diseases of certain long extinct animals."

Tiana's eyes glowed like emeralds as she reached for the rubies.

Pyre made them vanish within his robe, in which she felt he could secrete an entire ship, should he desire. "I foresee that Bjonn Northman shall—"

"Bjaine," she corrected.

"—shall very soon marry, and this shall be my wedding gift to his bride."

Tiana's eyebrows rose as she considered. A smug look came over her face.

"Come come, Tiana. I said Bjaine's bride, not you."

"But Jiltha is wed, and I am the only other woman around."

"There is Morna . . ."

"As I said," Tiana said, standing tall, chest out, "I am the only woman about!"

"Nevertheless the Nor'man will wed her. Nor could you possibly be happy with him."

"He is a strong, strong man and unintimidated—I can respect him!" Tiana stamped her foot. "The flames destroyed your wits, Wizard! Morna is a nothing—less than nothing! I have felt Bjaine's eyes on me! He and I are magnificent! He can take Bardon's place as second mate, and Caranga grows older by the day. . . ."

Pyre looked at her with amused contempt. "Is it infinite, your capacity for shamming and lying to yourself? Not Bjaine, Tiana Highrider! Not for *you!* Besides—fortunately, in view of your present muddled state of mind, the matter is out of your hands. Do you think such as Bjaine could forget that you knocked him senseless with a blow—and skinned him?"

"Stop pretending you know everything!" Tiana practically shouted, with sublime disregard for the fact that Pyre, apparently, did. "I also saved the life of that magnificent big hunk of maleness with his yellow hair and arms like oaks! I am a skilled surgeon, and the skinned patch on his belly is only a minor wound. He's suffered scores worse. Probably hundreds."

Pyre sighed, nodding, nodding. "Yes," he said, "Yes, yes. He also has a great need to dominate women, Tiana. He cannot forgive you for being what you are: a better warrior than he! Your skill as a surgeon would merely provoke morbid fears. Too, you mis-remember him because of Sarsis's illusion. Morna, in contrast, went out of her way to let him enslave her. She will love his protection and his whip."

"Oh, all that would change, with *me!* Scabs on the Back and mould in the Cud! He is a strong valiant man, and Tiana must have someone worthy of her!" Tiana stormed, sounding a bit plaintive. "Bjaine is the nearest I have found—why, I even said No to a *king,* up in Collada!"

"Tiana," Pyre began quietly, but a great jovial bustling voice interrupted, and Caranga came storming into the temple that now entombed the last of Sarsis.

The reunion was joyful and triumphant, and while Tiana was busy tending her foster father's wounds and telling all she had done, Pyre walked away into the night without a rustle.

Vixen sailed from Sonul somewhat short-handed, as many of the crew elected to bide in that city with a need for new lords. Tiana was glad of the extra space since it enabled her to provide a honeymoon cabin for Jiltha and a no-longer remotely morose Bardon. A few days out to sea, Morna came glowing on deck, wearing the necklace Pyre had promised she would have. She announced her sword-marriage to Bjaine and only smiled slyly when the ship's master asked haughtily if she'd got the sword's flat across her backside.

Well, Tiana told herself, *at least I didn't really want the big ugly oaf with his stringy wheat-beard hair!*

Thus ended the Eyes and the menace of Sarsis and the menace, to Tiana, of life with Bjaine. And thus, while Pyre bided alone and strove to test his new gemstones of sorcery and Ekron doubtless plotted in Naroka, Tiana Highrider returned to Reme in considerable public triumph and considerable private frustration.

It occurred to no one, save perhaps Pyre, that he had sworn the Oath by the World Fires, and of that swearing there must be consequences.

So ends Book II of three of
the War of the Wizards